IMMIGRANTS LAND

The Tangeman and Schiedt Families
in America
1848-1880

CHERYL D. CLAY

Immigrants Land
The Tangeman and Schiedt Families in America 1848-1880

Copyright © 2022 Adventure Six Press
www. adventuresix.com

ISBN: 978-0-9971515-2-7
Library of Congress Control Number: 2016933295

Cheryl D. Clay

Editor: Elizabeth A. Green
Designer: Lisa Snider
Cover photograph: Patricia Smith

To my husband, Jim,
without whose encouragement and good sense
this book would not exist.

✦

Contents

Prologue

Tens of thousands of northern Europeans immigrated to America in the mid-1800s. The flood of newcomers spread west across the continent looking for promised opportunities in the United States. Many of them boarded river boats that funneled down the Ohio River, and crowded through Cincinnati on their way to a better life in states further west.

In Prussia, Tangeman family members endured food shortages and threats of war and, subsequently, emigrated from Prussia to the United States. George and Wilhelm Tangeman left Europe in 1846 to avoid fighting an unpopular war. Their brother, Carl, also faced food shortages along with the menace of war before he emigrated in 1847. Following a harrowing journey across America (see *Immigrant in Peril: Carl Tangeman's Heroic Journey Across America 1847-1848*), Carl Tangeman joined his brothers, George and Wilhelm, in Cincinnati in 1848. Their three sisters, Louise, Wilhelmine, and Marie Dorothee, followed their brothers to Cincinnati in the early 1850s. These "immigrant orphans" clustered in proximity to one another in Cincinnati for physical safety, help to find jobs, and a sense of belonging.

Four Schiedt siblings, Anna Barbara, Margaretha, Heinrich, and Johann, arrived from Bavaria to America in the early 1850s with high hopes for a better life. Although shipping clerks in Europe and land developers in the United State touted financial opportunities, they overlooked other inherent dangers of imigration. Immigrant families struggled to cope with different languages, unfamiliar customs, and threats from local inhabitants. Nativists blamed immigrants for taking their jobs and reacted with violent attacks. Further, immigrants faced the perils of childbirth and strange diseases. Through great effort, the Tangemans and Schiedts survived the tumultuous social and political upheavals of the 1850s and 1860s and rapid technological advances in agriculture in the 1870s.

Immigrants Land: Tangeman and Schiedt Families in America 1848-1880 is a work of historical fiction. It weaves together the genealogical facts of my immigrant families of Tangemans and Schiedts along with actual historical events of the time period, 1848-1880. The story begins in Cincinnati, Ohio, with the immigrant generation of six Tangeman and four Schiedt siblings. It ends with the migration, and landing, of Tangemans and Schiedts in Kansas in 1880. It is a sequel to my earlier book, *Immigrant in Peril: Carl Tangeman's Heroic Journey Across America 1847-1848*.

Introduction

They were uprooted, dislocated, and forced away from their homes or drawn to adventure, religious freedom and a dream of a better life abroad. The alien newcomers arrived as strangers, foreigners seeking safety. They found a bewildering refuge. In their new country the old ways of greeting, speaking, showing affection, negotiating, or settling disagreements splintered apart. Like a tree felled in an angry storm leaves jagged, broken slivers on both the trunk and root stump, the immigrants' lives split from their ancestral homes. Family ties and friendships were shattered. They grieved over losses while hoping for a better life. They reached back across time and space endeavoring to keep a feeling of wholeness alive. In the face of these obstacles, new immigrants in the 1850s insisted they be allowed to exist in their new homeland. In the mid-nineteenth century in America the first immigrant generation clung to old ways while sparing no effort to learn new ones. Worry, fear of misunderstandings, and rejection colored everyday transactions. Even the smallest spaces carved out by the newcomers threatened locals' chokehold on power. Immigrants insisted they be allowed to exist in their new homes, their new land.

The immigrant generation of Tangeman and Schiedt siblings married and gave birth to many children. As was the custom, different individuals share similar names. Readers may refer to the Tangeman and Schiedt Family Rosters in the back of this book to clarify famiy relationships.

chapter 1

COURAGE

"Whatever you do, you need courage.
Whatever course you decide upon, there is always someone
to tell you that you are wrong. There are always difficulties arising
that tempt you to believe your critics are right. To map out a course
of action and follow it to an end requires some of the same courage
that a soldier needs. Peace has its victories, but it takes brave men and
women to win them."

– Ralph Waldo Emerson

DECEMBER, 1853

A wall of wood and plaster separated the young people harmonizing German Christmas carols in the Alemania Club from risks on the streets of Over-the-Rhine. Anna Barbara Schiedt and Carl Tangeman felt safe with fellow German friends in the crowded Alemania Club. Loosened up with beer and bratwurst, the Tangeman brothers, Carl, George, and Wilhelm danced polkas all afternoon with Anna Barbara, Elizabeth, and Margaretha. Carl's cheeks glowed from the beers he imbibed, while Anna Barbara's cheeks shone with her love of Carl.

Preoccupied by the Christmas festivities, Carl and Anna Barbara had not noticed the afternoon slip away. Carl helped Anna Barbara into her coat, "My dear, we are late to visit Mrs. Stolz." He opened the front door of the Alemania Club.

"Congratulations, on your wedding this week," and "Best wishes in your lives together," followed them onto Twelfth Street along with shouts and cheers for their engagement. In the Over-the-Rhine section of Cincinnati, a dusky mist sifted through the dim twilight. The pavement stones glistened with miniature ice crystals that had drifted aimlessly, uncertainly, almost as if suspended from the law of gravity. Increasingly, gauzy snowflakes dusted the uneven cobblestone street with a deceptive mask of purity.

Carl breathed in the damp, piercing air. It cleared his head and brought Carl's attention back to the darkening street. With Anna Barbara at his side, Carl set off toward Mrs. Stolz's Boarding House on Walnut Street.

In the five years since he arrived in Cincinnati, he had learned immigrants often abandoned their personal safety to walk the shadowy streets north of the Miami and Erie Canal. Wary of the dim street scene, Carl's eyes darted back and forth, searching for menacing contours in doorways and stairways along Twelfth Street. He set a brisk pace, eager to avoid conflicts after their joyful afternoon celebrating the Christmas season and their upcoming wedding. He was eager to share their news with Mrs. Stolz, his oldest and dearest friend in Cincinnati.

"Carl, I enjoyed our time with George, Elizabeth, Wilhelm, and Margaretha," expressed Anna Barbara. "The three of you brothers are close, just like Margaretha and I are close. And, I like George's wife, Elizabeth, very much. Perhaps Wilhelm will find a wife and Margaretha will find a husband, too." As with young couples in love, Anna Barbara hoped the whole world would find the love she felt with Carl.

"No doubt, they will. But they are still young. They have much time," replied Carl. He squeezed Anna Barbara's woolen-gloved hand draped in the crook of his arm, and his gaze fell into her smiling eyes.

At the intersection of Twelfth and Walnut Streets, the betrothed couple turned left at the corner portico of St. Mary's Church. They heard the choir singing a German Vespers Christmas service through the carved wooden outer doors. The melodious rendition of "Silent Night" followed them down the street and stimulated memories of Christmas celebrations in Sulingen and Ehningen.

"What a beautiful choir. It sounds like the vespers I heard back home in Ehningen," commented Anna Barbara.

"Yes, the music appeals to me, too. Perhaps we can attend another time. It is too dark to be on the streets this evening," responded Carl with an apprehensive glance down the street before them. On the pourly lit brick sidewalk, Carl quickened their pace toward Mrs. Stolz's boarding house.

In the middle of the block past the church, four dark forms stepped slowly out of the shadows onto the uneven sidewalk directly ahead of the young German couple. At first the figures were barely discernible. Then one of them slouched into the yellow mist of a gas street light and cocked his head toward the immigrant couple. He wanted to be seen, to provoke fear and to make his German adversaries withdraw. The troublemaker made it his point to seek out conflict with "krauts."

Harkening back to his Prussian military training, Carl surveyed the danger from the hoodlums and assessed how to prevail in an ensuing clash. *Should he stand his ground or attempt to flee and avoid a conflict altogether?* The thugs eyed the young German couple approaching on Walnut Street with obvious contempt. This was not the first time Carl had faced the taunts of local Irish nativists who resented newcomers to "their" city. But this time he had Anna Barbara at his side. His usual confidence was tempered by the responsibility he felt for her safety. How could he separate her from this danger and handle a physical altercation alone, if necessary?

Carl's gut churned. He searched the gray-shaded shapes for signs of their intentions and their capability to carry through. Then the four silhouettes slouched closer together and slowly approached Carl and Anna Barbara.

Carl fought to conceal his fear with a practiced, calm demeanor. He inhaled and exhaled to a silent, rhythmic chant. *Slow down, breathe easy. Slow down, breathe easy.* Meanwhile, adrenalin dispersed soundlessly through his limbs like smoke at dawn. Logically, he felt both calm in his resolve and confident in his skill to endure the clash, if it came. Prussian army training had taught him how to engage in physical battle. But, he was not prepared for the fear he felt for Anna Barbara's safety.

While smiling outwardly, Carl whispered to Anna Barbara, "You must run back to the church we just passed. Stay there until I return." Discretely, Carl moved one foot in front of Anna Barbara. His form blocked the view of his adversaries enough to give her a few seconds head start. Carl was relieved when he saw all four antagonists remained to harass him rather than to pursue Anna Barbara.

In those few seconds, Anna Barbara turned on her heel and ran as fast as her high-button, black leather shoes and long skirts allowed. She reached the stone-edged brick entrance to St. Mary's Church breathless. Glancing back toward Carl, she opened a tall wooden door and entered the vestibule. Anna Barbara sensed the danger only steps outside the doors of this church. Her back tensed and her fists clinched involuntarily. *Will Carl survive an assault by four troublemakers? Will they come for me next?*

She heard Carl's voice trying to calm the thugs who appeared to have the upper hand. The tones of their voices revealed a confidence they would "teach this kraut a lesson." In spite of his medium stature, Carl was not easily bested in a street brawl. For the last five years Carl's work had been intensely physical, both as a cargo hand on the Ohio River docks called

The Bottoms and when bending iron with heat and hammer at Eagle Iron-works. His body was strong and agile, especially his upper body. He preferred to avoid a pointless fight, but he was determined to protect himself and his fianceé from harm at the hands of these angry nativists.

"I have no quarrel here. You seem like fine fellas to me," said Carl in a low, soothing tone of voice. But the gang of four would have nothing of his "nice talk." Hearing a wooden door creek behind him, Carl took a quick look back as Anna Barbara opened the door under the arched doorway into the church. Then, Carl straightened and flexed his hands and arms, preparing to stand his ground.

"You krauts need to get outta here. You take our jobs. You work for nothin', then we have to work for nothin'. You don' belong here."

"And you don' mind livin' like sardines," snarled his comrade.

"Them apartments 'n Over-the-Rhine—they're a disgrace," taunted the leader.

"You krauts are a filthy lot. You spread cholera like wildfire," sneered the goon on Carl's left.

Suddenly, the tallest of the scoundrels lurched forward, awkwardly. His weight shifted from left to right, as he lumbered toward Carl, gathering negligible speed with each step. Carl side-stepped, grabbed his adversary's tattered jacket by the collar and one lapel in a smooth motion, sending him sprawling into the gutter. Carl's foe sputtered disgusting profanity while spitting out filthy street trash. He brushed off his jacket and pants and scrambled to move out of Carl's range of motion. His hoodlum pals laughed at the sight of their compatriot covered in slimy street muck. He withdrew from the fracas and sauntered down the street swearing loudly with each step.

At this point, Carl wanted the encounter to end with innocuous embarrassment and good-natured razing. Instead, the three remaining Irishmen became enraged at the thought of their friend being bested by someone even lower in the social scheme. "You dirty, rotten kraut!" grunted two of the thugs. They both charged Carl at full tilt, rushing headlong toward each side of his body with arms extended toward Carl's shoulders.

Carl took a calculated step backward while simultaneously grabbing the coat collars of both opponents. Ramming them downward and inward, he smashed their heads together leaving both men reeling and struggling to stay upright. They lost the battle to remain on their feet, groaning as they seized their throbbing heads and spun down to the brick sidewalk. The leader of the gang smirked, sized up the risk of continuing this fight by himself, and concluded it was time to withdraw.

"Hey, Kraut. Take yer lady-friend fer a walk somewheres else. I don' want to see you in this neighborhood again. Git it through yer thick heads – you don't belong here! Ye hear me?" shouted the tall, lanky leader as he turned and ambled away.

Carl did not respond. Instead, he leaned over to retrieve his hat from the sidewalk. Feigning confidence, he listened to the moaning troublemakers retreat into the distance. Carl turned casually toward St. Mary's Church without looking back. He found Anna Barbara waiting for him in the wood-paneled vestibule between the outer doors from the street and the inner doors to the sanctuary.

Anna Barbara whispered anxiously, "Carl, are you all right? Did those fellas hurt you?"

He pulled his fiancée into his arms. For a few moments, Carl squeezed Anna Barbara tightly to his chest. His pumping heart betrayed the fear he felt that this beautiful, sincere, loving young woman would ever be hurt, especially while in his company. Then his muscles relaxed, and his beating heart gradually returned to normal. They were both safe from harm, for now. She noticed him wipe a tear of relief from his eye. Though he was not one to verbalize his feelings, this street fight revealed Carl's deep feelings for her and the new life she suspected had begun within her.

Carl felt excruciating fear of losing Anna Barbara. He had lost his first wife, Elizabeth, and their two offspring to fever after crossing the Atlantic Ocean. Carl feared being alone again if he lost Anna Barbara. His greatest fear was to his conscience. The goodness of her soul would haunt him with shame if she were lost to dreadful violence on the Cincinnati streets. Too many of the locals feared and hated immigrants, especially German immigrants.

"Ja, I am fine. But I cannot say the same for those other fellas. They will nurse a few black eyes and broken noses," Carl chuckled as they slipped out of the vestibule. "But they won't stop harassing us immigrants. This is a free country, but those fellas don't care about our freedoms, only their own. They don't think immigrants have the same freedoms as they do. Somehow we must learn to get along, but it is hard. For this evening, we will walk the few minutes to Mrs. Stolz's boarding house, then take a carriage back to the parsonage a different way."

"Carl, should we notify the police? Isn't it their job to protect us from harm on the streets?" asked Anna Barbara.

"I doubt the police will help us. They don't come into Over-the-Rhine very often. Until we elect German politicians, there won't be much help from the police. They keep the peace for those who hire them to do so," explained Carl warily. "For now, we need to be careful and keep ourselves safe."

On the way to Mrs. Stolz's boarding house, Carl and Anna Barbara withdrew to their own thoughts. Anna Barbara thanked God for bringing her Carl, whose strength and cunning brought them through this attack by nativists. As she and her sister, Margaretha, had dreamed and prayed for, she had found a steadfast, reliable German man with whom to build her future.

Anna Barbara and Carl reached Mrs. Stolz's boarding house in time for dessert. "Welcome, welcome," Mrs. Stolz greeted the young couple. "Please come in and join us for a piece of *badischer zwetschkuchen* (plum cake)."

"Thank you, Mrs. Stolz," Carl responded as he grasped the hands of his oldest, dearest friend in Cincinnati. "We are happy to see you again." Carl's eyes glistened with relief to be off the street, back in the safety of his first home in Cincinnati.

"Anna Barbara, I'm so glad you came with Carl," continued Mrs. Stolz. "How have you been since I last saw you? How do you feel about America now that you have been here for a couple of years?" She gestured for her guests to have seats next to the coffee table in the parlor.

"There is much I like about life in Cincinnati. There are so many different kinds of people. I feel less German than in the old country, but not yet the way I imagined it would feel to be an American," explained Anna Barbara. She felt suspended from her past life, and not yet attached to her new life with a new language and culture.

"Have you learned some English by now?" asked Mrs. Stolz.

"I know some English, but I have little occasion to speak to the Irish with their thick brogues and angry ways. I know the words to make purchases at the Findlay Market and pay for laundry services. At home I speak German with my sister, Margaretha, and my sister-in-law, Wilhelmina," replied Anna Barbara. Then she took a bite of dessert and commented, "This *badischer zwetschkuchen* is delicious."

Carl nodded his agreement. "Thank you for making it for us, just like the dessert you made when I was one of your guests. I will never forget what you did to help me when I first arrived in Cincinnati."

"Carl, you are welcome. Now, how did you spend your afternoon? At a social club having a beer? Or at a Christmas party?"

Carl still felt anger at the thugs they met on the street in the afternoon. "We spent the afternoon at the Alemania Club with my brothers, George, his wife Elizabeth, and Wilhelm and Margaretha, Anna Barbara's sister," Carl said. "On the way over here we were accosted by four Irish thugs. We are safe now, but I don't like to fight off threats in the street. We need to be watchful and wary of our surroundings and the local people we encounter, especially after dark," continued Carl. Far from feeling diminished or defeated by the hostile nativists, he felt an indomitable drive to survive and protect himself and Anna Barbara.

"Carl sent me to St. Mary's Church for safety while he faced the four bullies," said Anna Barbara, blushing when she thought of Carl's love and courage to protect her. When her eyes met Carl's, they silently agreed it was time to share their news with their friend.

"Mrs. Stolz, we have wonderful news. We have decided to be married, and we would like you to attend the ceremony."

"That is wonderful news, and not a surprise," exclaimed Mrs. Stolz as she clasped her two hands together. "You two are good for each other. I hope you will live a long, happy life together. When will this happy event take place?"

"We will be married December 26, in the parsonage next door to Saint Paulus Deutsche Evangelische Kirche," replied Carl, beaming with love and gratitude for his first friend in Cincinnati when he arrived in 1848.

"That is where I have lived with my sister, Margaretha, brother Heinrich, and his wife, Wilhelmina, since I arrived in America," explained Anna Barbara. "I hope you will attend. The ceremony will begin at two o'clock."

"It will be my pleasure," responded Mrs. Stolz, with a tearful smile and robust hug around them both.

On the carriage ride back to her home in the parsonage, Anna Barbara reflected on how her German ways had already changed since she arrived in Cincinnati. People from the different German-speaking regions lived close together in Over-the-Rhine. Breaking bread with neighbors, sometimes they ate *bockwurst* or *weisswurst* sausages with *spatzel* from Bavaria, and at other times *pinkelwurst* and cabbage from Lower Saxony near Bremen. She discovered she enjoyed eating German foods she had never known before she came to America. Now that she would marry Carl in a matter of days, she would be drawn further from her old life near Wurttemberg and obliged to make adjustments to her new life with him. At this moment Anna Barbara felt detached from her life in the old country, weightless and floating like wisps of clouds above a landscape where she glimpsed her new life. Possibilities for her life were immense. To her structured way of thinking, this uncertainty was unsettling. She believed her marriage meant she will feel attached again to the earth she walked upon, moving steadily toward a distinct point on the horizon. She longed to live, work, and love Carl Tangeman as they built their future together.

chapter 2

THE WEDDING

December 14, 1853

Dear Carl,

With joy I received your letter last month about your upcoming marriage to Anna Barbara Schiedt. She sounds like a lovely young woman who has much in common with you. You have my whole-hearted blessing for future success, happiness and many healthy children. I have sent a token of my well wishes to help begin your lives together.

My life is good here with Hermann and his family. I help with the saddlery shop and play with my grandchildren whenever possible. At the same time, I miss you, your brothers and sisters in America. May God be with you all as you find a place to call your own in your new country. . . .

. . . . Congratulations to you and Anna Barbara. On behalf of your family in Sulingan, please welcome Anna Barbara to our family.

Your Father,
F. T.

◆———●———◆

DECEMBER 26, 1853

"Carl, are you leaving for your wedding so soon? Let's walk over together," offered Wilhelm as he closed his newspaper and took notice of his brother reaching for coat, hat, and gloves. "The apartment is as clean as this bachelor can manage. And I have taken my things over to Mrs. Stolz's boarding house."

"Thanks, Will," declined Carl, donning his oilskin coat, fur hat, and wool gloves. "Ordinarily, I welcome your company. Today, I need to stretch my legs, and clear my head, before I join all of you at the parsonage." Carl paused at the doorway, looking back into the apartment the three brothers had shared from their 1848 reunion until last summer. He thought of

George's marriage to Elizabeth Heimers in July 1853, after which the new-lyweds established their own home in Over-the-Rhine.

Carl struck a steady pace in a circuitous route through Over-the-Rhine. On this day after Christmas, few people were on the streets. The blustery morning mist assaulted his beard and outer garments, leading Carl to increase his pace to fend off humid, frigid breezes. His destination was the home of Heinrich Schiedt, the parsonage on Race Street next to Saint Paulus Deutsche Evangelische Kirche. Carl used this time to clear his mind and focus completely on his wedding to Anna Barbara.

Dare Carl hope for another loving life mate with whom to start a family and build a future? Taking him by surprise, memories of his first marriage to Elizabeth rose from the shadows of his mind. On this day of his wedding to Anna Barbara, it was not fair to compare the two women or to anticipate that life with Anna Barbara would be the same as with Elizabeth. Other thoughts of his first wife came to Carl. *Elizabeth, you know I have loved you since our childhoods in Sulingen. Life was easy with you. You understood my thoughts and my heart, because we were raised in the same spirit. We raised our children that same way, too. And you agreed to come to America, to make a new home for our family here. My life shattered when you, Dorothee, and David perished in New Orleans. You have taken every tortuous step with me since then. Going forward, my path is now with Anna Barbara. I will never forget you and our children but now I lay those memories to rest.* At this moment Carl moved one step closer to making peace with the loss of Elizabeth and their two children in New Orleans six years earlier.

Thoughts of life in Sulingen drew Carl's mind to the old country. He had taken his upbringing for granted before he left Sulingen. Now that he had experienced other ways of life, he cherished countless daily happenings that lived in his memory and in the letters he received from his father. As with the letter Friedrich wrote when Carl and Elizabeth left Sulingen for New York in 1847, Carl treasured the recent letter he received from his father. His blessing helped free Carl to fully embrace his marriage to Anna Barbara and their life in America.

On his way to the parsonage, Carl walked through the northern part of Over-the-Rhine past Findley Market. Retracing his many steps across this German-speaking enclave, he thought back over his time in Cincinnati since he reunited with George and Wilhelm. First, the three brothers found an apartment and jobs. As soon as possible, Carl pursued citizenship with zeal. He believed citizenship was a prerequisite for success in America. He was granted naturalized citizenship in the United States of America on September 16, 1852. Since that milestone, Carl pursued a friendship, then courtship with the blue-eyed, resolute young woman from Ehningen, near Boblingen and Wurttemberg in the Black Forest of Bavaria.

Carl asked the permission of Heinrich Schiedt, Anna Barbara's brother, to begin this courtship. Carl spent Sundays in her company sharing conversations about their values and aspirations, aims and expectations in America. Often, Heinrich and Wilhelmina invited Carl to join their household for Sunday dinner after morning services. Without parents in America, Heinrich and Wilhelmina fulfilled the role of providing parental support for his sisters.

Carl felt sad he would never know Anna Barbara's parents, and he regretted they would not know him either. He knew Anna Barbara felt the same about his family members who stayed in the old country. He thought fondly of his mother who had passed away in Sulingen before he left for America, and Mother Schiedt who was not well. Thankfully, both of their fathers were in good health, living out their lives with siblings who remained in the old country.

On his way to the parsonage, Carl splashed through puddles and carefully avoided rubbish that remained after a nighttime of drenching rain and rioting in the streets. German protesters took exception to the visit of Cardinal Bedini with a riot five days earlier. They left the streets of Cincinnati strewn with rocks, sticks, and broken bottles.

Adding to the street debris was the muck that remained after the annual "running the meat" on Christmas Eve. Hundreds of cattle, sheep, and pigs shipped from outlying towns ran through downtown Cincinnati toward meat packing plants, followed by the biggest meat sale of the year. Carl purchased beef and pork roasts from the Fifth Street Market for the wedding reception and had them delivered to the parsonage on Christmas Eve day. Wilhelmina Schiedt had roasted the meats for the reception planned to follow the wedding ceremony.

Early in their courtship, Carl and Anna Barbara wanted to know everything about each other. They had much in common—similar dialects of the German language, the *evangelische* faith and a sense of thrift and attention to detail. Anna Barbara described her home town of Ehningen, and spoke of the beauty of the

Black Forest. The mountainous area near Ehningen was laced with alpine hikes and hot spring-fed baths. Then Carl described his home town of Sulingen, situated on the northern Prussian plains, a grain producing area near Hanover, west of Berlin. The rolling hills were nearly flat, well suited for tilling the soil, planting, and harvesting wheat, rye, and oats.

Carl drew close to Anna Barbara in ways he had not experienced with Elizabeth. Although reserved with family and friends, Carl and Anna Barbara talked for hours with each other. She listened and encouraged Carl to share his thoughts and feelings about his past and their future together. His warmth and respect encouraged her to open up to him, too, and bridged their age difference of nine years. She accepted Carl's mix of integrity and industriousness along with the scars of grief from the loss of his first family. He admired her youthful courage to immigrate to this new country without her parents. They planned their wedding with the confidence they were prepared to face the dangers and possibilities open to immigrants in America.

In private moments, Carl felt trepidations for this new marriage. *Will we have children, and, if so, will Anna Barbara survive the risks of childbirth?* He vowed to himself to love and protect Anna Barbara and their children, if they were blessed to be parents. Having lost a spouse, Carl felt a deeper commitment to Anna Barbara in a way he had not known in the naive confidence of his youthful first marriage.

Anna Barbara Schiedt wanted to marry Carl Heinrich Tangeman. In the fifteen months of their courtship, Anna Barbara had fallen in love with this handsome, confident young man from northern Prussia. For nearly two years since their arrival in Cincinnati, Anna Barbara and her sister Margaretha had hoped, dreamed, giggled, and longed for loving marriages. Now it was happening for Anna Barbara.

Anna Barbara woke up early in the guest room of the parsonage with Margaretha at her side. She slid out from under heavy quilts onto the cold floor that curled her toes and propelled her toward the crocheted rag rug in front of the wash stand. She quickly poured frigid water into a ceramic bowl and splashed it on her face.

"Br-r-r, so cold."

"Mama and Papa should be here. I miss them so much. And we won't have her with us when we have babies," lamented Margaretha, tears oozing from her hazel brown eyes.

"Gretly, you silly goose, why do you say that? I'm the one getting married. If you want babies, you need a fella first. How about that tall, bearded fellow we saw in church a couple of weeks ago? Have you seen him since?" rejoined Anna Barbara.

"No, I think he was just passing through Cincinnati, on his way out west," replied Margaretha, seriously. "But he seemed all right. . . . Oh Anna Barbara, you're getting married . . . today. It won't be as good as having Mama here, but I will help you dress . . . as best I can. Next week I will write a letter to Papa and Mama telling them all about you, your dress, Carl, and the wedding ceremony."

Gretly removed the muslin wedding dress from a wooden hanger in the wardrobe closet.

"This dress is beautiful. I like the embroidery on white muslin and the way the tiered flounces will fluff when you move."

She laid the dress across the bed they had shared since their arrival in Cincinnati nearly two years ago. *My life is changing almost as much as Anna Barbara's. She is beginning her married life today, but I feel I am losing my older sister, my best friend, and confidant.*

Following his extended walk across the city, Carl arrived at the parsonage shortly after noon with a clear head and full heart. He was eager to marry Anna Barbara. Wilhelmina Schiedt heard his knock, answered their front door and insisted Carl join them in the dining room for soup and dark rye bread. He smelled the spicy, sweet aroma of traditional beef and pork roasts. When Carl glanced around the dining room looking for Anna Barbara and Margaretha, Wilhelmina explained she had taken a lunch tray upstairs for her sisters-in-law.

"Please, Carl, have a seat. The other guests will arrive soon enough."

Carl was too nervous to actually eat more than a few bites. But he appreciated having time for conversation with Heinrich and Wilhelmina.

"Earlier this month, Anna Barbara tried on a wedding dress that remained here from a wedding last year. With a few nips and tucks, I was able to make it fit your beautiful bride," explained Wilhelmina. "Now Gretly is weaving her hair in time for the ceremony at two o'clock."

"I can't express how much I appreciate all you have done for Anna Barbara and our wedding. We will never forget your kindness," choked Carl.

His emotion came to the surface without warning. After all, this was not his first time to declare his love and commitment to marriage with a woman who returned those feelings. He felt worried and vulnerable having suffered the loss of his Elizabeth and sober with the seriousness of intertwining his life with another. Carl took a deep breath and relaxed enough to gather his thoughts, ready to greet their close family and friends who had been invited to the wedding.

"You are entirely welcome, Carl. Anna Barbara and Gretly are dear to our hearts. They have been a joy to have in our home. And now it is time for Anna Barbara to be married and establish her own home with you. We see a bright future for you both. And we expect you to come back to visit often," responded Heinrich with a broad smile.

Carl relaxed as the conversation turned to a lighthearted examination of the topic of weddings, family life and Carl's ideas of how he would make a living.

A knock at the parsonage front door shifted Carl's attention. Wilhelmina answered the door and welcomed Louise (Carl's older sister) and Otto Otten and their children, Friedrich, Sophia Louise, and Bettie. They hung their coats and umbrellas on the hall tree and ambled into the parlor. Wilhelmina (Carl's younger sister) and Dietrich Otten came in next and followed the other guests into the parlor. Dietrich and Otto were brothers who had married the two Tangeman sisters. In a few minutes, Carl's brothers, Wilhelm and George, and George's wife, Elizabeth, arrived, along with Marie Dorothee, Carl's single younger sister. Finally, the last knock on the door belonged to Mrs. Stolz, Carl's faithful friend from his early boarding house days when his only desire was to locate and reunite with his brothers.

✦

"Anna Barbara, you are beautiful. When I get married, I want a dress like this one," Gretly mused as she finished tying her sister's braids high on the crown of her head, weaving in sprigs of holly and berries.

"Marriage to Carl is what I want, but you have plenty of time before you think about taking this step. Marriage changes a woman's life forever, even more than a man's," said Anna Barbara.

She sat still while Gretly finished intertwining holly sprigs in the braids in her hair. The way Gretly swept braids back from Anna Barbara's face revealed her defining high cheek bones and clear, blue eyes.

"*Ja*, it is too soon for me to think of marriage. It is difficult enough for me to think of you being off with Carl. I'll miss you so much . . . ," Gretly's voice trailed off as she struggled to stifle her tears.

"Now, now," soothed Anna Barbara. "I will be eight blocks away, right here in Over-the-Rhine. Walking that far will be good for both of us."

In spite of these reassuring words, Anna Barbara and Margaretha would never again share as much closeness as this time since they arrived in America nearly two years ago. The Schiedt sisters depended on each other, laughed and cried together, and strategized how to survive immigrant challenges in the worldly city of Cincinnati.

"There, your hair is ready. Do you want something to eat before I help you into your dress?

"Wilhelmina brought this tray with cold meats, bread, butter, dried apples and tea," said Gretly with forced cheer.

"I can't think of food. My stomach is churning already from the excitement of the wedding. A sip of tea is all I want. But you should have something to eat," responded Anna Barbara with deep affection. The Schiedt sisters shared a long, tearful embrace.

✦

At a few minutes past 2:00 pm, Anna Barbara Schiedt descended the creaky oak staircase of her home in the parsonage. Gretly followed three steps behind. In the parlor a hush fell over the gathering of family and friends of Carl and Anna Barbara as they heard the Schiedt sisters on the stairs. Wilhelmina stepped from the kitchen into the hallway, then followed her sisters-in-law into the front parlor. Gretly took a seat next to George's wife, Elizabeth, on the edge of the settee while Anna Barbara walked toward the far end of the parlor past their guests to stand with Carl. Carl's eyes never left those of Anna Barbara. They expressed his love, respect, commitment, and longing for their two lives to be bound together in matrimony.

In front of the blazing fire in the fireplace, Pastor Heinrich Schiedt held the Evangelical Catechism open to the holy sacrament of marriage. "Dearly beloved," began Pastor Schiedt. He extolled the sacred nature of marriage followed by a prayer of words of support for the young couple.

On this moment at the brink of exchanging wedding vows, Carl's mind flashed back momentarily to his childhood and early adult years in Sulingen. Watching Anna Barbara make her way toward him, those memories fled to the remote recesses of his mind. Instead, Anna Barbara's presence dominated his consciousness. He clung to the conviction that his love for Anna Barbara, and her love for him, would overshadow his past losses and bring their dreams and plans to fruition.

✦

Following the exchange of matrimonial vows in the German language, Pastor Heinrich Schiedt pronounced the new couple husband and wife and ended the ceremony with a prayer of blessing. Smiles of love and applause of congratulations overflowed the parlor. Wilhelmina slipped out to bring refreshments to the dining room table. Louise Otten joined Wilhelmina to arrange the trays filled with traditional German foods. Wilhelm and George slapped their brother on the back with good-hearted congratulations. Carl's sisters and brothers and Anna Barbara's brothers greeted the new couple, clasping their hands warmly.

"What a beautiful bride you are," exclaimed Elizabeth. She was beaming as she welcomed Anna Barbara into the Tangeman family. She was pleased to have a sister-in-law close to her age, and she anticipated many family gatherings with their next generation of Tangeman children growing up together.

Otto Otten shook Carl's hand, "Congratulations, Carl. We wish you a long and happy life together."

Carl slipped over to Mrs. Stolz, who stood at the edge of the group grasping a lace handkerchief to dab tears of joy from her eyes.

"Thank you for coming," said Carl as he took her hands in his. "You have seen my worst times. Now you have seen my best. I have long awaited this day, and I'm glad you could be here with us."

For Carl, she was not only a trusted friend. She was a generation older, beloved in ways similar to his mother who had been gone eight years. By her presence, Mrs. Stolz affirmed this marriage. She seemed to stand in for absent parents who otherwise would have bestowed the blessing of the past on the promise of the future by their presence at their children's weddings.

The wedding reception for Carl and Anna Barbara Schiedt Tangeman continued with a meal of traditional sauerbraten, pork roast, potato salad, and apple strudel in the dining room.

George rose and offered a toast to his brother and sister-in-law. "To Carl and Anna Barbara, to your eternal happiness. Carl, we thought you were lost on your trip to America, but now you are on the threshold of happiness with your beautiful bride, Anna Barbara. *Prost, prost, prost* to you both!!!"

Following the wedding dinner, guests and friends danced to polkas in the parlor played on the piano by Wilhelmina. Many robust beer toasts were made to their health and happiness and many children to come from this union. For a wedding gift to their brother, Wilhelm and George passed around the best cigars from their tobacco business to the men in attendance.

Later in the evening, after the other guests departed, George and Elizabeth drove the newlyweds in a carriage back to the apartment Carl had previously shared with Wilhelm. And Wilhelm walked Mrs. Stolz back to her boardinghouse where he would live for the foreseeable future.

chapter 3
BECOMING MARRIED

"What greater thing is there for two human souls, than to feel that they are joined for life–to strengthen each other in all labor, to rest on each other in all sorrow, to minister to each other in all pain, to be one with each other in silent unspeakable memories at the moment of the last parting?"

— **George Eliot**

✦———————●———————✦

JANUARY 2, 1854

"I will miss you all day, Carl Tangeman," lamented Anna Barbara, holding Carl's hand as she followed her husband to the door for one more embrace. The newlyweds had spent the past week together. "This has been the best week of my life."

"And for me, too. I will miss you every minute I am away, Mrs. Tangeman," replied Carl as he swept her into his arms one last time.

With a full heart, Carl left their apartment taking long strides toward Eagle Ironworks. The owner of the firm, Mr. Greenwood, liked Carl, especially his work ethic. Carl quickly learned how to shape iron to the customers' specifications using heat and the force of mallet on metal. Two weeks earlier Carl had asked Mr. Greenwood for a week off after their wedding. Mr. Greenwood granted his request, hoping his generosity would build Carl's loyalty to Eagle Ironworks.

Meanwhile, Anna Barbara took a deep breath to relax. Nearly swooning from their emotional farewell, she sat down for a few moments to finish her breakfast coffee. She paused to reflect on her first week of marriage, before she redirected her energies to the tasks of the day. She felt even more sure of her marriage to Carl than before their wedding ceremony. The closeness, the way Carl made her feel loved and cherished. For precious uninterrupted hours, the newlywed couple talked about their homes and families in the old country. Their earlier years only lived in the memories they shared with one another. Their family members in the old country and in Cincinnati occupied their attention as they shared recent letters from Tangemans and Schiedts back home. Of course, they talked over the latest happenings of their family members in Over-the-Rhine, too.

In every way he could imagine, Carl showed Anna Barbara his love and gratitude for agreeing to be his wife. He listened with sincere interest in her thoughts and dreams. At the end of their week together, Carl felt happy. It was the deep, cautious happiness of a man who knew tragedy and fully appreciated his second chance to start a life with Anna Barbara.

Before her marriage, Anna Barbara had not often been alone with her own thoughts and her own work. At first she wondered what Margaretha may be doing this Monday morning. Then a certain pleasure and a sense of responsibility to her new station in life dominated her feelings. Her first task was to organize their home similar to her mother's way of keeping her childhood home. She washed the kitchen dishes, and put them on the wooden shelf next to the cooking stove. In the bedroom she dusted the window sill and wiped out the floor of the wardrobe closet. Finally she swept the floor with her new woven grass broom and deposited the debris in their one waste bin. With her house in order, Anna Barbara turned her attention to the laundry.

On this first laundry day as Mrs. Tangeman, Anna Barbara gathered their soiled clothing and bed linens and bundled them into a laundry basket. With a bar of homemade lye soap tucked into the bundle she carried the wicker basket down the stairs of their apartment building and out to the street. In the damp, chilly air, Anna Barbara tramped five blocks to Rutschmann Laundry.

When she stepped through the wood-framed doorway, Anna Barbara welcomed the warmth of moist steam billowing from the open-air laundry.

"Good morning, Mrs. Rutschmann," Anna Barbara said cheerfully as she approached the matronly proprietress bending over her stove with pots of heated water.

"And what may I do for you today," replied Mrs. Rutschmann, lifting her head. She ruled her laundry with a clear head and strong, thick back. Her rosy cheeks framed a broad grin. It was hot, sweaty work shared by up to twenty-four laundresses using twenty-four wooden washtubs at a time. Some were housewives like Anna Barbara, and others were poor or immigrant women employed by wealthier families in Cincinnati as laundresses.

"What is this I hear about you getting married?" Mrs. Rutschmann asked with an inquisitive lilt in her voice. She liked to hear the news of the day.

"Yes. It is true. I married Carl Tangeman the day after Christmas," Anna Barbara replied with a touch of pride in her voice and a blush on her cheeks. She looked across the laundry and did not see either Wilhelmina or Margaretha. *This is my first laundry day on my own.*

Anna Barbara selected a wooden washtub near the outer half-wall of the laundry building, and Mrs. Rutschmann filled it with steamy, hot water. Anna Barbara rubbed lye soap on the worst soiled spots of shirts, dresses, pants, underthings, and bed linens. She scrubbed each piece of clothing on the gray, corrugated washboard attached to the side of her washtub. Dirt and grease yielded to Anna Barbara's firm, determined scrubbing action. With all pieces washed, she removed the cork plug allowing the soapy water to drain into the floor gutter that carried it out to the street. She signaled to Mrs. Rutschmann for more hot water, which she delivered from the boiling vat in the center of the laundry. Anna Barbara stirred the clothes with a long, wooden laundry stick to rinse out the soap. Sweat beaded across her forehead. She carefully inserted pieces of clothing and linens, one at a time, between the rollers mounted on the side of the wooden tub. She turned the hand crank to squeeze out the excess water. Finally, she folded the damp pieces into a bundle, tucked them into her basket, and paid Mrs. Rutschmann for the use of the washtub and hot water.

On her walk home, Anna Barbara welcomed the cool, moist breeze blowing northward across the Ohio River, up the hillside to downtown Cincinnati and through the streets to Over-the-Rhine.

At the apartment, Anna Barbara lugged the basket of damp laundry up the stairs. She stretched clean homespun sheets and hung the pieces of clothing over the heat register, chairs, and four corner posts of their bed. Even though the sheets hung directly above the heat register, it would take today and tomorrow to dry all of the laundry. Anna Barbara stretched her reserve set of homespun sheets straight and flat and tucked them under the straw mattress. On the top she smoothed out a top sheet, woolen blanket and thick quilt.

Anna Barbara ate her lunch of black rye bread and butter, an apple, and tea while she planned what to purchase at the Fifth Street Market for supper. After a short afternoon rest, her energy was restored for afternoon shopping and supper preparations.

Anna Barbara donned her black cloak. Her steps quickened out of the apartment and on to Fifth Street Market, her favorite shop for Bavarian sausages. On her way home, she planned to visit Margaretha and Wilhelmina. This was the first time she would see them since her wedding. She felt the ache of loneliness for these two women, especially her sister. It was the longest period of time she had been separated from Margaretha since her younger sister was born. Had they not immigrated, their relationship may not have been this close. In this new land, they had shared every daily problem, every puzzlement and every discovery. Neither sister could imagine her immigrant life without the other.

Margaretha answered Anna Barbara's knock on the parsonage front door with a shriek and outstretched arms. "Anna Barbara, I'm so glad to see you. How are you? How is Carl? Are you happy?" asked Gretly with questions tumbling out of her mouth, surrounding Anna Barbara with sisterly love. "Wilhelmina, Wilhelmina! Look who is here. Anna Barbara has come to visit," Gretly exclaimed loudly toward the back of the house.

Wilhelmina emerged from the kitchen to see the Schiedt sisters in a long embrace. After a moment, she said, "Anna Barbara, I am so happy to see you." Anna Barbara turned from her sister to greet Wilhelmina.

"As am I to see you," replied Anna Barbara, and she embraced her sister-in-law.

"You look well," said Wilhelmina, stepping back to quickly take the measure of Anna Barbara. After their greeting, she gestured, "Please come into the parlor. I will bring coffee and apple strudel."

While Wilhelmina returned to the kitchen, Gretly took Anna Barbara's hand and led her into the parlor where she had exchanged marriage vows with Carl one week ago. This simple gesture of formality to share refreshments in the parlor spoke to Anna Barbara of her status as a guest. Formerly, this was her home, her first home in America. Going forward she would be welcomed with the respect extended to a guest.

As the sisters sat next to each other on the settee, Gretly looked intently for the answers to her questions in Anna Barbara's eyes. She wanted to confirm that Anna Barbara was happy, that she had made the right decision to marry Carl. Gretly wanted her sister to settle in with Carl and be on the path to the future their parents believed would be theirs in America.

At first Anna Barbara looked down at her hands, fingering her gloves. She felt a rush of emotion she was reluctant to share fully with Gretly and Wilhelmina. In due time, Anna Barbara looked up, tears of happiness rolling down her cheeks. "Yes," affirmed Anna Barbara speaking from her heart. "I am happy. Carl is a wonderful person. He is a good husband, kind, and generous. He works hard and makes a good living."

With a sigh, Gretly relaxed, now that she could see Anna Barbara's happiness with her own eyes. "How is the apartment? Do you have everything you need in your new home?"

"For now, we are fine in the apartment Carl shared with George and Wilhelm. Maybe in the spring we will move into a larger place. We have enough money saved to live comfortably, and I want to live in a safer neighborhood."

"Where would you like to live?" asked Margaretha.

"I'm not sure. For today, I want to hear all about you. How are you? I love Carl, but I miss you so much. Carl works long days. I hope you can visit the apartment and keep me company," suggested Anna Barbara.

"I want the same," affirmed Gretly, as tears spilled from her eyes. She held Anna Barbara's hand and blurted out, "I have missed you. Heinrich and Wilhelmina are kind and loving, but they are not you. I am so glad you came today."

Wilhelmina carried a tray into the parlor with coffee pot, cups, saucers, plates, forks, napkins, and apple strudel. She placed the tray on the coffee table and pulled up a side chair. "Anna Barbara, would you like coffee? Cream or sugar?"

"Yes, please, coffee with sugar and cream," replied Anna Barbara. Wilhelmina served the coffee and strudel, then they settled back to take pleasure in this reconnecting moment.

Details of the past week poured out of Margaretha, reclaiming that bond the sisters shared. "And what about you? What can you tell us?"

"I can tell you married life is different from being single," began Anna Barbara, and all three women chuckled. "I like having someone else to care for. I remember all that Mama did for us when we were at home—cooking, cleaning, gardening, sewing. I want to have an organized home, orderly and clean like hers. It takes a lot of work. I can't imagine doing all of this and caring for children, too, if we are so blessed."

"Perhaps it will be some time before children come to you," offered Wilhelmina. After several years of marriage, Wilhelmina had not lost hope for a child of her own.

"Yes, of course," agreed Anna Barbara. "I was so excited before our wedding that I skipped my menses. I'm sure it will return in the next couple of weeks."

Wilhelmina suggested, "I've heard of that happening. You were greatly stirred up, and sometimes it happens in reaction to a strong emotional experience such as marriage." The conversation turned to friends the three women had in common.

"This has been the best visit. Thank you for coming," exclaimed Margaretha when Anna Barbara reached for her shopping basket.

"I must be on my way," said Anna Barbara thinking of how she would prepare Bavarian sausages for dinner. "Let's do this again on Thursday. I will be baking tomorrow."

"Yes, yes. May I come to your apartment to help with the baking?" asked Gretly.

"I would very much like you to come help me. And you may bring back fresh bread for this household, too," replied Anna Barbara as she donned her cloak and picked up her basket with Bavarian sausages.

ABOUT SIX WEEKS LATER

The aroma of potatoes and bratwurst baking in the cast iron oven filled the apartment and wafted down the stairway. Carl sometimes heard German coworkers complain about the cooking of their non-German wives. Today, Carl's heart overflowed with appreciation for the home Anna Barbara created for them to share. Here he relaxed in warmth and safety. On the streets, he watched every encounter for danger, especially those with native Cincinnatians. At home he let down his guard.

Anna Barbara heard Carl pounding up the stair steps, taking two at a time. She was eager to see him after a long day of baking and cleaning. His pace of arrival suggested he had news of something compelling to share with her.

"Anna Barbara, I missed you," Carl exclaimed as he came through the door and hung up his cap and jacket. In three long strides Carl was at her side, sweeping her into his arms.

The apartment sparkled from being swept and scrubbed, and Carl smiled as he noticed Anna Barbara's efforts. "M-m-m, I smell fresh bread and something else," Carl commented. "Coming home to you and our home is the best part of my day." In contrast to his bachelor life with his brothers, this home reminded him of life in Sulingen growing up with his parents and siblings. He wondered about his brother Hermann in the saddlery business with his father. How were they faring as conflicts continued among the principalities of Prussia? *Will I ever get over the pain of leaving my homeland? Will my immigrant heart ever be completely at peace in Amer-*

ica? In this apartment in Over-the-Rhine with Anna Barbara, he came close to the peace he longed for.

"Carl, Carl. I'm glad you are home," responded Anna Barbara, with a lilt in her voice and a flush in her cheeks. Her face flushed more than from the heat radiating from her Eagle stove where dinner was roasting.

"I must wash up. Then I have something to tell you," Carl tossed over his shoulder as he ducked into the bedroom and poured water from pitcher to basin. With the bar of lye soap he lathered up his head, neck and arms. Then he changed his sooty shirt and trousers and emerged from the bedroom, clean, hungry, and ready for conversation over supper. Carl could not imagine feeling any happier than he did at that moment, in that place with Anna Barbara.

Carl and Anna Barbara sat down on their two wooden ladder back chairs beside a table barely big enough for two. Following grace, Anna Barbara invited, "What is your news? Please share with me," she said, barely taking a breath before continuing. "Margaretha came over and helped me bake bread and an apple cake for dessert. The apartment is so quiet when you are at work. She helps me and keeps me company."

"Everything smells delicious," Carl said. "You and Margaretha are a good team." Carl smiled as he savored the bratwurst and dressing.

"Thank you. We had a lovely day together. And how was your day?" asked Anna Barbara, eager to hear Carl's news.

"Today, I had the opportunity to meet a new customer for the foundry. Mr. George Miller brought in a wagon that had slipped off a country road in a rainstorm near Springfield. The iron wheel rims needed to be straightened along with the tongue of the wagon. It will take another day to finish the job. I hope to have another conversation with him before he leaves Cincinnati for his home in Loudonville."

"Why do you want to visit with Mr. Miller? And where is Loudonville?" asked Anna Barbara.

"Mr. Miller stayed at the shop all afternoon watching me repair his wagon. He asked lots of questions about my methods and where we source our iron. When I asked him his interest, I found out he had purchased a foundry in Loudenville two years ago. That is a town on the other side of Ohio, much closer to Cleveland. That part of Ohio is in need of a good foundry. In fact, he has enough business already to put another blacksmith to work with him. He wants to talk to me tomorrow, probably to offer me a job," responded Carl with a broad smile.

Anna Barbara sat back in her chair, "This is a surprise, one I had not thought may happen so soon," she commented with a dumbfounded look on her face.

Carl was bewildered by Anna Barbara's response. "I thought you would be more excited about the prospect of leaving Cincinnati. There have been epidemics of cholera that took thousands of lives, especially people who live in Over-the-Rhine," Carl reminded his wife. "And I know you have been concerned about the danger we feel on the streets, especially after dark."

"Yes, Carl, I have said those things about Cincinnati," admitted Anna Barbara. "Perhaps this small town of Loudonville is an opportunity to move to a safer place." She realized how seriously Carl took her words.

"I may not actually receive an offer, but I wanted to tell you about Mr. Miller. He is a fine fellow. I think we should consider this opportunity, if it comes to pass," continued Carl.

Anna began to think in rapid streaks of thought the reasons this may or may not be a good opportunity. *Will Carl make more money? Will the business expand? We may be able to afford a bigger home, perhaps purchase land and build a house. On the other hand, we will be far away from the rest of our family.*

"Mr. Miller said there is a new railroad that runs from Mansfield, through Perrysville and Loudonville. And there will likely be a new canal built close to Loudonville with plenty of iron work for the docks and locks. His foundry will build a secure future for his family. Anna Barbara, you are so quiet. Is something the matter? Do you not want to find a safer place?" Carl asked as he looked carefully at Anna Barbara's face to discover her true feelings.

With a face full of emotion, Anna Barbara pushed back her chair and walked quickly to the bedroom. Carl followed close on her heels. "My dear Anna Barbara, what is the matter? Do you not want to move? I thought this was our hope and dream. Please tell me what is wrong . . . ." Carl sat on the edge of their bed with his arm around her shoulders.

Anna Barbara sobbed, "*Ja*, I want to move to a safer town, someday. But, Carl, I may be pregnant. I have missed two periods, one in December, another in January. And my body feels different, fuller." Between sobs and sniffles, Anna Barbara watched Carl for his reaction to her news.

His face lit up with joy, "My dear, dear Anna Barbara. This is the best possible news. I didn't think it would happen so soon, but you make me very happy. We are starting a family," Carl exclaimed as he hugged her firmly, yet gently.

"How are you feeling? Are you well?" Carl asked. He remembered Elizabeth's feelings of sickness and tears during her two pregnancies. One minute ecstatic and joyful; the next minute worried, even despondent. Of course, her mother and sisters were close by to help her through those ups and downs. Without her mother and a circle of female relatives, Carl would need to be even more supportive of Anna Barbara than he had been with Elizabeth.

Carl smiled through tears and awkwardly reached out to Anna Barbara, gently caressing her shoulders. Gesturing with his hands, he spoke of his thankfulness and reverence for the life she carried. Anna Barbara took in a deep breath and sighed with relief. She lifted her eyes to see Carl's tears reveal his profound longing for this child. Carl took her hands in his, "Anna Barbara, this is the happiest moment of my life." And it was. Even more than his children with Elizabeth, now he took nothing for granted about his future. He felt exuberance and caution, joyful anticipation matched with careful attention to mother and child. The intimacy of this moment bound Carl's sense of purpose to Anna Barbara's drive to provide a loving home for their children.

"Would you like this?" Carl asked as he offered his red handkerchief. She blew her nose and looked up into his crystal blue eyes. His love and respect washed through her heart, affirming her new sense of womanhood. As she stood up, he said, "Now, let's finish our supper. The bratwurst is delicious, just like in the old country." He embraced her again.

For the rest of supper, Anna Barbara and Carl talked of their future and the coincidence of a possible job offer and a child coming to their family.

✦

March 2, 1854

Dear Mama and Papa,

Greetings from America. I hope the two of you are well. Please give my greetings to Anna Marie, Jacob, Johann and Elizabeth and our other relatives. I miss each one of you.

Carl and I have lived in an apartment in Cincinnati since our wedding in December. I have kept the house, remembering how you taught me to cook and clean. Carl likes the foods from our family, and I have learned how to make some of his family dishes from his sisters who live here in Cincinnati.

I am glad to know that Johann and Elizabeth plan to immigrate to America. There are many more opportunities here for jobs and land. There are many new things to learn in America. We look forward to welcoming them to Cincinnati when they arrive. It helps to have family members close by.

Now that I am this far along, I want you to know that we are expecting our first child, God willing, in September. Carl is very watchful over me. He helps with heavy things and he wants to know that I am healthy every day. So far, I feel fine except when I eat onions. I know some other German women who are pregnant in our neighborhood. Sometimes we get together and mend our clothing together. We loan clothes to each other as we get bigger and need larger sizes. At these times I remember how you gathered with your sisters to sew clothes for your husbands and children. I will always remember the stories and laughter coming from our dining room table on those days.

Margaretha lives nearby, only eight blocks away, about as far as you and Papa are from Anna Marie and Jacob's house. We see each other to do laundry or cook together every week. This is the first time we have lived in different houses. It is easier for me, because I have Carl.

Every day I think of you and pray for God to grant you good health and happiness.

Your loving daughter,
Anna Barbara

chapter 4

SCOUTING OUT LOUDONVILLE

*"America was indebted to immigration for her settlement and prosperity.
That part of America which had encouraged them most had advanced most
rapidly in population, agriculture, and the arts."*

— President James Madison

EARLY MARCH, 1854

"Anna Barbara, Will is here with the carriage," Carl called to the bed-room, as she picked up her bonnet and cloak. "May I help you with your wrap?" Carl offered. On their way out of the apartment, he picked up their well-worn carpet bag filled with clothes and bread, applebutter sandwiches and dried fruit for their train trip to Loudonville.

"Good morning, Carl. How are you today, Anna Barbara?" Wilhelm greeted his brother and sister-in-law with mixed feelings at the thought of their trip to Loudonville. He wanted Carl and Anna Barbara to prosper, but he did not relish the thought they may move away from Cincinnati. He kept these thoughts to himself as he clicked the carriage horse reins, and started driving to the Cincinnati, Columbus and Cleveland Railway passenger depot. They had plenty of time, barring an unforeseen event, to arrive at the depot well before their 9:15 am departure time.

Anna Barbara was both dazzled and unnerved by the sights and sounds she encountered close up in the train depot. The steam engine belched and hissed and forced hot steam to circulate through a maze of curving, merging, and straight pipelines. Carl had been curious about the new mode of travel when the CCC Railway Company began service for cargo and passengers in 1851. Now he wholeheartedly embraced the notion of train travel. In newspaper accounts he had read that railroads were destined to replace canals and rivers as a faster, safer, and more cost effective means to convey passengers and cargo.

"All aboard, Crestline Station," proclaimed the conductor in a voice trumpeting above the animated crowd flowing toward passenger cars. Carl picked up their travel bag in one hand and helped Anna Barbara up the steps to Passenger Coach Number Three with his other hand. Turning left, they walked down the aisle between double seats to the middle of the train car. Anna Barbara settled into the window side of the high-back, oak bench seat, while Carl lifted their bag onto the overhead luggage shelf. They sat back and admired the smooth oak paneling on the seats, side walls, and ceiling.

Turning to face her husband, Anna Barbara asked, "Carl, is train travel safe? What if the train goes too fast? They move faster than horses. What if the train flies off the tracks?" Worry scattered across her face.

"Yes, trains are perfectly safe," reassured Carl. "George rides a train to Dayton to deliver tobacco to customers every month. Even though the train car is moving, inside we are not affected by the speed, except if we try to walk from car to car. Then we must grasp the seat backs and be careful to keep from falling in the swaying train car." He chuckled and placed Anna Barbara's hand through the crook of his arm and squeezed her hand. She grasped his arm, looked into his crystal blue eyes and endeavored to appreciate the thrill of train travel.

The train lurched forward, then slowly emerged from beneath the rounded glass roof of the Cincinnati passenger depot. The steam-powered locomotive gathered speed and moved past small, yet respectable, homes of meat-packing workers and tumble-down shacks of ne'er-do-wells. Beyond the city limits of Cincinnati, they coursed swiftly through the hilly countryside, generally northeast toward Columbus. Anna Barbara settled back in her seat and began to enjoy rapidly appearing forests, farms, and open fields. From a distance she saw a buckboard guided by a young man. He struggled to control the sweaty black stallion careening down the country road straight toward the train. She stiffened when the stallion reared up, struggled to slow down, and nearly lost its footing. The train intersected the path of his forward movement in a noisy rush. The driver was barely able to rein him in safely before the train clacked past, rattling the iron rails.

◆

The train screeched to its first stop of the morning at the Hamilton Station at the north edge of Hamilton County. Anna Barbara asked, "Is it all right for us to leave the train? I would like to walk around and use the facilities."

"Of course, let's go this way," Carl replied with a gesture in the direction of the conductor. The conductor explained this was a stop to take on water and coal. They would have about twenty minutes before the train left the station. Carl watched the water and coal transfers to the reservoir and coal car, respectively, while Anna Barbara followed his gesture toward the outhouse.

The next three stations of Dayton, Urbana, and Marysville, were also coal and water stops. At noon, Anna Barbara opened their carpet bag to share lunch with Carl. Lulled by the rhythmic movement and clacking of iron rails and wheels, she napped on Carl's shoulder until they reached Crestline Station.

Crestline Station displayed few signs of human habitation. There were two small homes huddled behind the station house, one for the station master and the other for the livery owner. Next to the livery was a small boarding house with cafe serving lunch to passengers. Seeing the conductor, Carl asked, "Excuse me, do you know why Crestline is such a small town?"

"Of course. This village is the crossroads for trains from Cleveland to Cincinnati and St. Louis to Cleveland. A couple of years ago, when this station was built, the town was platted. There will be more homes and businesses in the coming years. This is the station where you will find the next train east to Mansfield in two hours. Good luck with your journey."

Unlike Crestline Station, Mansfield Station was near the center of a bustling town of a few thousand residents. Absent an afternoon train to Loudonville, Carl noticed two hotels on Main Street. The first one they came across had vacant rooms, and Carl registered "Mr. and Mrs. C. H. Tangeman" at the front desk. He felt proud and settled to have Anna Barbara at his side.

The following morning, Carl and Anna Barbara boarded the first train bound for Loudonville. With only one stop at Perrysville Station, they arrived in Loudonville before noon.

About three miles before the train arrived in Loudonville, the tracks turned gently to the right and sloped gradually downward. The steam engine pulled into the brick Loudonville Station to the accompaniment of shrieking brakes and billows of smoke and steam. Situated in the center of town, everyone heard the familiar commotion and knew the morning train from Mansfield had arrived.

"Can you see the station? Mr. Miller said he would meet us on the platform," said Carl as he leaned toward the window for a better view of the platform. "There he is. I see him," Carl declared. He waved to a man in his forties, medium height, dressed in a tweed waistcoat and matching hat. Next to him stood a middle-aged, matronly woman in an apple green velvet shirtwaist dress trimmed in forest green piping.

Carl took down their travel bag, then held Anna Barbara's hand as they stepped onto the platform of the Loudonville Station. Mr. Miller smiled broadly, "Greetings, Mr. and Mrs. Tangeman. Welcome to Loudonville." Carl and George Miller shook hands firmly. "And this is my wife, Catherine Miller," introduced Mr. Miller.

"How do you do?" greeted Carl with a gentle handshake. "It is good to be here in Loudonville. This is my wife, Anna Barbara." Anna Barbara smiled quietly and accepted Mrs. Miller's outstretched hand.

"How do you do?" greeted Mrs. Miller.

"Very well, thank you," replied Anna Barbara feeling warmly toward this woman, who was nearly old enough to be her own mother.

Beyond the station, Carl and Anna Barbara glanced across the town of one- and two-story brick buildings. Three church spires pierced the low cloud ceiling hovering above the town.

"Come, let us all have lunch, then we will see the town and visit the foundry this afternoon," Mr. Miller suggested. He led the foursome to the Grand Hotel on Water Street. They were seated near one of the front windows for their noon meal.

"Mr. Miller, this is a beautiful town. It is almost hidden in the trees along the river. I expected a town situated on one of the beautiful fields we passed on the way into town," Carl said to open the lunch talk.

Mr. Miller smiled and explained, "Originally, the tracks were to be laid about a mile north of Loudonville. When the town fathers learned of that plan, they applied as much influence as they could muster with the railroad investors. In the end, the railroad tracks were built with a swerve down through the town of Loudonville, over the Blackfork River then back up and east toward Wooster."

Anna Barbara offered, "This seems like a solid town. The brick buildings are very attractive and prosperous looking."

"There are more shops than I expected," commented Carl.

"Please keep in mind that more people live in the surrounding townships than live in the town. These shops serve a few thousand farm families in the area, too," replied George Miller.

Following lunch, the Millers and Tangemans strolled along Main Street past Black's Bakery and Confectioner next door to the old American House, an old-time roadhouse and saloon from bygone frontier days. "T. J. Henderson just opened a harness and saddlery on Main Street a few doors east," motioned George. Continuing their tour of downtown Loudonville, the two couples passed Larwell Dry Goods, Openheimer Clothing, Booth Grocery Store, and two taverns, a shoe store, tinshop, gunsmith, watchmaker, and jeweler around the town square. Completing the tour, Carl and Mr. Miller continued east on Main Street toward Miller Foundry while Catherine and Anna Barbara walked to the Millers' home. Carl and his prospective employer toured the foundry and discussed equipment and methods to work with iron for various purposes. Mr. Miller was restrained, yet eager to show Carl the advantages of moving to Loudonville and working in his foundry.

✦

On their walk to her home, Anna Barbara asked, "Mrs. Miller, do you have children? I am interested in how it is to raise children in Loudonville?"

"Please, call me Catherine," she replied with warmth in her eyes. "Yes, we have four children, two daughters and two sons," replied Mrs. Miller. "You will meet them this evening."

"Is Loudonville a safe place for children?" offered Anna Barbara.

"This is a safe town for us and our family, and I believe it will be so for your family as well. There is hardly any crime. Not only do we welcome newcomers, we need people to help grow our town. Most businesses are looking to hire, like we are. Newcomers come and stay a while, then move on out west. Many believe they want to be pioneers. They build a house, start the farm or new job, then sell and move on. These departures create opportunities to other newcomers to find farms or jobs."

✦

Carl and Anna Barbara stayed overnight with the Miller family. They met their four children, ages seven through fourteen. "Mr. Tangeman, are you going to move to Loudonville? I think Cincinnati would be more interesting," said fourteen-year-old Rebecca.

"I agree," replied Carl, taken aback by this bold comment. "There is a lot going on in Cincinnati with thousands of people. But some of those people want to cause trouble for immigrants like us."

"What is the most terrible thing you have ever seen happen?" asked twelve-year-old Robert.

"Robert, that is not a polite thing to ask our guests," inserted his mother.

Carl smiled to his host family. "Thank you, Mrs. Miller. Actually, Robert, I have a story about something that almost took my life," replied Carl. "Perhaps you will allow me to tell it after supper?"

His words met a chorus, "Yes, yes," and general excitement from all the children. Their enthusiasm lent credibility to the general notion that Loudonville was a safe, enjoyable place to make a living and raise children. For the children, the excitement of city life was attractive compared with their uneventful small town.

Following dinner, the Millers and Tangemans settled into the parlor to hear Carl's story. He began, "Several years ago I left Prussia with my first wife and two small children on our way to New York. Unfortunately, our ship encountered a ferocious storm on the Atlantic Ocean, that blew us off course to New York. Eventually, we landed in New Orleans, far from our destination. Do you know where New Orleans is located?" Asked Carl.

Robert answered, "Yes, I think it is in Louisiana, at the mouth of the Mississippi River.

"A few days later my first wife and children died of a fever. Subsequently, I had to decide what to do with my life. Should I make my way across the country and look for my brothers in New York, or give up and move elsewhere? What do you think I did?" asked Carl.

"You went to New York!" exclaimed Robert.

"Yes, that is exactly what I did," affirmed Carl. "My next problem was to decide how to travel across country to New York. There were only a few railroads at that time. Traveling by foot or horseback would take a very long time. The fastest way to travel was to take a river steamer up the Mississippi River, then on the Ohio River all the way to Pittsburgh, Pennsylvania. Something happened on the Mississippi River that almost took my life. I was on a river steamer named *The Talisman* for several days. Then very early the next morning there was a crash. *The Talisman* smashed head-on into the *Tempest*, another river steamer, moving downstream. River water poured onto the deck of *The Talisman*. In just a few minutes that deck tipped downward causing dozens of people to slide into the cold river. Most of them drowned."

"What happened to you?" asked seven-year-old James.

"That is the scariest part of the story," continued Carl. "I slid into the water, in the dark, and I didn't know how to swim. I moved my arms and legs trying to stay on the surface. I kicked off my leather boots and sloughed off my water-logged woolen jacket. Then I sank below the surface of the river. At that moment, I had to choose between giving up and sinking to the bottom of the river or fighting to get back to the surface. In that second, I decided to fight hard—for my next breath and, indeed, my life. All of the muscles in my arms and legs strained to lift me up through the murky water. I was totally alone, no one to help. Finally, I bumped against a floating chunk of wood, probably from the side of *The Talisman*. It was big enough to keep me and one other fella afloat. We held onto the wooden debris with one hand and paddled with the other until we came close enough to the shore to let go and crawl out of the water."

The Miller children broke out in applause. "That was a fine story. Thank you, Mr. Tangeman."

"Yes, that was an exciting story, Mr. Tangeman," enthused Mrs. Miller. "Children, now it is time for bed. I will come join you for prayers in a few minutes."

Meanwhile, Mr. Miller, Carl, and Anna Barbara stayed in the parlor to discuss his offer of employment in Loudenville. "Carl and Anna Barbara, you have seen our town and the foundry. I hope you have discovered this is a good opportunity for you and Anna Barbara."

"Anna Barbara and I have enjoyed visiting your family, your foundry, and the town. How do you see this town and your business expanding in the future?" asked Carl.

Mr. Miller replied, "Let me share what we know at this time. Ashland County was formed mostly from a portion of Richland County to our west in 1846. At that time, the county seat became Ashland, and Loudonville was promised to be the county seat of another new county to be formed with three nearby townships. And the Walhonding Canal was authorized by the state legislature to come up from the Blackfork River to Loudonville. In the very near future we expect great demand for our foundry to help build the canal locks."

"I am favorably impressed with all I have learned about Loudonville and your foundry. Anna Barbara and I have much to discuss. If you will excuse us, it has been a long day for Anna Barbara." Although Carl was intrigued with the possibility of moving to Loudonville and working for Mr. Miller, he did not want to express his feelings until he and Anna Barbara made their decision.

"Of course. Good night Carl and Anna Barbara," said Mr. Miller.

"Goodnight, Mr. and Mrs. Miller," replied Carl.

After they were in bed, Carl asked, "Anna Barbara, how was your day? What did you learn about Loudonville from Mrs. Miller?"

"My day was enjoyable. Mrs. Miller and I became acquainted, and she showed me around the town and answered my questions," explained Anna Barbara. "The schools are well established, and the Miller children are thriving as students. We walked by three churches including the Hanover Evangelical and Reformed Lutheran Church, similar to your church in Sulingen, and Zion Lutheran Church almost next door. What did you learn at the foundry?"

"The foundry is only a few years old. It has excellent equipment, and a good reputation. I think Mr. Miller's offer of employment is a sound opportunity for now and the business is likely to grow. I am ready to give notice to Mr. Greenwood at Eagle Ironworks and move here as soon as possible," continued Carl enthusiastically.

"Loudonville is a safe and welcoming town. It may be a fine town for us, but I am still thinking through the details of such a move," commented Anna Barbara.

The next morning at breakfast, Mr. Miller said, "Carl, I hope you have made a decision to work for our foundry. Catherine and I would like to be your sponsors as you settle into your new home."

Carl replied carefully, "Mr. Miller, you have made us a generous offer. And we can see ourselves living in Loudonville. At the same time, we will further discuss this momentous move on our trip back to Cincinnati. You will receive a telegram from me before a week has passed." The Millers and Tangemans shook hands cordially before Carl and Anna Barbara walked back to the train station in time to leave on the eight o'clock morning train west bound for Mansfield.

✦

"Anna Barbara, tell me what you are thinking about Loudonville. You said you were not ready to make a decision. What do you need to know? Or have you already decided this is not what we should do? I need to understand your thoughts, please," implored Carl. He was grateful for this job opportunity, and he believed his family would thrive in Loudonville, but he would not make this move without Anna Barbara's agreement. Anna Barbara seemed drawn into herself, and Carl could not read her expressions to know her thoughts and feelings.

Anna Barbara was silent for a few minutes. She thought positively about all they had seen and learned in Loudonville, but she was reluctant to simply say, "Yes," to this opportunity. She took a few moments to put her thoughts and feelings into words.

"Carl, I enjoyed our trip to Loudonville. Mr. and Mrs. Miller were warm and kind. They would likely become our best friends. And I could see our children in the faces of the Miller children. They were capable students and sincere young people. We will be pleased if ours become the same caliber of human beings. But something holds me back from this decision. I am feeling like I did when Margaretha and I left Ehningen, leaving Mama and Papa behind. We knew we would never see them again, and there is a part of me that stayed in the old country. I feel the same about leaving Cincinnati. I am sad about leaving Gretly behind. My first child will be born without my mother or Gretly with me. That feels like too much to bear," sniffed Anna Barbara, tears spilling from her eyes. She looked down at her hands that held a twisted linen handkerchief.

Carl thought over Anna Barbara's words. *This opportunity is so much to give up, but Anna Barbara will have to give up Margaretha, an enormous source of support in Cincinnati. The birth of her first child will be a time she will need support in a special womanly way.*

"My dear Anna Barbara. Thank you for telling me how you feel. This move will change our lives as we move away from Cincinnati. How can I make this move comfortable and good for you?" Carl asked. She had trusted him and their relationship enough to open her heart and share how she felt when she left her parents, other family, friends and her life back in Ehningen. Now he was asking her to move away from her family in Cincinnati.

After several minutes of silence, looking but not seeing the passing countryside, Anna Barbara turned and faced Carl. "Carl, if we bring Gretly with us to Loudonville, I will gladly come. She will keep me company while you are at work, and help keep house after the baby comes. If anything happens, . . ." Anna Barbara spoke the fear of her heart. "I need to have her with me when this child is born. I know I have your love and support, but I need Gretly to be with me and help me face whatever comes." For Anna Barbara who was still learning how Carl thought through family decisions, she was not sure how he might respond to her desire to have Gretly actually live with them. *Will he want to share our home with Margaretha? Will he be willing to support another family member?*

To her surprise, Carl's eyes lit up, and he responded almost immediately. "Yes, of course. You will need to have Gretly with you for the birth. And I know she will be a great help and comfort as we get settled in Loudonville. It will be difficult to move away from everyone we know in Cincinnati. If we do, I believe we will find a better life in Loudonville."

By this time, there were tears in the eyes of both Carl and Anna Barbara, as they faced their first sharp disagreement and came through to the other side with an agreeable solution. Carl had Anna Barbara's support to further the family's fortunes, and Anna Barbara learned that her well-being and protection were uppermost in his mind, especially through her first pregnancy. Finally, Carl learned the bond between Gretly and Anna Barbara was strong enough to influence where they choose to live during their lives in America.

✦

Carl and Anna Barbara arrived in Cincinnati late Saturday afternoon. They climbed into a waiting carriage that delivered them to their apartment. While Anna Barbara stretched out on their bed to rest up from the tiring train journey, Carl excused himself and walked quickly to the Saint Paulus Deutsche Evangelische Kirche parsonage.

"Carl, please come in," gestured Heinrich Schiedt. "Is Anna Barbara all right?"

"Yes, she is quite well, Brother Schiedt. I came to ask you and Wilhelmina for a great favor. Are you willing to host coffee and dessert for our siblings here at the parsonage next Sunday afternoon?" asked Carl.

"Yes, of course," replied Heinrich. "It is time for us to see the Tangemans again. We are happy to host your family."

"Thank you, Heinrich. I appreciate your help, Wilhelmina," replied Carl. "I will invite George and Elizabeth, Wilhelm, Louise, Wilhelmina, Marie Dorothee, and their families. Will you please invite Margaretha, too?"

"Yes, of course," agreed Heinrich.

Stretching out his legs, Carl moved quickly to George's and Elizabeth's apartment, then on to see Wilhelm at Mrs. Stolz's Boardinghouse. On his way back home to the apartment, he visited his sister Louise, who promised to pass along Carl's invitation to their other sisters.

✦

By three o'clock on Sunday of the following week, Carl's siblings arrived at the parsonage and found a seat or place to stand in the parlor. They had not been all together since the wedding of Carl and Anna Barbara the previous December. They brought one another up to date about their daily lives and news. Margaretha had received a letter from her parents. Wilhelm and George had their eye on another tobacconist shop in downtown Cincinnati. They had accumulated enough capital to expand their business.

Finally, Carl and Anna Barbara arrived and found their places in the parlor to the expectant glances of the rest of the family. George stood and spoke first, "Everyone, since we are all together, Elizabeth and I have the very best news. We are expecting a child. God willing, Elizabeth will be well and our first child will arrive this fall." Cheers erupted, and everyone offered congratulations to the happy couple. Being the first Tangeman brother to be married the previous summer, it seemed fitting that he and Elizabeth would welcome the first child, too.

The good news settled on the family gathering, then Carl stepped forward holding Anna Barbara's hand. "We have some good news, too. I am happy to announce that Anna Barbara and I are also expecting a child in the fall." Again, the room erupted in joyful applause and well wishes.

Elizabeth reached for Anna Barbara's hand, her face bright with anticipation, "We will have our babies together and raise them together. What wonderful news." Anna Barbara smiled faintly, reluctant to hear reactions to their next piece of news.

"That is not all," began Carl as he held Anna Barbara's hand. "Anna Barbara and I have decided to move to Loudonville. I have received an offer of employment with the Miller Foundry. It is more money than I can make here in Cincinnati. And Loudonville is a beautiful and safe small town in Ashland County. We can afford a house with a place for a garden. This is a good opportunity for our family. At the same time, we will miss seeing all of you as often as we do now. Of course, we will come back to Cincinnati for holidays. It takes about a day to travel by train. We will see all of you as often as possible."

By this time everyone had questions, but the mood and conversation level were much subdued. Gretly slipped to the back of the room where she struggled to grasp the news that Anna Barbara would soon move to the other side of Ohio. The thought of this separation from her sister left her empty, like sails that have lost their wind. Then she heard Carl call for their attention one last time.

"Dear family, I have one more announcement. Anna Barbara has a great task ahead. She will oversee this move, nurture our growing child and settle into a new community. Gretly, we will be forever grateful if you come with us to Loudonville. Anna Barbara and I invite you to help us both in this new endeavor. We will have a house big enough for all four of us. Will you come to help us in Loudonville?" he asked, beaming in anticipation for her response.

Gretly was stunned. Her fears of separation and loneliness vanished with Carl's invitation. Tearfully, she moved across the parlor and fell into Anna Barbara's arms. All was well again for the Schiedt sisters from Ehningen who would be together for as long as they could see into the future.

chapter 5

LEAVING CINCINNATI

LATE MARCH, 1854

Sporadic drizzle baptized the day with gloom adding to Wilhelm's forlorn mood. Up to this day he had denied the reality that his brother Carl, Anna Barbara, and Margaretha were moving to Loudonville. Not prone to feelings of pessimism, Wilhelm felt an unexpected sadness at the thought of remaining behind in Cincinnati.

His mood brightened as he drove the tobacco business buckboard to collect Margaretha at the parsonage. She answered his tap on the door knocker and smiled broadly, showing that she welcomed this move with Anna Barbara and Carl. She was also pleased to see Wilhelm, and she welcomed the time she spent with him, as they drove the eight blocks to Carls and Anna Barbara's apartment.

"Good morning, Gretly," greeted Wilhelm, struggling to keep regret from his voice and face.

"Good morning, Wilhelm," replied Margaretha spiritedly. "Thank you for coming for me and my belongings."

Looking at Margaretha's small trunk and canvas bag, he said, "I see you are ready for your move to Loudonville. Here, may I carry your bags?"

"Thank you, Wilhelm. I have these two items," replied Margaretha. She checked for her handbag and umbrella, then turned toward her brother and sister-in-law. Wilhelm removed the trunk and canvas bag to the buckboard. As was the custom of chain immigration, Margaretha and Anna Barbara had been sheltered and sponsored by their brother and sister-in-law while they settled in Cincinnati. Heinrich and Wilhelmina Schiedt gave Margaretha a warm hug and tried to hide their tears. It was a comfort to them that the sisters were moving to Loudonville together.

Margaretha was quiet with her own thoughts on the rainy ride beside Wilhelm to her sister's apartment. She dabbed her eyes, then blew her nose on an embroidered handkerchief and tucked it into her handbag. At the apartment, she took Wilhelm's hand and climbed down from the front seat. Carl offered his hand to Anna Barbara, then Margaretha, helping them step onto the black trunk and then the floor of the wagon bed. Finally, Carl and Wilhelm heaved the black and camelback oak shipping trunks onto the back of the buckboard.

"Anna Barbara, will you be comfortable sitting on this trunk? It is only a few minutes to the train depot," asked Carl.

"Yes, I will be fine," Anna Barbara nodded her agreement and moved closer to Gretly under the umbrella they shared.

On the rain-soaked streets, the buckboard slipped through soupy mud. It made for a softer ride than when the mud was baked hard on a sunny day. Carl was concerned that Anna Barbara would have a smooth ride for the sake of her pregnancy. He wanted to be settled in Loudonville as soon as possible for her health.

Wilhelm carefully guided the team of horses and buckboard to the front entrance of the Cincinnati train depot. After Carl helped Anna Barbara safely to the sidewalk, Wilhelm put his hands on Margaretha's waist and lifted her down to the ground. She turned to thank him, and his eyes held hers for several seconds. They were warm and lively, and Wilhelm would miss seeing Gretly in Cincinnati. He did not realize at the time that Margaretha had similar feelings. She was too shy to reveal herself to him directly, and he was not accustomed to reading subtle cues to the feelings of a young woman.

◆

Margaretha had listened intently when Anna Barbara described Loudonville. Still, she was apprehensive and on edge until she actually saw her new home in this remote, rural Ohio town. Perhaps life would be more like their Bavarian hometown, Ehningen, near Boblingen. If so, she might like it more than the agitated city of Cincinnati.

Compared with travel by horse and buggy in the spring mud season, the train trip to Loudonville was luxurious. Even so, Anna Barbara was weary from the jiggling and jostling in train cars by the time they arrived at the Loudonville train station. As promised, Mr. Miller met Carl, Anna Barbara, and Margaretha with a wagon to transport them and their belongings. Carl introduced Margaretha to Mr. Miller, who announced, "Mrs. Miller and I insist you stay with us until you secure housing. And I have a few possibilities for you to visit at your convenience."

"Thank you, Mr. Miller. We appreciate your hospitality very much," said Carl. Then he turned to his wife. "Anna Barbara, would you like to go to the Millers' home or accompany me to look for our home in Loudonville?"

"I am weary from the train trip. Can you look for a house without me?" Anna Barbara spoke in low tones into Carls' ear.

"First, let's take the women to your home," said Carl to Mr. Miller. "Then I will look for a house while we still have some daylight."

Carl looked for a house the way he approached a metalwork task, with energy and diligence. Mr. Miller accompanied him to see three houses for rent. Carl chose the four-room house that was midway and walking distance between the Miller Foundry and the shops on town square. The following day he delivered their trunks to the new house.

For two days, Anna Barbara and Margaretha scrubbed floors, walls, and ceilings in their bungalow on North Adams Street. They hung green muslin curtains lent to them by Mrs. Miller. Working together, the Schiedt sisters transformed their new house into a clean, comfortable home. Carl began his new job with the assurance his wife and sister-in-law were happily immersed in settling into their new home and community. Already, he felt grateful that Gretly came with them to Loudonville.

"Gretly, how do you find our new home? And Loudonville?" asked Anna Barbara as she scrubbed the kitchen floor.

"Loudonville seems fine to me. There are more shops than I expected. Best of all, we are together, and you are expecting your first child," replied Margaretha with excitement, and the sisters embraced.

"I was afraid of the nativists, and avoided them in Cincinnati. Here, I don't feel signs of tension with nativists or Catholics," commented Anna Barbara. "The locals welcome us. They are hopeful and helpful. Apparently, they need newcomers to work in the chair factory and other businesses like Mr. Miller's foundry."

"Oh, Anna Barbara, I already enjoy this town. And I enjoy keeping house with you. Now that the house is clean from top to bottom, let's begin our garden," suggested Margaretha. Before the daylight receded, Margaretha had raked and staked out a garden plot.

chapter 6
ESTABLISHING ROOTS

"The glory of gardening: hands in the dirt, head in the sun, heart with nature. To nurture a garden is to feed not just the body, but the soul."

– Alfred Austin

LATE MARCH, 1854

Yellow-green buckeye flowers burst to life only to hide beneath a morning's mist. The stems and blossoms of these native shrubs sheltered beneath a forest of oak, hickory, and birch along the Black Fork of the Mohican River circumnavigating Loudonville. On a pristine day dawn overspread the forest with light and warmth. Soon enough shafts of sunshine pierced fog and penetrated to budding leaves, coaxing them to awaken and uncurl.

"Anna Barbara, the house is clean, and neat. This is the kind of day Mama planted her garden. I remember the sunshine and fresh air. She bought her seeds from *Schwartz' Baumarkt* in Ehningen. Let's start our garden, too," suggested Margaretha with a lilt in her voice. "It may be muddy from the rain last week, but I think we should begin today."

"I agree. Let's go buy seeds from Stout Hardware Store on the town square. Corn, lettuce, beans, carrots, and seed potatoes," Anna Barbara responded enthusiastically. The sisters returned from the hardware store with their seeds, a garden hoe, and spade. All afternoon the sun shone through low, patchy clouds and evaporated droplets of moisture that clung to compacted clumps of soil in the backyard.

Later in the afternoon, Margaretha peeled potatoes for supper while her sister scraped carrots and cored apples. "I think the seed potatoes should be planted near the back of the garden in mounded hills, like Mama's," began Gretly.

45

"Don't you think the corn will grow best at the very back of the garden?" responded Anna Barbara.

"Yes, of course, it will form a frame for the potato mounds and smaller plants nearer the house," said Gretly.

"We will enjoy our garden from the kitchen, just like Mama could always see hers," said Anna Barbara.

"It will be like sharing the garden with Mama," replied Margaretha thoughtfully, as she wiped perspiration from her brow. Carl's footsteps on the back porch diverted their attention.

"Carl, welcome home," greeted Anna Barbara in a lilting voice. "We have something to show you."

"What have the two of you been doing? Cooking? Baking?" asked Carl, teasing his wife and sister-in-law.

"Yes, of course, my dear," said Anna Barbara, "and something much better." She took Carl's hand and led him through the back porch. "We bought seeds and tools for our garden. The soil is too wet right now. Maybe in a day or two you could help us prepare the soil?"

"By this Saturday, if the soil is dry enough, I will use that beautiful spade to break up the clods and turn the earth over. Would you like me to ask Mr. Miller if he knows where to get decayed farm manure to enrich the soil?" asked Carl.

"Yes, please," replied Margaretha. "I remember Mama always asked Mr. Neuerbauer for his oldest, crusty sheep manure."

Two more days provided enough sunshine to dry out the soil to the point it was more loose than sticky. On Saturday afternoon, Carl brought home a third gunnysack full of dried manure from Mr. Miller's neighbor, who kept three horses. First, he turned over the soil in the garden plot Margaretha had marked off. He drove the shovel tip downward, lifted upward and released a thick layer of dark, loamy soil. Next, he used the shovel tip to slice straight down and break up each clump. This rich, worm-digested dirt showed promise. He spread out the dry clumps of manure and turned over the soil once again to thoroughly mix in the enrichment.

On the following Monday after breakfast with Carl, the Schiedt sisters gathered their tools, seeds, and supplies and trooped out to their garden plot. "Gretly, let's stake out the rows. Here, take this twig and tie on the twine. I will tie the other end to another twig," suggested Anna Barbara. Margaretha used the hoe and carefully drew an indentation beneath the twine guide. The sisters repeated this process four times. They planted lettuce, carrots, beans, and corn in the rows and seed potatoes in hills in front of the corn row.

It was more than the anticipation of crisp, fresh vegetables to enrich their meals and sustain their bodies, that drew the two women to invest this time and effort. The garden was a connection to their lives in the old country. Margaretha and Anna Barbara remembered hours spent in the company of their mother while they planted seeds and discarded weeds from arrow-straight rows of vegetables in Ehningen. The garden was where they heard stories of their grandmother's garden, pesky rabbits who stole the lettuce, and years when bounteous crops came with seemingly little effort.

Through April, the womb of the Ohio earth bulged with expectation, not unlike Anna Barbara's expanding midsection. Invisible at the lacy surface of the garden, life-sustaining corn, carrots, lettuce, and bean seeds absorbed droplets of moisture from recent rain. Life-beginning rays of spring sunshine pierced the earth and warmed the droplets, imperceptibly releasing a life force from the heart of each seed. In this way life began below the surface of the earth and inevitably stretched upward. In a matter of weeks, embryonic plants, warmed and nourished by manure-dressed soil, valiantly broke through the crust of the earth.

Above the surface of the earth, meadowlarks and mourning doves swooped through the half-light of dusk and sang triumphant anthems of spring to herald the new growth. At the brim of dank, dark garden soil, molecules of steam ascended through a crooked ladder of minuscule hollow spaces and escaped to freshen the air. Fragrances of the vegetable garden and apple blossoms wafted through bedroom windows each night, invading Margaretha's, Anna Barbara's, and Carl's nostrils and stirring their dreams.

The awakening earth was only one aspect of their existence that supported new life in 1854. Anna Barbara felt with pleasure her twenty-four--year-old body adjusting to the belly bump that now filled out her frame in an unmistakably pregnant manner. Carl noticed her physical changes from across the room and close by. When he came up behind her, wrapped his arms around her belly and nuzzled his affection into the side of her neck, Anna Barbara felt completely loved and comfortable in her new home.

✦

Springtime in Cincinnati agreed with Wilhelm. He relished the balmy days that began with a walk down Race Street to the tobacco warehouses near the Ohio River. On Saturday afternoons he played the new game of baseball with a group of fellows from the warehouse district. Often he joined George for lunch at their favorite outdoor *biergarten* in Over-the-Rhine. And Mrs. Stolz welcomed his help preparing and planting her vegetable garden at the boarding house. Foregoing those appealing pursuits, Wilhelm eagerly boarded the Cleveland, Columbus, and Cincinnati Railway passenger train to visit Carl, Anna Barbara, and Margaretha in Loudonville.

As the train prepared to depart, steam hissed, swirled, and belched from the noisy locomotive. Wilhelm likened the commotion from the matte black iron horse to a thoroughbred flexing restless muscles for a strenuous race. He compared his own fidgety mood to a two-year-old worked up to run his first serious horse race.

Wilhelm missed Carl and the Schiedt sisters after they relocated to central Ohio in March. Their letters supplied newsy bits about settling into life in their new home, but it wasn't like seeing them regularly on weekends and sometimes during the week. Wilhelm missed having a beer with Carl when his brother stopped by Mrs. Stolz's boardinghouse after work. On weekends, the three brothers, Carl, George, and Wilhelm, had often met at the Alemania Club. Of course, George brought Elizabeth, Carl brought Anna Barbara, and Margaretha came too. These times were what Wilhelm missed the most now that his brother, his wife and sister-in-law lived in Loudonville. He still talked with George at the warehouse daily. He sometimes stopped by the Alemania Club, but he found no one he enjoyed as much as the camaraderie of all three brothers, their wives, and Margaretha.

The iron wheels of Wilhelm's train lurched, then slowly turned, a signal for him to run the few remaining steps and leap from the platform onto the steps of a moving passenger car. Pulling away from the dome-covered depot, this daily train passed through the outskirts of Cincinnati, and across hardwood-covered hillsides in full leaf. Within the hour Wilhelm's train sped past thriving farms where wheat stems and beginning corn stalks carpeted spring green fields.

Wilhelm had time to think through how unsettled he felt about his future. Since Carl and the Schiedt sisters moved to Loudonville, he had felt alone and increasingly distant from Carl and George. Both of his older brothers were now married to beautiful German women with whom they shared language and a history from the old country. And both couples were expecting their first children. Their lives were moving forward with growing families while he felt that his life was standing still. Although he earned a good living in the tobacco business, he saw the happiness of his brothers and began to wonder if such good fortune could ever be his, too.

That evening, Wilhelm arrived in Loudonville at the depot and spotted Carl on the platform. Carl's eyes lit up to see him step off the train. They shook hands vigorously, and Carl grasped his brother's shoulder warmly. "Welcome to Loudonville. I am glad you are here. Come, it is only a short walk to our house. Are you hungry? I smelled a beef stew cooking for supper."

Wilhelm smiled, "Yes, I will enjoy a home-cooked German meal. And a walk feels good after sitting on the train all day. It was a beautiful trip past farms with good stands of wheat and corn. Are you still thinking about farming? The farms look prosperous in this area," said Wilhelm.

"*Ja*, I think about buying land, but I don't want to take out a mortgage to do so. For now, I have a good job, and we are saving to eventually buy a place," responded Carl. "I have been learning everything I can about farming here in Ashland County. This weekend there is a demonstration of the new McCormick Reaper in Hayesville. Would you like to come with me to see it?"

"Yes, very much," said Wilhelm with a grin. "I know crop prices have been high, and farmers are making money on wheat and corn. Let's go see how the new machinery works."

Fifteen minutes later the Tangeman brothers arrived at the home of Carl, Anna Barbara, and Margaretha. It was a one-level, square house with front and back porches, situated within a fenced backyard. Wilhelm noticed a small garden behind the house with carrots, lettuce, and green beans already coming up.

"Anna Barbara, Gretly, we're home," Carl called as he opened the front door. The two women emerged from the kitchen.

"Wilhelm, it is good of you to come for a visit. We can't wait to hear the news from Cincinnati," declared Anna Barbara as she grasped his outstretched hands in both of hers.

"Anna Barbara, it is good to see you again, too. I noticed your garden in the back yard. I see it is not the only thing growing for you," replied

Wilhelm with a smile and a wink. Anna Barbara was clearly showing the child she was carrying. He turned to her sister, "And Margaretha, it is good to see you too. How do you like living in Loudonville?" he asked. Their eyes met and held a few seconds longer than needed for politeness. Carl and Anna Barbara noticed, but looked away.

"Loudonville is a fine small town. It reminds me of the town we came from in Bavaria. It is easy to get to know people, especially those who speak German," replied Margaretha.

"Is there a special part of town for those who speak German, like we have in Cincinnati?" asked Wilhelm.

"Not really. Loudonville does not have a section like Over-the-Rhine. The Hanover Evangelical Church is where we have made friends with other German folks. Most of our neighbors are friendly, too," answered Margaretha.

Anna Barbara withdrew to the kitchen to check the beef stew. It was ready to serve in wooden bowls at the small corner table which was barely big enough for four people. She delayed an announcement of supper for a few minutes to allow Margaretha and Wilhelm a little time to themselves.

Away from the large family gatherings and weekend visits to German social clubs in Cincinnati, Margaretha and Wilhelm now had time to spend with each other. Carl and Anna Barbara were pleased to allow for the possibility his brother and her sister might develop feelings for each other.

◆

On Saturday morning, Carl and Wilhelm awoke before seven o'clock. When they finished breakfast, Carl cheerfully previewed their morning, "Wilhelm, I have hired horses from the Lancombe Livery. It is a little over an hour's ride to Hayesville. Thank you for breakfast, Anna Barbara. We are off to learn about McCormick farm machinery."

Carl and Wilhelm rode ten miles north on the Hayesville Road through the village of McKay and past green fields of grains. Within a mile of the Hayesville crossroads, they noticed a crowd gathered around a reaper machine on the west side of the road. The brothers secured their horses on the hitching rail and joined the rest of the onlookers. "I remember seeing farmers in the old country cut wheat and other grains by hand with swings of a scythe. Then, they tied shocks of wheat stems together and left them upright to dry in the fields. It was exhausting work," commented Carl.

"This McCormick Reaper is even more impressive in person than in the newspaper articles," added Wilhelm. The machine was pulled by two horses and controlled by a rider on a seat above the cutting platform. With the reaper, one man could do the work of five men cutting wheat by hand with scythes.

On their ride back to Loudonville, Wilhelm declared, "That reaper was impressive. If I had a farm, I would buy that machine."

"I am inclined to agree with you," replied Carl. He hoped Wilhelm would turn to farming sometime in the future, perhaps in this part of Ohio.

✦

Anna Barbara and Margaretha tended their new garden together, usually right after breakfast, when the earth was slightly cool to the touch. Free from the distractions of learning English and navigating foreign influences and cultural changes, they drew comfort from tending their traditional German garden.

Often in May rainy drizzle kept Anna Barbara and Margaretha indoors. They did not see the first carrot sprigs break through the soil. The carrots were visible in a straight green row by the time the garden soil dried out enough to accept visitors near the end of the month. Carl brought home scrap boards from the foundry and laid them as walkways between vegetable rows. Margaretha carefully stepped between rows to cut the first tender lettuce leaves and pull slender, moist carrots.

JUNE, 1854

June arrived packaged in a thunderstorm that cracked the sky with lightening and invaded the air like tumbling boulders crashing down from on high. Although similar to summer storms in the old country, this Ohio storm was louder and blew punishing winds and unruly rain throughout the night. The garden survived, but lost stems and leaves of some plants. Three corn stalks were left bent as if reaching to touch the ground. Carl tied the damaged stalks to head-high wooden stakes. The corn continued to live and grow, emitting squeaky, stretching sounds at night that were audible from the bedroom windows.

✦

On a summer evening late in June, Carl arrived home especially hot, sweaty and hungry. He washed up on the back porch, then joined Anna Barbara and Margaretha at the kitchen table relocated into the shade of apple trees in the back yard. A merciful breeze cooled their skins and carried familiar fragrances.

Spicy, sharply vinegary meat sauce spilled over the edge of the beef roast, the aromas tickling their noses with memories, surrounding the three of them like a mother's quilt. "This sauerbraten is the best I have ever tasted. Are these fresh vegetables from our garden?" exclaimed Carl.

"These are the first potatoes of the season," Anna Barbara replied with a twinkle in her eye. "I reached into the sides of the potato hills, felt around and slipped out the bigger ones," she gestured with her hand sneaking into the side of an imaginary potato mound. "I never knew a potato that smelled so sweet," she said with a smile.

"In the next couple weeks the potato hills and onions will be ready to dig," added Margaretha enthusiastically. "The root cellar will be filled for winter." She clapped her hands excitedly.

"Will you let me dig the potato hills?" offered Carl with a sheepish grin. He understood the pleasure the two women derived from their garden and felt he should ask permission to join the vegetable harvest.

"Yes, if you have time, perhaps one evening next week," replied Anna Barbara smiling shyly and feeling Carl's playful love and gentle care.

On mid-July evenings, Carl dug the hills of potatoes while the sun seemed to hesitate momentarily, then slip below the horizon. Carl filled their largest garden basket with the lowly vegetable that sustained thousands of lives in the old country during times of famine. His satisfaction with their garden vegetables was boundless.

chapter 7

ANNA BARBARA'S BABY

The summer heat of 1854 invaded Anna Barbara's body like an unwelcome stranger. Sultriness prickled her skin and fired up her body. She perspired continuously. Sweat drenched her linen tent dress multiple times a day. While she stretched out to escape in a nap, the relentless heat seemed to stretch minutes into hours. Anna Barbara could not imagine coping with this oppressive heat without Margaretha at her side.

As each summer week passed in the relentless heat, Anna Barbara felt ever more ready for her delivery day. At the same time she thought of the inherent dangers and women who had died in childbirth. Her mother had survived multiple deliveries, but her aunt in Bavaria died during her first pregnancy. Anna Barbara would need an experienced midwife to help her first delivery.

Anna Barbara's physical discomforts accumulated to a tipping point of intense yearning to welcome this baby into her arms. A sense of urgency replaced her earlier feelings of apprehension for delivery.

On her five-foot-four-inch frame, Anna Barbara's baby had no place to go except extending her belly straight forward. She moved carefully through doorways and slid gingerly into the chair at the kitchen table. She planned her movements and tried to avoid sudden belly shifts.

Anna Barbara was almost, but not completely, comfortable resting on her bed. On a particular late August afternoon, time crawled more slowly than the moving speck that crept diagonally across the ceiling above Anna Barbara's face. At first, the speck moved so slowly, she was not sure it actually moved at all. An hour later she awoke from a nap, a brief respite from the robust kicking within her ripening belly. The speck had moved a full three inches. She recognized the moving dark brown spot as a spider! In her clean house!

"Gretly, Gretly!" she shouted for her sister.

"Whatever is wrong? Are you all right?" Margaretha inquired as she rushed into the bedroom.

"Yes, I am fine. There is a spider," she explained and pointed to the mobile eight-legged speck on the ceiling. "Can you get rid of it?"

Margaretha dispatched the spider with one mighty swat of her cleaning rag.

Through the summer, Wilhelm's visits to Loudonville broke the monotony of heat-saturated days. He brought news from Cincinnati with characteristic enthusiasm and good humor. When Wilhelm visited, Carl enjoyed talking about farming and sharing his insights. Sometimes they rented horses and rode out to peruse pieces of land for sale. Wilhelm reserved his evenings for neighborhood walks with Margaretha.

Two rows of corn grew majestically along the back of the garden, standing watch over the drying remains of potatoes, carrots, onions, beans, and lettuce of the bounteous garden. Pearly tassels crowned the tubular corn stalks and stretched like fingers reaching toward the sun. August crawled toward fall, and the tassels bent and leaned downward, a signal the corn was nearly ready to be harvested.

In the intense summer heat Anna Barbara stayed inside during the middle of the day and wiped her skin with a cool cloth and fanned herself. Meanwhile, Margaretha harvested the vegetables and packed mature potatoes into wooden boxes, separating them with newspapers. Then she braided together onion stems to be hung from hooks in the root cellar below the house. Carl carried the boxes down to the root cellar and stacked them neatly along the cool walls.

Carl noticed how slowly Anna Barbara moved around the kitchen with one, then the other hand on a hip. "Anna Barbara, that was a delicious supper, especially the corn on the cob," commented Carl with sincere appreciation for a fine supper following a long day of work.

"Thank you, Carl. I'm glad you enjoyed Margaretha's cooking this evening," replied Anna Barbara.

"Are you feeling well enough to take a walk after dinner or would you prefer to rest?" asked Carl.

"I am feeling fine, but this wee one has been very active today. Yes, I would like a short walk in a gentle breeze," replied Anna Barbara.

"I will clean up the dishes while you two take your evening stroll. The moon is just coming up to light your way," interjected Margaretha.

The evening breezes cooled Anna Barbara, and she relaxed in the company of her husband who was also her best friend. *My time must be drawing near, or perhaps that is wishful thinking. I feel large enough to have a healthy baby this evening.* The thought of having Margaretha and Carl by her side buoyed her spirits and briefly overshadowed the aches and stretches she felt most of the time. Then she thought of Mama and Papa and how much she missed them. Her immigrant self alternated between anticipation of this growing life in her belly and memories of her parents and her old life in Germany. Her childhood in her family of origin did not prepare her to be an immigrant in America; it barely gave her the courage to step on the ship that carried her to the new world.

"What are you thinking?" asked Carl.

"Oh, Carl, I was thinking about Mama and Papa. I miss them," replied Anna Barbara with a catch in her voice.

"Of course you miss them. From everything you have told me, they love you very much," replied Carl. "Do you see how beautiful the moon is this evening? Your parents see this very same moon. They are thinking of you and praying for you and your baby," he said as he took Anna Barbara into his arms and soothed her quiet tears.

On the first Friday in September, Wilhelm arrived by train from Cincinnati. He came to see Margaretha and to support Anna Barbara and Carl as they prepared for the arrival of their first child. Anna Barbara was in good spirits, eager to meet her very active son or daughter. Wilhelm returned to Cincinnati on Sunday afternoon.

On Tuesday, September 5, 1854, Anna Barbara awoke at dawn with a dull back ache that wrapped around her sides. In a few minutes the telltale back ache subsided, leaving Anna Barbara relieved. In several minutes the back ache returned as Carl rolled toward her and opened his eyes. "Anna Barbara, are you all right? Why are you awake? Are you having pains?"

"Carl, I am fine. I have a backache that comes and goes. Otherwise, I feel fine, really good. I will get up and prepare breakfast. Later this morning I will go shopping at the dry goods store," replied Anna Barbara with a broad smile. While Carl washed and dressed for the day, Anna Barbara felt another creeping backache. Again it stopped. She washed and dressed and helped Margaretha to prepare breakfast.

"Anna Barbara, is it your time? Should I stay home today?" asked Carl. He set the table for his wife, sister-in-law and himself.

Anna Barbara replied, "There is no need for you to stay home. The backache is gone. It may not come back for hours or days according to Mrs. Miller. I feel better than I have for several days. You should go to work. Margaretha is here with me. She will find Mrs. Watson, the midwife, if need be. Mrs. Miller will stop by to check on us after lunch."

Margaretha stayed with Anna Barbara as contractions started, then stopped, throughout Tuesday. They decided not to visit the dry goods store. When Carl returned home early from work, Margaretha met him at the front door, "Carl, please go find Mrs. Watson. The contractions are steady, about five minutes apart. Anna Barbara is fine, but she will need Mrs. Watson this evening."

Carl could not help making comparisons to his first wife's labors which were long and difficult. The sooner he found Mrs. Watson, everyone would feel better. A prayer for a safe delivery passed his lips as he slipped out the front door.

✦

Anna Barbara was stronger than the demands of her labor through the night. Margaretha and Carl took turns being with her as the contractions prepared her body for delivery. The first light of day filtered through the linen curtains, and Mrs. Watson commented, "Anna Barbara, you are made for having babies. Listen for my instructions. Your baby will be here in a few minutes."

Anna Barbara, with the support of Margaretha and Carl, pushed, then stopped, at Mrs. Watson's directions. With care and skill she led Anna Barbara safely through the delivery of her first born. "You have a healthy baby boy," announced Mrs. Watson. And he sang to his mother's heart with his first breath and bleating cry.

Carl beamed with joy and relief to know his son had arrived safely and Anna Barbara had survived her ordeal. When Mrs. Watson placed the new babe in Carl's arms, tears streamed down his face. This moment of haunting euphoria did not erase his memory of the two children he lost in New Orleans, but it grew and filled Carl's heart to overflowing throughout his life.

Anna Barbara rested and nursed her son while Margaretha and Mrs. Watson replaced the bedsheets and tidied up the bedroom. Mrs. Watson stayed to be sure Anna Barbara was healthy before she returned home. Carl thanked Mrs. Watson, paid her for her services and bid her farewell. He walked quickly to Anna Barbara's side, tears still in his eyes. "Anna Barbara, this moment is like no other. You have survived and we have a healthy son," Carl murmured contentedly, and they both made over the wonder of this fresh human being.

Paul George Tangeman was born September 6, 1854. Carl sent a telegram to his brother, George, announcing the birth of his son, his brother's namesake. George joyously shared the news with the rest of the Tangeman and Schiedt family members.

Wilhelm returned to Loudonville on September 16 to attend his nephew's baptism. With adequate sleep and Margaretha's tender care, Anna Barbara felt stronger each day, walking gingerly around the house and garden. Paul George was an easy baby who ate and slept and basked in the attention of his parents and aunt and uncle.

Paul George Tangeman was baptized on the afternoon of September 17, 1854, at Hanover Evangelical and Reformed Church, on North Union Street in Loudonville, Ohio. The baptism was attended by Carl, Anna Barbara, Margaretha, Wilhelm, Mr. and Mrs. Miller, their children, and a few other congregants. After the baptism ceremony, attendees were invited to the Tangeman home for a reception.

Wilhelm raised his beer stein and offered a toast, "Carl and Anna Barbara, congratulations on your healthy, strong and handsome new son, Paul George Tangeman. All of us join you to celebrate his birth and baptism. May you all enjoy long, healthy lives together. *Prost, prost!*" Friends and family raised their steins and cheered, "To Paul George!"

chapter 8

THE COURTSHIP

After the last reception guests stepped into the faltering afternoon sunshine, Carl, Anna Barbara, Margaretha, and Wilhelm sat down in the parlor in weary contentment. Paul George slept in his cradle, affording his parents the opportunity to rest following a festive baptism and celebration.

"Anna Barbara, your son was a perfect gentlemen. He slept through his baptism even as the water trickled down his forehead," began Margaretha.

"Ja, he could not have been more cooperative," Anna Barbara replied as she remembered the ancient ritual that marked the acceptance of this child into the community of the church.

"Would you like to lie down, dear sister? This day was taxing for us all," offered Margaretha. Anna Barbara gratefully withdrew to the bedroom to rest. Margaretha proceeded to clear the table while the brothers remained in the parlor.

"Carl, your family appears to be thriving in Loudonville," began Wilhelm after he settled on a side chair. "You have a good job, a loving wife. Paul George is healthy, and I'm sure, happy to have survived his baptism. It seems like this small town life is beneficial for your family."

"I enjoy my job at the Miller Foundry. Business is very good and Mr. Miller needs to hire another blacksmith," replied Carl, not sure where Wilhelm's line of thinking was leading. "Perhaps more important than my good wages is the sense of safety we both feel. There have been no attacks from nativists, perhaps because there are plenty of jobs for everyone. Now that we have a child, it is even more important that we live in a safe community."

Wilhelm leaned forward, hands clasped and head bowed in deep thought. In a few moments he lifted his gaze and spoke directly to his brother. "Carl, I have decided it is time for me to begin courting Margaretha. Last week I spoke to Heinrich, and he gave his blessing for our courtship to begin. If it is all right with you, I plan to visit Loudonville about every other weekend this fall," Wilhelm spoke with a catch in his throat that betrayed his strong feelings for Margaretha. Wilhelm stood up to break the moment of intense emotion. Carl rose from his chair, too.

"Willhelm, I am so pleased for you. Yes, of course, we welcome your visits and wish you well in your courtship," Carl replied as he shook Wilhelm's hand heartily, then embraced his brother.

After supper, Wilhelm and Margaretha asked to be excused for a walk around the Loudonville town square. Wilhelm rested his hand gently on Margaretha's waist as they swished their shoes through oak, maple, and chestnut leaves. On this warm, fall Sunday evening the only sounds to be heard were the crinkling and crushing of dry leaves under the couple's rhythmic foot falls.

Carl and Anna Barbara relaxed in their parlor and played with Paul George while Wilhelm and Margaretha enjoyed a long walk. Carl asked, "What do you think about Wilhelm and Gretly? Might they be getting serious?" He hoped Margaretha had shared her feelings about Wilhelm with her sister."

Anna Barbara replied thoughtfully, "I can see that Margaretha enjoys Wilhelm's company. And she likes the way he is outgoing, always thinking of ways to advance his business interests. I think he has a sense of humor that makes her happy to share his company."

"My brother gets along well with most people, but he has never had a close relationship with a woman. He has never courted anyone."

"Have you noticed how they almost block out everyone else when they are together?" asked Anna Barbara thoughtfully. "And I think he likes to hear her sing lullabies to Paul George."

"Wilhelm spoke with me this evening about his intention to court Margaretha. Perhaps we should be ready for a wedding. They seem to be a good match," concluded Carl.

"Carl, what wonderful news. Yes, they will be very happy together," said Anna Barbara with a smile.

Through the fall of 1854, Wilhelm visited Loudonville and courted Margaretha about every other weekend. Carl and Anna Barbara welcomed him to their home while Margaretha welcomed him to her heart. Wilhelm easily fell deeply in love with Margaretha. Her beauty, her sincere interest, and her warm personality convinced Wilhelm he wanted this courtship to end in their engagement and marriage. On neighborhood walks, they shared their dreams and and hopes for the future. Underlying his feelings was an appreciation for the language and German culture they shared. In this land of people from many different traditions, Wilhelm was attracted to a life with Margaretha that would be a comfortable extension of their lives from the old country. The more time they spent together, the more he imagined marriage and his future with Margaretha.

Margaretha was charmed by Wilhelm's quick wit and playful personality. And he had a successful tobacco business. Finally, the fact that Margaretha's sister was married to Wilhelm's brother boded well for a lifetime of close associations between the couples.

Carl, Anna Barbara, Paul George, and Margaretha boarded the train in Loudonville on December 23, 1854 for their first visit to Cincinnati since Paul George's birth. They were all anxious to see George and Elizabeth and their new baby boy, Charles. Wilhelm and the other Tangeman brothers and sisters would all attend Christmas dinner at their sister Louise's home. They planned to call on Heinrich and Wilhelmina Schiedt and Mrs. Stolz during the visit, too.

Three days before Christmas, Wilhelm met his brother's growing family and Margaretha at the Cincinnati train depot with a hired carriage. Anna Barbara, Carl, and baby Paul George occupied the back seat, while Margaretha joined Wilhelm on the front seat. In low tones, they shared the private musings of a couple in love. He delivered Carl and family to the home of their older sister, Louise, which had plenty of room for guests. Margaretha accompanied Wilhelm to return the carriage. Then he escorted her on a leisurely walk to her former home at the parsonage.

The first generation of Tangeman siblings in America (Carl, George, Wilhelm, Louise, Wilhelmine, and Marie Dorothee and their families) gathered for Christmas dinner at the home of Louise and her husband, Otto Otten. Beneath their surface happiness were memories of holiday times back in the old country. They spoke German and feasted on *lebkucken, sauerbraten* and dumplings, potatoes, and apples, and sang the traditional German hymns, "Silent Night" and "*O, Tannenbaum.*"

Throughout the day, Charles Otto and Paul George, the three- and four-month-old Tangeman sons, respectively, were passed around, tickled for smiles and held high in celebration. These two were the first generation of

Tangemans born in the United States, a good omen of the family's continued well-being and future prospects.

After dessert was served, Wilhelm asked for the attention of his family, "I have an announcement for all of you. I am pleased to tell you that Margaretha Schiedt has agreed to marry me." She rose and he raised her hand in his to the cheers of everyone. This declaration was of little surprise to the extended Tangeman family. Many noisy congratulations, winks, and nods ensued. "When is the wedding?" "Where will you live?" "Now we know why you made all those trips to Loudonville." It made official what family members had suspected for the past several months.

"*Probst, probst*! Now I understand why you sent over your favorite dark beer! We need another round to celebrate my brother Wilhelm's engagement to Anna Barbara's sister Margaretha!" declared George.

Later in the afternoon, Friedrich Otten, Louise's older son, played traditional German polkas to the joyful dancing of younger and older Tangemans alike.

✦

Now that their engagement was official, Wilhelm and Margaretha needed to decide where to live after their wedding, Cincinnati or Loudonville? The cigar business was thriving in Cincinnati, making that city the obvious choice for financial reasons. Alternatively, Margaretha preferred to live in Loudonville, close to her sister. Not only did they share many conversations over their daily work, Margaretha also wanted to stay close to Anna Barbara whenever her own first child arrived if she and Wilhelm were blessed with children. This was the first conflict faced by the young couple who were compatible in most other ways.

Margaretha spent every day of her Christmas visit to Cincinnati with her fiancé. They took long walks when the weather permitted, and visited the Alemania Club to see friends and share a meal during times of rain or snow. As much as they cared for each other, they felt stuck when it came to the topic of where to establish their home after their wedding. At the same time, they were each optimistic the other partner would have a change of mind, given enough time. Carl, Anna Barbara, Paul George, and Margaretha returned to Loudonville before the new year, without a solution to the dilemma. Wilhelm was hopeful for a solution to their stalemate when he realized Margaretha had packed Anna Barbara's wedding dress for the trip back to Loudonville.

chapter 9

COMPROMISE

The day after New Year's Day, Wilhelm returned to work at the cigar warehouse with mixed feelings. His heart soared when he thought of Margaretha. When she agreed to his proposal of marriage, he felt his life move forward at last. At the same time, he was glad for the distraction of work, a break from his gentle, yet earnest and exhausting, efforts to persuade Margaretha to move back to Cincinnati.

"Wilhelm, are you all right? Are you not pleased to be engaged?" George asked his younger brother. At the Christmas celebration, Wilhelm and Margaretha were the picture of happiness. Now Wilhelm looked tired and somber.

"I am very happy to be engaged to Margaretha. She is the person I want to marry as soon as possible," replied Wilhelm. "We have an unfortunate problem to solve before we plan the wedding."

"I can't imagine what that could be," commented George. "The two of you are so well suited, and you both obviously care deeply for each other."

"Oh, yes. Gretly is a wonderful person. We enjoy our time together, very much," said Wilhelm, smiling at the thought of seeing her again. "The problem is this: Gretly would like me to move to Loudonville, and I want her to move here, where our business is doing so well. Anna Barbara and Gretly are very close, and I understand how difficult it was for two young women to immigrate without their parents. These two women want to live close to support one another."

"I see," replied George stroking his beard thoughtfully. "Wilhelm, do you remember Mr. Lehman, who used to buy tobacco from us every couple of months?"

"*Ja*, he was a good customer. He used to have a tobacco shop on the west side. Whatever happened to him?" asked Wilhelm.

"I heard that he opened a tobacco shop in Mansfield a couple of years ago. Now he is trying to come back to Cincinnati. He may have a tobacco shop he would like to sell in Mansfield. Are you interested?" George asked and watched for his brother's reaction to this possibility. As in their first immigrant year in New York, George continued to watch out for his younger brother's business and personal interests.

Wilhelm's mind raced. From his courtship trips to visit Margaretha in Loudonville, he remembered Mansfield was only an hour away from Loudonville by train. *Would Margaretha be willing to live in Mansfield? If I agree to her visiting Anna Barbara in Loudonville as often as she wishes, is this the compromise solution both of us could embrace?*

The following weekend, Wilhelm traveled to Loudonville to make final arrangements for their wedding and to propose Mansfield for their first home together. Margaretha enthusiastically agreed to Wilhelm's proposed compromise. Wilhelm bought and took over Mr. Lehman's tobacco shop, and the young couple planned to begin their married life in Mansfield, Ohio.

Carl, Anna Barbara, and Paul George accompanied Margaretha by train to Mansfield on April 14, 1855, for her wedding day. They gathered at the Evangelical Lutheran and High German Reformed Church in downtown Mansfield, Ohio, for the marriage ceremony.

"Margaretha, you are a beautiful bride. Wilhelm is a lucky man to have won your hand in marriage," Anna Barbara said as she helped Margaretha slip into the same wedding dress she had worn when she married Carl. "Let me braid your hair this way," said Anna Barbara as she held the braids up to show her sister's high cheek bones and clear complexion.

At a few minutes past 3:00 in the afternoon, Margaretha walked down the church aisle carrying a nosegay tied to her personal Bible with blue satin ribbons and a heart full of love. She was eager to marry Wilhelm Tangeman.

Following the evangelical ceremony, the wedding guests moved to the Munich Biergarten to celebrate this joyously anticipated marriage. "This marriage is a double joy for Anna Barbara and me. We have all known each other well. Now we will live out our four lives together. May you both find great happiness as we have in holy matrimony. *Probst, probst!*" Carl toasted.

Following their wedding dinner, Wilhelm and Margaretha retired to their new home amid well wishes and good-hearted jesting. Carl and George and their families stayed overnight at the Grand Hotel, then returned to Loudonville and Cincinnati, respectively, following breakfast the next morning.

Anna Barbara was elated when her sister married Carl's brother, Wilhelm. They were well matched and very happy together. At the same time, she missed seeing Margaretha every day, sharing time and the work of his house. Even Paul George missed his Aunt Gretly. He could not use words to express his feelings. Instead, he crawled from room to room looking for her, a forlorn expression on his face.

A few days after the wedding in Mansfield, Carl returned home with the *Cincinnati Enquirer* under his arm and a furtive look on his face. "Welcome home, Carl," Anna Barbara greeted her husband. Paul George crawled to his father and stretched up his chubby arms. Carl leaned down and picked up his son, eliciting a broad smile. His son never failed to cheer and distract Carl's attention from any cares left over from his work day.

"I am glad to be home. This was a busy work day, and some pieces of iron did not cooperate with my mallet," Carl replied. "And I read some disturbing news in the *Cincinnati Enquirer.*"

"What is that?" asked Anna Barbara, hoping there were not further riots in Cincinnati threatening their families.

While Anna Barbara finished supper, Carl related, "I just read what is happening out west since the Kansas-Nebraska Act that passed last year in Washington, DC. Pro-slavery and anti-slavery settlers are moving into both states. Citizens are authorized to vote whether or not to allow slavery in their state. In the Kansas Territory people are fighting with each other over the question of slavery. I never imagined we would have these forces threatening war in America."

"*Ja*, there is much going on here in America, and there is much going on in this household. I miss Margaretha, but I'm getting used to doing the work by myself. In a few weeks, I hope we will go visit Gretly and Wilhelm in Mansfield, if they don't come here first," related Anna Barbara. Her keen attention to the matters of their family gently diverted Carl from dwelling on the affairs of the nation.

✦

"Carl, I need to talk with you about something I overheard today," said Anna Barbara.

Carl looked up from his newspaper and smiled. "What is it, my dear?"

asked Carl.

"Today I was shopping at the dry goods store when I overheard two new-comers talking in German. They did not realize that I understood their words. They were speaking about Africans moving through our town under the cover of night. They spoke of how dangerous it was, and how some white people helped them move north toward Canada where they will be free," explained Anna Barbara. "I remember your friend, Mrs. Stolz, in Cincinnati. Was she in the group that is helping people escape from slavery?"

"Yes, you remember correctly. Mrs. Stolz sometimes hid Africans in a secret room in her house. It was dangerous work, but she believed she was doing the right thing. So she was willing to accept the risk to herself and those she was helping. Hundreds, perhaps thousands, of individuals have moved through Ohio seeking freedom. As long as there is a federal law allowing slave owners to recapture slaves in the United States, they are forced to flee to Canada," responded Carl.

"Carl, who is right, the slave-owners who want to regain their property, or the Africans who want to be free?" asked Anna Barbara. She understood the arguments for each side of this conflict, and she wanted to understand Carl's viewpoint, too.

"First, I came to this country to get away from senseless wars back home. I don't want this conflict to become our conflict. On the other hand, I don't believe one person should enslave another, buying and selling people like animals. That part is clearly wrong. I met African slaves on the river steamers on the Mississippi River. We will hear many opinions in Loudonville and from our relatives in Cincinnati. I try to stay out of the controversies. But if someone asks for my help on their journey up north, I cannot turn an African family over to authorities to be returned to their masters in the south. What do you think?" asked Carl.

"I think I agree with you. I don't want to be in the middle of these conflicts over Africans either. But if they ask for our help, I will try to do so," replied Anna Barbara.

"I may have helped Africans last week without realizing at the time. A fella brought in a wagon for repairs to a wheel and axle. Mr. Miller asked me to do the work right away before I started other jobs. Before I finished, Mrs. Miller came to the foundry with a basket. She quietly put it in the wagon and returned home. I think it was filled with food, but she didn't speak to the wagon owner. If Mr. Miller is a man of conscience who helps Africans move on to Canada, I am glad to work for him," affirmed Carl.

Anna Barbara nodded her agreement, glad to be married to a man with clear convictions.

Married life suited Margaretha and Wilhelm. Through the summer and fall of 1855, they shared every waking moment, except when Margaretha traveled by train to visit Anna Barbara in Loudonville about twice a month.

"Are you sure?" Wilhelm responded when Margaretha told him she was pregnant. She revealed the changes to her body with Anna Barbara during her January visit. Both women concluded Margaretha was expecting her first child at the same time Anna Barbara was expecting her second.

"Yes, Anna Barbara agrees with me. My body feels different and I have missed two periods," Margaretha explained enthusiastically. "I am with child!"

"You look so happy. Are you feeling well?" asked Wilhelm as he twirled her around to express his joy.

"Yes, I am very well. Some mornings I feel a little queasy. Anna Barbara tells me it will likely end soon," continued Margaretha. "We are both expecting at the same time. Nothing could be better."

Henry William, second son of Carl and Anna Barbara, arrived on May 26, 1856. Margaretha stayed with Anna Barbara and Carl several days before and after the birth of Henry. This time Anna Barbara delivered her baby confidently, almost routinely. Meanwhile, Aunt Gretly tried to keep up with a very active, twenty-month-old Paul George. He was in motion every waking minute, curious, climbing and asking for names of everything. Margaretha took her nephew outside often to run and explore their fenced-in back yard. Even so, both women thanked Carl for the time he spent playing with Paul George each evening.

Margaretha's pregnancy progressed throughout the hot summer months. When her sister was close to delivery, Anna Barbara boarded the train in Loudonville with baby Henry and arrived in Mansfield before noon. For the week Anna Barbara spent in Mansfield, Paul George stayed with Mrs. Miller and enjoyed the attentions of her four older children.

✦

"Will! Will! Margaretha's water broke a few minutes ago. Her labor is underway," Anna Barbara greeted her brother-in-law calmly, yet earnestly when he returned early from the tobacco shop.

"How is she? Should I find the midwife?" asked Wilhelm over his shoulder as he walked quickly to Margaretha's side.

"Labor will still take a few hours," replied Anna Barbara. "You have time to visit your wife for a few minutes before you leave to fetch Mrs. Teinert."

Wilhelm was grateful when Anna Barbara arrived. It gave the expecting couple confidence in a safe delivery of their first child. Through the afternoon and evening labor progressed with the practiced assistance of Mrs. Teinert. It culminated ten hours later with the birth of Charles William Tangeman, on September 10, 1856, in Mansfield, Ohio. Both sisters took pleasure in knowing they had been present for the births of each other's first babies. Margaretha wrote to her parents to announce the birth of Charles William, as she knew Anna Barbara had done after each of her sons was born.

The Tangeman brothers felt fortunate to have married the Schiedt sisters from Bavaria. Their bond of love and support stabilized both households with help through their inevitable daily struggles. Unlike the isolation many immigrants, especially women, felt, their husbands understood how language, culture, and family ties bound these two sisters to each other. Their first generation immigrant relationship was a source of comfort, confidence, and hope for themselves and their families.

chapter 10
SEPARATION

Frigid, snow-laced winds blew incessantly across Ohio in the winter of 1856-57. On January 12, Carl measured an accumulation of a foot of snow on Loudonville streets. Temperatures plunged below zero many nights in January 1857, and they barely rose above zero even on deceptively clear days.

By January 15, snow had reached a depth of two feet in Loudonville. Throughout Ohio, snow accumulated, and the Ohio River froze, halting the shipment of supplies and products. The severe winter weather was devastating to Wilhelm's tobacco business. In February, while he sold nearly all of his stock, only a few meager shipments arrived by train from Cincinnati to re-fill his shelves.

The sustained bitter cold and mounds of snow on the tracks disrupted train travel, and in some locations, the rails even curled and snapped from the effects of extreme cold. Essentially, Margaretha and Anna Barbara were isolated from each other in Mansfield and Loudonville, respectively. Finally, near the end of February, normal temperatures allowed Margaretha to take baby Charles for a visit with Anna Barbara, Carl, Paul George, and Henry.

Upon her return to the Mansfield Train Station, Margaretha was relieved to locate her husband. "Wilhelm, here, please take Charles. He's getting so big and wiggly," pleaded Gretly, as she handed her five-month-old son to his father at the train depot. "It was good to see Anna Barbara for the past three days. Now we are both exhausted," she continued. This was her first visit with her sister since Christmas.

"I'm so glad you are home. I have missed you both," replied Wilhelm, jiggling his son to see him smile.

Later that evening after Charles was in bed, Wilhelm opened a conversation he dreaded to have with his wife. "Gretly, there is something we must discuss. Please don't be too upset," he began.

"What is wrong?" asked Margaretha, a worried look crossing her face.

"While you were in Loudonville, I reviewed the books at the shop. This winter was devastating for the business. We missed three shipments of tobacco during January and February. As you know, the severe cold broke the rails and stopped trains for several weeks," Wilhelm paused to swallow and deliver his conclusion.

"If we continue to depend on the tobacco shop for our living, we will need to cut back our expenses, perhaps move into a smaller house. Or we could move back to Cincinnati and go into business with George. Now that we have a child, I believe we should move back to Cincinnati as soon as arrangements can be made," said Wilhelm.

"I understand what you are saying. I know the shop is not doing well. As much as I would like to stay close to Anna Barbara, I agree it is time to move back to the city," Gretly replied reluctantly. Wilhelm showed his gratitude for Margaretha's calm acceptance of their situation by taking her in his arms and holding her close to his chest.

In the summer of 1857, Wilhelm rejoined his brother, George, in the wholesale tobacco business in Cincinnati. At the time of their move back to the city, Margaretha was expecting their second child.

The Schiedt sisters were immigrant orphans. Living an ocean away from their parents, they relied on themselves and each other with no daily help from their family who had stayed behind in the old country. In their new country, they had no legacy on which to build their own families, only the memories of voices, breadboards, an arm around a shoulder, smells of *apfel kuchen,* and a thousand bits of lived moments left behind but carried with them in their minds and hearts.

On their last visit before Wilhelm and Margaretha moved back to Cincinnati, Anna Barbara and Margaretha mused over their upcoming separation. They felt their lives tied together in real, mysterious, and enduring ways. "Gretly, I will miss you when you move back to Cincinnati. The only problem with this move is how far away you will be," confessed Anna Barbara.

"I feel the same way, dear sister. You were with me when Charles was born. I will always be grateful for these years together," said Margaretha, using a handkerchief to dab her eyes. She thought of how they confided in each other to let off steam as they adjusted to life in America. They laughed at their mistakes learning English. They bought garden seeds by sight and repeated their curious English names while planting them. She would miss sharing these daily moments with Anna Barbara now that they would live a day's train ride apart. The sadness of separation was balanced by the joy of their own growing families.

Far from disparaging the physical strain of pregnancies, raising children, cooking, and cleaning, the Schiedt sisters gave thanks for their good fortunes in America. They had married the Tangeman brothers, decent men who loved them, who were eager to work hard for the better life their parents wanted for them. Unlike the old country with its cumbersome regulations, limited opportunities, and food shortages when the crops failed, these fresh immigrants embraced their opportunities to create financial and family legacies for generations to follow. The Schiedt sisters had settled into an agreeable rhythm of domesticity, of babies arriving every couple of years. They hoped Elizabeth and George would be similarly blessed with a house full of active, curious offspring.

Maria Barbara Klein Schiedt would have liked to embrace her four grandsons and one granddaughter born in America, before her death. She read each letter from her daughters in America many times over, relishing every detail of their children, physical descriptions, fussiness and sleepiness, milestones, facial expressions. She imagined what they looked like and even the sounds of their voices. These visions warmed her heart through the days of her last illness in October, 1858. She died after learning of the birth of Wilhelm's and Margaretha's daughter, Sophia Louise Tangeman, her first American granddaughter.

November 4, 1858

To my dear sisters, Anna Barbara and Margaretha,

Sadly, I must tell you that Mama passed on to her heavenly father on October 10, 1858. She received each of your letters announcing the births of Fred and Sophia. She read them often, and they brought her much joy to know your lives are blossoming in America as she and Papa had hoped for you both.

Her last days were peaceful with thoughts of her family here and in America.

Papa is living with Jacob and me now. It is good to have him close, where he can spend time with our children. He continues to farm his land, and contribute to our household in many ways. Without Mama, he was very lonely on his own. Jacob's nephew, his wife and children have now moved into Papa's house.

I miss Mama tremendously, as I miss each of you. I am occupied caring for our house and family as Mama taught us. Jacob works long hours in his new tailor shop now that Mr. Bergman can no longer see well enough to do this kind of work. Our son helps his father when he is not in school. Perhaps he will join the family business in a few years.

While Mama was so ill, Johann and Elizabeth welcomed twins to their family, John F. and Eliza. Mama was gratified to meet them and hold them before she passed away. They plan to immigrate to America as soon as the twins are old enough to withstand the voyage.

I hope this letter finds your family in good health and spirits. We pray for you and cherish your letters about your lives in America.

Your sister,
Anna Marie Schiedt Schwan

chapter 11
MR. ROTH

"All can now understand that outrage and violence have done their worst in Kansas, and that the game will not win. The American idea of free government will vindicate itself in Kansas over every obstacle. We may say it has already vindicated itself. Kansas will be a Free State in one way or another. She has fought her way through persecution and slaughter, and now holds a position she will not surrender. She may have to fight for her freedom yet, but that freedom she will surely have whether peaceably or forcibly yet remains to be seen."

– New York Daily Tribune
Monday, January 11, 1858

◆———●———◆

The Miller Foundry thrived as Carl and Anna Barbara welcomed each addition to their growing family. In the first six months of Carl's employment, business orders for iron castings more than doubled. His detailed workmanship reinforced a reputation for quality at the foundry and attracted repeat business. George Miller and Carl Tangeman could barely keep up with the demands for metalwork in their local community. Consequently, Carl worked long hours, when necessary, and his corresponding wages added to their savings for future land purchases.

Foundry work was hot and sweaty. The forge was designed to apply extreme heat to iron to make it malleable and shape it for a new purpose. The mechanical bellows forced air to the fire increasing the temperature inside the forge. Manipulating the air and heat to bend metal to exact specifications satisfied Carl's mind and muscles and his sense of responsibility to support his family.

At the foundry, Carl become friends with many of his customers, including a number of area farmers. Eager to learn about agriculture in Ohio, Carl welcomed these associations. Herman Roth, a newcomer who farmed

73

in Hanover Township, quickly became a friend. He had much in common with Carl and appreciated the quality of his work.

June 23, 1858, had been hot and sweltering long before noon. Mr. Roth arrived at the foundry late in the blistering afternoon sun. In a state of mild urgency, he quickly dismounted from his wagon seat and strode directly to the foundry workshop. "Mr. Roth, good afternoon," greeted Carl. He laid down his tongs and mallet to give his attention to this customer who was also his friend.

"Mr. Tangeman, it is good to see you. How are you and how is your family?" asked Mr. Roth politely.

"We are fine. Anna Barbara is mighty busy with another baby and two toddlers," replied replied Carl. "What did you bring in today?" He followed Mr. Roth to his farm wagon not wanting to waste more time in small talk.

"I brought in my McCormick Reaper for your expert repair service," stated Mr. Roth. "Harvest is upon us, and I need this repair in order to bring in the rest of the crop."

"I understand the urgency. Let me take a look," replied Carl. He climbed into the back of the wagon, and mentally planned how to form a metal brace and attach it to the reaper.

"Yes, I can make the repair. Let's lift the reaper off the wagon bed," directed Carl. He enjoyed the company of Mr. Roth, another recent immigrant from northern Prussia. Carl turned his mind to repairing the broken fly wheel. For a few moments he concentrated so completely that he lost himself in the details of heating and hammering iron, shaping it for the repair at hand. Foundry jobs such as this came under his mental and physical control in a deeply satisfying way.

"As you know this is the middle of harvest. How soon may the repair be completed?" asked Mr. Roth allowing a sense of urgency to creep into his voice.

"It should be ready for you to pick up tomorrow evening," replied Carl. "If you have time, would you like to have supper with us when you return? Anna Barbara would enjoy meeting you, and she is a very good cook," Carl smiled his invitation.

"Thank you, Carl. I accept your offer," replied Mr. Roth with a smile and firm handshake. On his way back home, the farmer relished the thought of a home-cooked German meal and spending time with Carl's family.

Herman arrived at the foundry late the following afternoon. As promised, the repairs were finished. He paid Carl for his metal work, then both men lifted the reaper back into Herman's wagon.

"Our home is a fifteen minute walk. Anna Barbara has prepared dinner for us, and I know she would like to meet you," said Carl. The men walked briskly along Main Street toward the Tangeman home. "I hear the harvest may be good this year," commented Carl.

"*Ja*, gentle spring rains came right after planting this year. Everything was favorable for the wheat crop to thrive. Then the last two weeks dried out the heads. If it stays dry for another week, the harvest will be finished in Ashland County. If the harvest is as good as it looks to be, I will pay off a small mortgage on my farm and have enough profits to live well for the next year," explained Herman. The men turned right on Water Street and smelled dinner at the Tangeman home drifting their direction.

"Anna Barbara, Mr. Roth and I are home," announced Carl as he entered through the front door. The familiar spicy smells of traditional German cooking caused Herman to breathe the tangy aroma deeply into his ample chest.

Anna Barbara approached the men from the back of the house. "Mr. Roth, I am pleased to meet you. Please come into the kitchen. You are just in time for supper. We have sauerbraten with dumplings and gravy," greeted Anna Barbara.

"I'm pleased to meet you, too. Please call me Herman. And who are these fine young fellows?" asked Mr. Roth.

"This is Paul George and Henry," she replied, gesturing to her older and middle son. "Baby Fred is in his crib."

"Thank you for including me for supper. It smells delicious." He welcomed the chance to have a German supper.

"Herman, come with me. We wash up on the back porch," invited Carl. Paul George toddled after the two men. With clean hands, Carl scooped up his son and held him high in the air. "What has my little man done today? Have you helped Mama in the garden?" Paul George gurgled and giggled and slobbered his response to the delight of his father.

"Mama, mama, . . . darden," Paul George repeated and pointed toward the back yard. Carl jiggled him back and forth until the toddler wriggled and slipped down to the floor to find his brother.

The Tangemans broke bread that evening for the first time with Herman Roth. His passion for agriculture captured Carl's imagination. In time, he hoped to purchase land and master how to plant and cultivate and harvest, too. Throughout the evening Herman shared freely from his storehouse of experiences making a living from the land.

"It seems most of us are newcomers to Loudonville," said Herman with a smile that turned up the ends of his dark, bushy beard. "It is a privilege to be invited into your home. This meal is the best I have had in months." As a single person, he missed having a conversation partner and relished the opportunity to recount his immigrant experiences and exchange perspectives on their adopted country with these new friends.

"I'm glad you enjoy it," replied Anna Barbara with a smile. She liked to cook, especially for a guest who appreciated the results of her efforts.

After offering thanks for this meal, Carl began, "How is it you came to Ohio and bought your farm in Hanover Township? I have known quite a few people who purchase a farm, stay a few years, then sell out for a profit. They move further west and buy more acres for the same money and do the same thing again."

"My story is different from those folks. Our intention was to establish a farm and live all our lives in Allegheny County, Pennsylvania," Herman began. "My wife, Edith, and I crossed the treacherous Atlantic Ocean in early '52. We bought a farm near Pittsburgh almost immediately, in time for spring planting. We were enthusiastic to learn English and the ways of our neighbors. Our dream was to work our farm and become part of the community. Many of our neighbors were also immigrants from German-speaking areas in Europe and they became our friends."

"Excuse me, Herman, may I serve you this delicious sauerbraten with dumplings and gravy?" asked Carl. "Please continue your story."

"Yes, please," Herman replied as he passed his plate to Carl. Then he continued. "After three years on that farm, Edith became pregnant. We were both pleased to have a little one on the way, due last November. Edith felt fine for the entire pregnancy, and we had never been happier. We arranged for a midwife who agreed to come attend her delivery. Unfortunately, Edith's labor was difficult. I left to fetch the midwife, and when we came back, it was clear there was something wrong causing distress for the baby and much discomfort for my wife. In the end, Edith bled to death, and the child never drew his first breath," related Herman in a matter-of-fact manner as if in a trance. His story touched Carl deeply and stirred feelings of grief for the death of his first wife, Elizabeth, and their children. This was an unfortunate experience they had in common.

"I am so sorry for your loss," consoled Anna Barbara tearfully. Unfortunately, stories of women dying in childbirth were not uncommon, especially first-born children. Although she smiled in sympathy to him, she was disturbed to be reminded of her own risk of slipping away, either she or her next child, or both of them failing to survive childbirth.

After these losses, Mr. Roth described how his life spun into profound grief. "By this spring, I could no longer abide living in the home I built for Edith and our family. I sold my farm to another immigrant family and moved west, to Hanover Township. I found my fresh start when I purchased a 78-acre farm in time for spring planting this year," said Mr. Roth, his voice dropping to signal the end to his story.

"We are pleased you moved here," said Carl. "If there is anything we can do to help you get settled, please allow us to do so."

"Thank you for your good work on my machine and your kindness this evening. This dish brings back happy memories of Edith's sauerbraten, too," replied Herman with sincere gratitude. For a few moments, he gazed out the kitchen window remembering his family. He swallowed hard and turned back to Anna Barbara with a fleeting smile.

This dinner was the first of many shared among Carl, Anna Barbara, their sons, and Herman Roth.

Carl's friendship with Herman Roth allowed each of them to revisit threads of their lives left behind in Prussia or during immigration. Their relationship was like family; feelings were expressed without prolonged discussion. Trust was built easily and quickly enhanced by nuances of their native language. For Carl and Anna Barbara, Herman was the kind of friend they would cherish for a lifetime.

Herman continued to live in Hanover Township through the 1858 and 1859 harvest seasons. He stayed partly due to his friendship with Carl and Anna Barbara. As much as he reached out to young women in Ashland County, he did not find interested prospects. Unfortunately, the wounds of his heart that remained when Edith and their son died never completely healed. After his farm sold in September, 1859, Herman Roth set out for points west, linking his fortunes with the multitudes streaming west from Ohio toward the Great Plains. Carl and Herman exchanged letters through the ensuing decades. Herman's letters were kept and reread by Tangeman family members over the years. They were treasured as a reliable source of first-hand information about frontier life.

Dear Carl and Anna Barbara,

February 27, 1860

   Greetings to you from Keswick, Iowa. My train trip across Indiana and Illinois took me past towns, fields, and farms with neat houses and barns. I met a family with four children moving to Chicago and they reminded me of your family. They were eager to move west and very optimistic to purchase a large farm. I hope you and your boys are well, too.

   Last week I crossed the Mississippi River over the railroad bridge at Rock Island, Illinois, to Davenport, Iowa. It was frightfully wonderful. The Rock Island Bridge had two single-track spans on the Illinois side of the island and three similar spans across the main channel into Iowa. We live in a time of engineering marvels.

   Now I am staying here with Mr. Gerhard Steinmark, a man whose farm is near Keswick, Iowa. I met Mr. Steinmark shortly after he escorted his wife to Davenport where she boarded a train to return to her people in York, Pennsylvania. She expected to come west with her husband to establish a farm in Keokuk, County. After two years living on 133 acres of homesteaded land, she seemed to lose her mind. She was found staring blankly out of windows. She seemed to lose interest in housework, becoming silent for hours at a time. Mr. Steinmark invited over neighborhood women to visit, but after they left she returned to her inward way. For her own health, he sent her back to her parents and familiar surroundings. So, here we are, two bachelors living on the prairie.

   Mrs. Steinmark apparently fell victim to "prairie fever," an affliction that most often affects women. The Steinmarks' farmstead is situated nearly two miles from their closest neighbors and even farther from the nearest town. Being isolated from other people, especially womenfolk, became too much for her to bear. By the end of the harvest season this summer, either Mr. Steinmark will return to York and join his father-in-law's business as a shopkeeper or Mrs. Steinmark will have recovered enough to return to Iowa.

   This country is vast. I am captivated by the land and the people who choose to adventure out to this frontier.

With fond memories of your family and kind regards to all,
Herman Roth

◆

1860

By the beginning of the decade of the 1860s, Carl and Anna Barbara welcomed two more sons; Fredrick on April 5, 1858, and August Charles on April 5, 1860. Meanwhile, Wilhelm's and Margaretha's family now included Charles W., Sophia and Otto, who was born in 1860. The Schiedt sisters weathered their separation when Wilhelm and Margaretha moved from Mansfield, Ohio, back to Cincinnati in 1857. Even so, they missed helping each other with daily tasks, sharing emotional support, and caring for their children together.

Anna Barbara received a letter from her brother Johann shortly after the birth of August Charles, announcing their plan to imigrate to the United States. Johann (John), Elizabeth, and their two-year-old twins, John F. And Eliza, planned to leave Ehningen and expected to arrive in Cincinnati in June. John was a jovial businessman gregarious in his dealings and adept at recognizing lucrative business opportunities. The Tangeman brothers and sisters, as well as, Heinrich and Wilhelmina Schiedt, welcomed the prospect of John and Elizabeth joining them in Cincinnati, Ohio.

At this crossroads of the 1850s and 1860s decades, the Schiedt sisters and Tangeman brothers reflected on life before and since their immigration to America. Their early days in Bavaria and Prussia were spent absorbing daily life within their families of origin. They brought those cultural ways, language, values, religion, foods, and dress, to their adopted country. Inevitably, those old ways were melding into a new country of the United States that was forming before their eyes.

The Schiedt and Tangeman immigrants lived their adult lives separated from their European roots, the source of their sense of self and German identity. Each year in Ohio the way they spoke, what they ate, how they dressed, and how they made a living necessitated changes and adaptations to survive and thrive in America. They felt the pain of separation when some part of their cultural roots was torn or peeled away or simply slipped away bit by bit. Those wounds of separation scabbed over, but the first generation immigrant scars remained throughout their lifetimes.

chapter 12

FROM DISCORD TO CIVIL WAR

*"The dogmas of the quiet past are inadequate to the stormy present.
The occasion is piled high with difficulty,
and we must rise with the occasion."*

– Abraham Lincoln

The roots of the American Civil War began years before hostilities erupted on April 12, 1861. On that day Confederate soldiers fired on Fort Sumpter in South Carolina's Charleston Harbor. Through the 1850s tensions between North and South had intensified over questions of property rights of slave owners, abolition of slavery, and western expansion. Would slave owners be allowed to legally recapture their slaves from free states? Would newly formed western states be admitted to the United States as free or allowing slavery? Should slavery be abolished altogether?

Millions of European immigrants who arrived in the 1840s and 1850s were minimally invested in the notion of free and slave states. In the northern states immigrants more often attempted to steer clear of political conflicts, instead focusing on seeking land for settlement or sale. Those who moved west added population pressure to western expansion states. According to the Missouri Compromise of 1820, slave and free states were to be admitted to the United States equally to maintain a precarious north/south balance of power in the US Congress. The Kansas-Nebraska Act of 1854 authorized new states to decide their own free or slave status by a vote of their residents. Subsequently, armed conflict broke out sporadically in the Kansas Territory until residents voted for Kansas to be admitted as a free state. That decision tipped the balance to a majority of free states in Congress where future laws were certain to favor abolitionist points of view. The confederate states seceded from the United States in a matter of weeks thereafter.

". . . all is quiet in Kansas. Sir, if there be quiet in that distant territory, it is not the quiet of contentment, it is not the calm repose of a people secure in their rights and happy in the enjoyment of them; it is the fitful lull which precedes the storm."

– *True American,* Steubenville, Ohio, Wednesday, February 24, 1858, p. 1

December 22, 1858

The Tangemans and Schiedts of Loudonville traveled to Cincinnati three days before Christmas. On Christmas Day, the Tangemans gathered at the home of Louise and Otto Otten. It was a noisy time with six children under the age of five in constant motion, all boys except Wilhelm and Margaretha's daughter, baby Sophia. On the day after Christmas, the Schiedt siblings (Anna Barbara, Margaretha, and Heinrich) met to celebrate Christmas at the parsonage home of Heinrich and Wilhelmina Schiedt.

Following the Christmas celebrations, Carl visited his long-time friend, Mrs. Stolz. He was interested in her perspective about the mounting tensions between North and South, amplified by the passage of the Kansas-Nebraska Act.

✦

"Carl, I am glad to see you. Come in, come in. Would you like coffee and *apfel kuchen*?" greeted Mrs. Stolz. It had been a year since he visited the boardinghouse where he lived during his search for his brothers, Wilhelm and George. Walking down the entry hallway, he remembered their reunion in 1848. Emotions of gratitude and relief again flooded his mind and heart. Mrs. Stolz noticed Carl wipe away a tear as they entered the parlor.

"Thank you, yes, a cup of coffee would be welcome," replied Carl, smiling as he settled into an upholstered side chair. "How are you? I hope you have been well." Mrs. Stolz had been a safe haven for Carl from nativist thugs on the street when he first came to Cincinnati in 1847. Now she was an emotional safe haven, a sensible voice who understood much of the swirl of local and national political conflicts.

"I have been well, but I don't do as much as I used to do. It is to be expected at my age," replied Mrs. Stolz. Of all of her boarders, she had stayed in touch with Carl over the years. She handed Carl a cup of coffee, and he noticed the toll of years on his friend. She moved more slowly and carefully now, revealing stiffness in her joints. Even so, Carl felt the familiar sense of being at home with Mrs. Stolz. "What is on your mind?"

Carl sipped the coffee and asked, "If you have time, I would like to know your opinion about the rumors of war we read about almost daily."

"Of course, I have as much time as you wish," said Mrs. Stolz.

Carl began, "There are violent conflicts in the Cincinnati streets. Abolitionists versus pro-slavery, nativists versus immigrants, Protestants versus Catholics. Since the passage of the Kansas-Nebraska Act, these conflicts have become more intense here in Cincinnati. Of course, I am concerned for all of us if war comes. Perhaps I should move out West, perhaps Kansas, to acquire land for farming."

"Ah, yes. I remember farming was your interest. But why are you thinking of moving so far away?" inquired Mrs. Stolz.

"That is simple. Since we have been in Loudonville for the past four years, I have seen many pioneers come, buy land, then sell it in a few years and move on west. The price of land has gone up and up. I can make a good living at the foundry. On the other hand, land is tangible. It can be passed on to one's children and grandchildren for their future security. Now that our family is growing, I want to provide land for each of them. That is only possible out West where land is less expensive."

"I see. You want to provide for your family, and our growing conflicts bring much uncertainty," added Mrs. Stolz. Since she had no children of her own, Carl had become the son she did not have. She shared his concerns for the future of his children.

"What do you know about 'Bleeding Kansas'?" asked Carl.

"I have read the Cincinnati newspapers and tried to keep up with events here and around the country. When the Kansas-Nebraska Act passed, most people believed Nebraska would vote to be free and Kansas would vote to be a slave state, thus keeping the balance of free and slave states in Congress. In the case of 'Bleeding Kansas,' pro-slavery raiders from western Missouri stirred up support for their cause with raids intended to intimidate settlers in eastern Kansas," explained Mrs. Stolz. "And abolitionist raiders from Kansas burned cabins and killed a few people in Missouri."

Carl was silent as he sipped his coffee and took in what Mrs. Stolz had said. "Is there a way to avoid war between the northern abolitionists and southern pro-slavery forces?"

"Probably not," responded Mrs. Stolz. "The abolitionist forces are determined to do away with the institution of slavery. At the same time, southern plantation owners say slavery is necessary to their way of life. Every new state that comes into the union going forward will become a hotbed of conflict over the slavery question."

"For now, it seems best to stay in Loudonville for our safety while the children are young. We can save money to move out West later when political tensions have settled down," concluded Carl.

"Yes, I agree. Now tell me about Anna Barbara and your children and life in Loudonville," Mrs. Stolz asked as Carl finished his slice of *apfel kuchen*. She laughed at Carl's descriptions of the antics of Paul George, Henry, and baby Frederick. Later, when Carl announced he needed to return to his family, Mrs. Stolz insisted he take the remainder of the *apfel kuchen* to share with them.

✦

Sooner than Mrs. Stolz envisioned, political tensions were fueled by the ardent abolitionist John Brown. He and his five sons supported Kansas entering the union as a free state. Earlier, they had ridden for freedom and retaliation after Quantrell's Raid in Kansas by Missouri militia in 1856. Fervent to incite a slave revolt in the South, Brown led an insurrection that blew up the arsenal at Harper's Ferry, Virginia, October 16, 1859. Before the end of the year, Brown had been tried, convicted, and hung by Virginia officials. The explosion of tensions around Brown's death blew away the last straw knitting the United States together.

Violent events in Kansas and Virginia, as well as riots in Cincinnati were unsettling for Carl and Anna Barbara. Meanwhile, August Charles arrived on April 5, 1860, exactly two years after Frederick's birth. With four sons to raise, all of their time was devoted to their boys' firm, yet loving, upbringing.

The streets in Loudonville were safe from nativist taunts but not other conflicts. There were two German language churches, the Hanover Evangelical and Reformed Church and Zion Lutheran Church, almost next door to each other. Carl and Anna Barbara were members of the Hanover Evangelical and Reformed Church along with numerous other immigrant families. The beliefs of the two congregations were very similar, but both groups stubbornly insisted they remain separate. The Loudonville community members were shocked and stricken when both Lutheran churches burned to the ground in 1860. Seeing how near the fire came to their house, Anna Barbara feared another fire could sweep through the town, threatening homes and lives.

Carl had joined local citizens who formed a bucket brigade after the fires were discovered in the early evening, to no avail. Before the ashes of the two churches were cold, congregants began earnest discussions about what to do going forward. In the years since Carl and Anna Barbara arrived in Loudonville, they had heard comments about the folly of having two Lutheran churches in a small town almost next door to one another. Perhaps now they would join together.

Carl returned home after dark, sooty and exhausted. Anna Barbara expressed her concern, "Carl, are you all right? You have soot everywhere. Is the fire out?"

"*Ja*, I am fine. I will wash up, then we will talk," replied Carl. He took off his work shirt and pants, heavy with smoke, and left them on the back porch. He used lye soap and warm water to rub his skin clean and dry with an old washcloth and towel.

Anna Barbara's worry echoed his own, "What can we do? If there is another fire in Loudonville, it could destroy the entire town. Do you think that will happen?"

"We are more comfortable here in Loudonville than anywhere else. The churches can be rebuilt. Remember, we recommended this town to your brother and sister-in-law, John and Elizabeth, when they immigrate to Ohio," reminded Carl.

"Do you think the two Lutheran churches could now join together and rebuild one sanctuary for everyone?" Anna Barbara asked, brightening at the thought of seeing all of her German Lutheran friends together.

"I don't know. Some of the church members were starting to speak of that possibility as the fire died down," replied Carl. "We know how hard it is for people to settle their differences from the old country. Don't you think we hard-headed Germans could learn something new here in America?"

In spite of discussions to rebuild the two destroyed Lutheran churches as one, there were too many hard feelings between the two groups to bridge the gap. The thought of saving the higher cost of two buildings was not enough to convince parishioners to put their differences aside. Carl understood the desire to maintain control over one's own religious life. At the same time, as a relative newcomer, he was not as attached to only one congregation as most of the other members. He and Anna Barbara were inclined to make peace with the issues of the past.

Other conflicts loomed larger than the church squabbles in Loudonville. Increasingly, Carl felt concern about the mounting tensions between northern and southern states.

◆

Lacking strong presidential leadership since 1856, Americans craved the possibility of a better president being elected in 1860. Following a hard fought campaign, Abraham Lincoln was elected President of the United States on November 6, 1860. Hopes were high that sectional conflicts could be ameliorated and war averted through Lincoln's folksy, humorous, intelligent style of leadership.

Following five years of conflict in "Bleeding Kansas," Congress admitted Kansas as a free state, January 29, 1861. This act fulfilled Lincoln's desire to create no more slave states in the nation. It also inflamed passions and solidified southern resolve to maintain the legal status of slavery in existing slave states.

For Carl, Anna Barbara, and thousands of other immigrants to the Midwest, Kansas became a "promised land" when it achieved statehood and opened to settlement as a free state. Carl began to learn as much as he could about the plains region and how to farm where buffalo thrived on prairie grasses.

◆

February 20, 1861

Dear Carl and Anna Barbara,

Congratulations on the birth of your fourth son, August. You are both fortunate to have these four healthy boys. Soon Paul George will be able to help with the younger ones and your garden.

This letter comes to you from Atchison in the new state of Kansas. I re-

member our conversations about "Bloody Kansas" before statehood. The settlers who came here put their lives at risk to join the northern or southern sympathizers. When Kansas residents voted to join the Union as a free state, the outcome settled the question of slave or free state status. Now that statehood is accomplished, the new residents are learning to get along. New settlers arrive every day with high hopes for a wet year after last year's terrible drought.

Yesterday, I drove a wagonload of merchandise west over a two-rut road to Lancaster, Kansas. The prairie grass was as high as the wheels, even in winter. It hid the small animals like rabbits and coyotes and most of a herd of antelope at a distance. By the time I drove the eight miles, the wind had whipped me into a frozen bundle of oiled canvas, ice, and snow shreds. The wind never stops blowing across these plains.

The settlers who arrive daily by wagon train or railway want desperately to succeed. They are strong in spirit and body to establish homes and farms in these harsh conditions. The winter weather is a challenge to survive when the wind drives snow to pit and scrape the skin. These folks are incredibly committed to building the new state of Kansas with perseverance to overcome every obstacle. This new state feels like home to me at last.

I hope your family continues in good health and good cheer.

Your friend,
Herman Roth

◆

Civil War clouds built up to a lethal storm that began April 12, 1861, with armed conflict followed by the secession of South Carolina from the United States. Four years of destruction were about to rain on the American homeland. The Tangemans, like other immigrants, dreaded being drawn into this war. Immigrants compared the American Civil War to European revolutionary wars in 1848 such as Italy, territories of German-speakers, and France. In Europe, individuals in positions of power made decisions and drew thousands of soldiers into military service for reasons profoundly detached from the common people. In contrast, those citizens born in America believed deeply in their chosen cause, defended by either the Union Army or Confederate Army. Ironically, the soldiers on the frontline of the Civil War came disproportionately from the legions of the poor, and most immigrants were poor during their first generation in America. The northern army, especially, filled its ranks with new arrivals, immigrants who lacked either passion for abolition or cash to purchase a deferment from active military service.

In the spring of 1861, Ohio's young men heeded Abraham Lincoln's call for 75,000 men to join the Union Army, some of whom were caught up in the revelry of a righteous war. They were excited by war fever to fight for the abolition of slavery. In their new uniforms and basking in the camaraderie of friends and neighbors, the newly minted Northern soldiers marched to the beat of local bands. In small towns and cities, crowds felt the holiday mood and cheered their own boys to a swift victory.

"Don't worry, Gretly, I will not join this war. Plenty of fellas have joined to knock out slavery quickly. They say the war will be over by the end of summer. I'm not so sure about that outcome, but I know I am needed here to take care of you and the children. I need to run the tobacco business with George. Besides, the army will be a good customer. I will help the war effort with tobacco for the troops," stated Wilhelm with a characteristic twinkle in his eye. He took satisfaction in seizing business opportunities, even at this grave time of civil war.

Margaretha took a dim view of the war saying, "I understand what you are saying. With this baby coming in a couple of months, I don't want you to go to war, either. It just seems like everyone your age is joining the army, and I'm worried. I can't imagine if anything ever happened to you . . ."

♦

"George, did you see the soldiers' parade on Race Street today?" asked Elizabeth Tangeman with a mixture of pride and apprehension.

"No, my dear, I was at the warehouse during the parade. But it was so long and noisy, traffic was stopped for over an hour. It slowed down our deliveries to tobacco shops all afternoon," replied George with impatience.

Elizabeth's day with women at Saint Paulus Kirche had been saturated with concern and a sense of duty as the Civil War began. "Mrs. Stauffer and Mrs. Reichert were astonishingly positive about their sons and nephews marching off to war. And poor Mrs. Bentz was simply frightened at the prospect her only son would join or be drafted into a local regiment. I must admit I will feel the same way about Charles if he is ever called to war. Being the only one makes a son's departure so much more impacting on a family. If only I could carry one of these pregnancies to full term. . . ."

"I'm not surprised to hear the mixed feelings of the women for this Civil War. All we can hope for is a swift end to the terrible business. So far, the news is not good from the front lines. The Battle of Bull Run was lost in Virginia last month," responded George.

Elizabeth's voice brightened, "Let's talk of more cheerful news. We received word that your niece, Sophia Otten, Louise's daughter, will marry Phillip Geier in September. Since it was Christmas when Carl and Anna Barbara last came for a visit, do you suppose they may come for the wedding? Perhaps we could send a telegram to forewarn them of the invitation so they have the opportunity to make plans. Their little one must be walking by now. Four little boys on the train will be a handful, but we would all like to see them. George, will you send a telegram and offer to have them stay with us? Paul George and Henry and our Charles are good friends, and I could help Anna Barbara with the younger boys," suggested Elizabeth, who smiled at the thought of a house full of young boys playing and laughing.

"Of course, I will send off a telegram tomorrow. Now, what is for supper? Something smells very good," replied George as he gave Elizabeth an enthusiastic embrace.

Northern war fever raged through the summer of 1861 and abated before the first winter. From the privates on the battlefields all the way up ranks to generals and President Lincoln, disillusionment and impatience replaced the early enthusiasm for the fight. In the beginning, both Union and Confederate soldiers believed they would achieve a quick victory. A second summer of war was unfathomable.

Sophia Louise Otten (daughter of Louise Tangeman and Otto Otten) married Phillip Geier on September 8, 1861, at the Saint Paulus Deutsche Evangelische Kirche. Pastor Heinrich Schiedt conducted the traditional marriage ceremony.

"*Ja*, it was a beautiful wedding. With the war all over the country, we need this joyful occasion. It reminds us of happier times to come," commented Margaretha as she held her infant son, Otto, to her shoulder. Wilhelm said she did not need to attend this wedding, but Margaretha did not want to miss the festivities.

Elizabeth commented, wistfully remembering her own wedding, "The dress was so elegant. Ivory satin with lace overlay, and the straight lace veil. Those full sleeves had satin cuffs."

Anna Barbara added, "Oh, yes, the dress was gorgeous. Did you see the embroidered roses on the satin weskit bodice? Unless my next baby is a girl, I may never need to have a beautiful wedding dress with crinoline underskirt in my house. I love my boys, but they are so active, some days they completely wear me out."

Elizabeth longed for a full life with many babies. Even one more, but she kept these thoughts to herself with, "Margaretha, may I hold your precious bundle?"

"Yes, of course. Otto is so quiet I hardly know he is here," replied Margaretha. Just then, Wilhelm came over to the women with a plate of food and a beer. He placed the refreshments on the table and took his wife's hand. They danced the polka and remembered weddings back home. Traditional celebrations in America were bittersweet. The Tangemans felt a sad undertone of separation from family in Sulingen, reinforced by a sense of being alien to the surrounding non-German community in Cincinnati.

The Homestead Act was signed into law by President Lincoln on May 20, 1862. It provided for 160 acres to citizens (or intended citizens) who lived on the land for five years, made improvements and paid an $18 filing fee. Land was available to virtually all citizens, as well as former slaves and women, except for individuals who had taken up arms against the US.

The dual news of Kansas becoming a state in 1861 and the Homestead Act in 1862 led Carl and Wilhelm to think land in the west might be within reach. Before they could make such a move, however, there were two obstacles to overcome. First, the Civil War must come to an end. Second, they decided the younger children should be old enough to be healthy travelers, at least one year of age.

Apprehension pervaded the summer of 1862 in Cincinnati. Families worried for the safety of young men who responded to President Lincoln's call to arms. Racial tensions between Africans and Irish mounted when the drought reduced shipping and stevedore jobs at The Bottoms became scarce. The sweltering heat in July 1862 seemed to strike a match to a tinderbox of antagonism among Africans and Irish, and the city suffered violence and destruction from over a week of riots. No one in Cincinnati felt secure from the roaming crowds of enraged men fed up being out of work on the Ohio River docks. Adding to the racial strife, if the North won the Civil War, most Cincinnatians believed freed slaves from the South would flood into this border city, creating even more friction and hostility.

With success in Louisiana and peril in Virginia, President Lincoln (strongly supported by Northern governors) called up an additional 300,000 troops on July 1, 1862. They were called to support the first 75,000 standing troops. William Tangeman was drafted in the summer of 1862 and ordered to report for duty in Columbus, Ohio, on September 3, 1862. Although he had the means to pay another young man to serve in his place, Wilhelm joined the Union Army.

"Will, you promised me. You said you would not join this war. Too many have died," pleaded Margaretha. Thoughts of being a widow and raising three children on her own filled her mind with dread. *How can Wilhelm even think about enlisting in this unwelcome civil war?*

Wilhelm pulled Margaretha close to his chest. She sobbed while he stroked her thick, dark auburn hair. "Gretly, I never thought the war would last this long. No one did. What it comes down to is this: This country is a democracy, where people are free to govern themselves. Slavery has no place in a democracy. We benefit from our freedoms, and we must also defend them. I have decided to respond to President Lincoln's call for soldiers, and I will fulfill my duty. Besides, when I return, and I will return to you and the children, there will be no question of my patriotism to the United States."

"All right, Wilhelm. I understand what you are saying. But I won't feel you are safe until you are back home," acquiesced Margaretha. She borrowed her husband's handkerchief and blew her nose. She took a deep breath to settle her emotions, ready to support Wilhelm's decision. In spite of her own misgivings, Margaretha was glad he opposed slavery.

"One more thing, Gretly. When I joined the army, I used my American name, William. From here on, that is my name," William concluded with a broad smile and another close embrace.

✦

July 12, 1862

Dear Carl and Anna Barbara,

Greetings from Dickinson County, Kansas. Last month I arrived in the frontier town of Chapman, Kansas, located about 15 miles southwest of Fort Riley, near Junction City. It is the outpost for provisioning army posts further west.

A few families live in this Smoky Hill River Valley. They have planted corn and wheat with high hopes of a good harvest. I arrived as harvest began. Mr. Pete Booth hired me to help with the harvest and turn some virgin prairie with a single steel plow shear. It was harder than any farm work I have ever done. It takes a strong ox with both of us straining every muscle to draw the first furrow. It's a little easier after that. Farmers want to plow a straight furrow, which is nearly impossible in virgin sod.

Mr. Booth left to serve in the Union Army after the wheat harvest was in. That left Mrs. Booth and the five children to keep the farm up and running. The winter wheat crop they planted last fall, only ten acres, came in real good, especially with a snow blanket in the winter and spring rains. They also planted corn and oats in the rest of their 140 acres.

The winter wheat crop was so rewarding, they saved all of it to plant this fall for next year's crop. Corn is a good crop, too. We will keep about half of it to feed the milk cow and a couple of bred sows and sell the rest.

I will stay here until Mr. Booth gets back from the war. I hope he comes back before another harvest is ready. Mrs. Booth is a good cook, and she knows enough about farming. But, working for her is like working for a bull-headed general. I will surely move on when Mr. Booth returns.

Your friend,
Herman Roth

chapter 13
HOSTILITIES

"Dawn approached slowly through the fog on September 17, 1862.
As soldiers tried to wipe away the dampness, cannons began to roar and
sheets of flame burst forth from hundreds of rifles, opening a twelve hour
tempest that swept across the rolling farm fields in western Maryland.
A clash between North and South that changed the course of the
Civil War, helped free over four million Americans, devastated Sharpsburg,
and still ranks as the bloodiest one-day battle in American history."

– Antietam National Battlefield
Sharpsburg, Maryland
National Park Service, U.S. Department of the Interior

"We have, as all will agree, a free Government, where every man
has a right to be equal with every other man. In this great struggle,
this form of Government and every form of human right is endangered
if our enemies succeed."

– Abraham Lincoln
August 22, 1864,
Speech to the One Hundred Sixty-fourth Ohio Regiment

William Tangeman reported for duty in the Union Army of the American Civil War, September 3, 1862. He brought with him four boxes of premium cigars intended to celebrate their first battlefield victory. The cigars symbolized confidence, for he believed his side would prevail quickly.

On his first day in the Union Army, Private Tangeman arrived with his fellow soldiers of the 8th Militia to their training campground near Columbus, Ohio. They were assigned to Company G, and training began immediately. Officers drove their troops hard to prepare for what they were told would be a major battle within weeks. For three days, the new enlistees marched and learned to carry out orders from daylight to dusk. They were only allowed breaks from intense marching for mealtimes and cleaning their weapons. On September 7, Company G boarded a train eastbound on the Baltimore and Ohio Railroad. After two days of riding through Ohio, and Wheeling, (West) Virginia, they arrived in Hagerstown, Maryland, where they set up camp and continued marching drills.

On September 15, 1862, Company G marched eight miles to a spot near Sharpsburg, Maryland. While General George B. McClellan and his cadre of Union generals strategized how to drive General Robert E. Lee's Confederate Army back to Virginia, their Union Army troops prepared for battle with battlefield drills, letters home, and clean guns. In the late afternoon General McClellan called his troops together and explained his plan to engage the Confederate Army the following morning. Through the rainy night, William and his fellow soldiers were restless. At first light of dawn, they were both anxious and apprehensive to meet the battle on September 17. According to General McClellan's plan, his soldiers were to be divided into three groups. The groups on the left and the right were ordered to attack the left and right flanks of General Robert E. Lee's troops respectively. Whenever one or both flanks of General Lee's army collapsed, General McClellan's center was poised to be sent through the breech to destroy the enemy.

For twelve hours of fierce fighting, Lee's forces were able to withstand the northern assaults and hold their positions well enough to maintain their lines of defense. For unknown reasons, General McClellan did not bring forth his reserve troops, of which Company G was a part, to attack the Confederate line.

During the damp night after the battle, General Lee withdrew his exhausted army to safety in Virginia, ending his first invasion into the North. On September 18, William and his fellow soldiers of Company G, Regiment 8, laid down their rifles and picked up shovels to dig graves for thousands who perished in the Battle of Antietam.

President Lincoln issued the Emancipation Proclamation freeing slaves in Confederate States on September 22, 1862. The proclamation would take effect, January 1, 1863. Some in the North declared the war was won, but it was not over. In the thrall of "war is won" fever, William Tangeman and Company G were held in Maryland to finish clearing the battlefields of Antietam. With that job completed, they were sent back home to Ohio. William Tangeman and the soldiers of Company G mustered out of the Union Army October 3, 1862. He returned to his family in Cincinnati, satisfied he had fulfilled his duty to his adopted country.

94

Six-year-old Charles W. recognized his father's footsteps on their front porch and shouted, "Mama, Mama! Papa is home!" Margaretha held baby Otto in her arms, and Sophia clung to her apron as she approached the front door. *Was it possible her husband was back home before the maple and sycamore trees turned to crimson and gold?* Looking much as he had when he left home five weeks earlier, Will stood before his family. He engulfed his wife and three children with hugs and kisses. When they learned the news of Will's return from the war, George and Carl were both proud of his service and greatly relieved to have their brother back home in good health.

Following the Draft Act passed on March 3, 1863, George Tangeman was drafted into the Union Army in June, 1863. Although men, twenty to forty-five-year-olds, were required to register, George at 41, may have been too old to be called into service. Or he may have paid a bounty of $300 to a substitute, a common practice of the day. In either event, George did not actively serve in the Union Army in the American Civil War.

✦

As the Civil War unfolded, Carl and Anna Barbara continued to reside in Loudonville. They welcomed a son, John, to their family in 1862, and their first daughter, Eliza, in 1864. Carl was thankful to be too old to be drafted, and the father of sons who were too young to be called.

Business was brisk at the foundry, where Carl worked through the war years. He continued to learn what he could about agriculture from local farmers: crop yields, grain prices, livestock, and markets. The war effort created demand, which pushed up prices for farm products, and, consequently, the values of land. When the war ended, he thought about taking his next step toward land ownership in Ohio, or perhaps out west. The war years were mild and wet on the plains, which encouraged him to consider farming in Kansas.

✦

On a particularly hot and humid day in the summer of 1863, Carl worked on a long lineup of orders for metal fittings of wagons, carriages, barrels, gates, and doors. The war was good for business; however, with more men called up to serve in the Union Army, Mr. Miller was unable to hire another metalworker. Thus, more work fell to Carl.

Carl walked home this particular evening more slowly than usual, yet eager to greet Anna Barbara and his five sons. After he washed off the sweat and dust of his day's work, Carl liked to play with his sons and learn about their day. On this day he could hear the boys long before he arrived at the back door of their home. One look at Anna Barbara revealed her exhaustion and exasperation with their sons. She was on the brink of tears, and her eyes pleaded with Carl to help to settle down the behaviors of their boys.

"Boys, boys!" Carl issued a command for attention. Momentarily, the older four, Paul George (nine), Henry (seven) , Fred (five) and August (three) stopped running and shouting. In spite of his own weariness, order was needed in his home. Unsure of how to bring his sons under his control, Carl fell back on his officer training in the Prussian Army. "Boys, follow me. We're going for a hike in the woods." Anna Barbara picked up baby John and watched Carl prepare their older sons to leave the house. She did not know what Carl had in mind, but she agreed that something must be done.

"Boys, come line up behind Paul George from oldest to youngest," Carl directed. With his four oldest sons in tow, Carl led the boys in single file out the back door, a short distance to the left and across Main Street into the wooded lots beyond. Paul George was first behind his father followed by Henry, Fred, and August. Paul George was the most important child to impress with his message this evening. If Paul George fell into line, the others were likely to follow his lead.

Weary to his exhausted bones, Carl marched through the woods and along the path toward the Black Fork of the Mohican River. The twenty-minute walk gave Carl time to prepare his message to his sons, while they used up some of their excess energy. Looking directly into Paul George's eyes, Carl began, "My sons, your fighting with one another has reached a point, it must be stopped. No doubt you have seen other boys fight in the schoolyard. It may seem like the thing to do if someone hits you first. But it is not. At home it is especially wrong to fight with your brothers. There can be no fighting in this family."

"Why not, Papa?" asked Fred. "When someone hits you first, you have to hit them back."

"No, Fred, you do not," replied Carl with his eyes directly on Fred's. "Your brothers must always be your best friends. You may play with them, but you must never fight to hurt one another. Families are strong when they support each other, not when they fight and tear each other down. Strong families sometimes save the lives of each other. That happened to me. My family saved me in a way they did not understand until much later."

"What do you mean, Papa?" asked Henry.

"When I first came to America from the old country of Prussia, my ship was caught in a terrible storm. It blew off course and did not arrive in New York where Uncle George and Uncle Will were waiting for me. Instead, it arrived in New Orleans, which was a very long way away. Every day I thought of my brothers and how much I wanted to find them in New York. It took me a long time, but finally I arrived in New York."

"Did you find Uncle George and Uncle Will?" asked Paul George.

"Yes, I did, but not until I came to Ohio. We finally found each other in Cincinnati. It was the happiest day of my life," continued Carl. "Brothers should always work together and support each other. There will be no better friend than your brother, if you are a friend to him. Do you understand what I am telling you?"

"Yes, sir, papa," responded Fred as he gazed down at the ground, his toe moving back and forth on the powdery trail dust. "My brothers are my friends."

"I wuv my brudders," lisped three-year-old August with a smile that melted Carl's heart and almost caused him to lose his composure.

Meanwhile, Henry and Paul George hung their heads, knowing their father was right. They had been teasing the younger boys and fighting with each other. It all started as good fun, but soon deteriorated into roughhousing. When someone was hurt, Mama came to soothe hurt feelings and resolve the conflict. The older two boys reveled in stirring up the household while trying to stay clear of the blame. Their father's message was aimed at them, and they knew it. If they continued in their rambunctious ways, they would have their father to reckon with at every turn. He was right, and they were wrong to be troublemakers. Typical of effective leaders, Carl commanded the respect and love, and a little fear, of his charges.

"Now boys, line up and follow me. Your mother has supper ready for us," ordered Carl in a firm, yet kindly tone. When Carl and his sons entered the house, Anna Barbara could see the boys' wild spirits had been tamed. All through supper they were respectful to each other and their parents. Anna Barbara's eyes met Carl's and conveyed her gratitude that he was able to "settle down" their sons.

✦

The American Civil War ended as violently as it had begun. The bloody war had engaged the northern and southern armies in more than 10,000 military battles and more than 620,000 soldiers died.

The war, a national convulsion of self-proclaimed, conflicting righteous causes, ended with the surrender of General Robert E. Lee at Appomattox Courthouse, in Virginia on April 9, 1865. Five days later President Abraham Lincoln was assassinated by John Wilkes Booth at Ford Theater in Washington, D.C.

Following General Lee's surrender, Congress added the thirteenth, fourteenth, and fifteenth amendments to the Constitution of the United States. These acts of Congress abolished slavery and granted citizenship and voting rights to male former slaves.

The United States had survived politically and geographically intact, but forever changed. Racial, sectional, and economic tensions at the root of the war continued at a slow boil with recurring eruptions of violence well into the twentieth century. Far from "returning to normal" after the war, the eyes of the nation turned to a future of reconstruction of the South and further settlement of the West.

October 15, 1865

Dear Carl and Anna Barbara,

Thank you for your letters with details of life in Loudonville. My years in Loudonville allowed me to heal, especially the time I spent with your family. You are in my prayers for good health and prosperity. Congratulations for having a little girl after your five mischievous boys. She will be the apple of your eye, a sweetness for your old age.

My first year with the Booths we lived in a two-room sod house. Before the sod was broken, the prairie grass roots were so tightly packed, blocks of sod were used to build a house. We sliced the sod into blocks (18" thick, 2' long and 18" wide,) from the area marked off for the house and used them to build up the walls. The children packed down the dirt floor with their bare feet where the sod had been removed. For the roof, we laid wooden planks from wall to wall, and then placed more sod blocks on top.

The weather in 1863 and 1864 was wet and mild, producing harvests good enough to purchase the supplies for a frame farmhouse. I helped Jeb Nelson, a carpenter from Chapman, build a farmhouse for the Booths. The frame farmhouse was built around the sod structure, which was kept as a root cellar for storage of potatoes, onions, and apples for the winter.

A month after the house was built, a prairie fire roared across the plains within sight of the Booth Farm.

On the day of the prairie fire, I heard a low roar from three or four miles west of the farm, then I saw the billows of smoke streaking ahead of the fire line. The wind whipped up strong and steady. If the direction had shifted east toward us, it could have wiped out the crops, farmhouse, barn, and corrals. As it was, the cows and horses were agitated and nervous trying to find a way out. The fences held fast, and, with God's help, the animals survived.

The wind on the plains is stronger than polecat spray. It blows for days at a time without letting up. When Mrs. Booth hangs out the laundry on a windy day, it is dry in a few minutes. But, if a piece gets loose, it lands in Nebraska within the hour.

Abilene is a growing prairie town. After Mr. Booth returned from the war, I found a job building a storefront hardware store on Main Street in Abilene. The owner, Mr. Bracken, asked me to work for him in his warehouse and, sometimes, as a clerk in the store. It is interesting work, and I get to hear the stories about homesteading from our customers. I found out not everyone stays on their land for five years. The crops may be poor, or they may run out of money to purchase the tools and supplies they need. In that case, there is another newcomer ready to buy them out. A lot of land changes hands every year or two.

The Homestead Act of 1862 has inspired a steady stream of homesteaders to try their luck farming on the prairies. With the exception of individuals who took up arms against the US, others may lay claim to a parcel of land, up to 160 acres, and register it for $18 at the local land office or county courthouse. If they live on the parcel for 5 years and make improvements such as house or barns, the land is theirs, free and clear. For newcomers trying to get ahead, this is an opportunity to own a quarter section of land. Of course, the land promoters invite settlement by pioneers from further east to bolster their own profits out west.

I think of you often and wonder if you might consider coming to Kansas to be homesteaders.

Your friend,
Herman Roth

chapter 14

AFTER THE WAR

As if holding their breaths for four years, Will and Gretly followed the decisive battles of the American Civil War, the great Battle of Gettysburg and Battle of Vicksburg on the Mississippi River. *Would this dreadful war never end?*

Like most other northern families, the Tangemans and Schiedts rejoiced when the Civil War ended. On the surface, the United States of America was reunited, a cause for optimism about the future. Thousands of fathers, sons, brothers, and friends returned to the drumbeat of bands marching down Loudonville, Cincinnati, and main streets across Ohio. Although the Tangemans were glad to see the Civil War end, they also mourned the loss of life in war. In the course of the conflict, half of the men in Ohio aged twenty to forty-five had gone to war and many did not come back, or they brought back obvious, as well as, invisible marks of battle.

The scars of a war fought on US home soil were deeply felt. In the southern states, former slaves were legally free. However, with little education and few skills within an environment hostile to their success, many southern blacks were vulnerable to terror groups such as the Ku Klux Klan. African Americans in northern states lacked capital to purchase land or housing. The few available jobs for low-skilled individuals paid low wages. Housing was limited to the poorest areas in cities where both former slaves and freedmen lived. Hostility toward African Americans was muted in the North compared to the South, but ever-present in both regions.

Will approached his brother over coffee in late May of 1865. "George, I'm thinking about moving to Ashland County to take up farming. Would you be interested in buying out my part of this business?"

"I suppose I could think about it. Will you make more money farming? The weather, the price of crops . . . It could be a riskier way to go," replied George. He knew the tobacco business was a reliable way to earn a living in Cincinnatti. Mostly, George questioned his brother's decision because he would miss Will as his business partner and best friend.

"I have given it a lot of thought. The land prices are better now than they will be in a few years, and the crop prices keep going up. The demand is there for crops to yield even more return on investment in the coming years. Yes, there is some risk, but that is part of the challenge and reward," Will replied, thinking about, but not voicing the thrill of the risk, the inherent pleasure of realizing profits from a wise business move.

"In that case, I will put together a contract to sell, see my banker and get back to you this weekend," stated George. Will was more of a risk taker, willing to follow his business hunches. He understood how the potential rewards of farming were pulling his brother toward a future in agriculture. With Carl and John Schiedt in Loudonville, they would support each other to begin this new venture. "Have you talked with your brother-in-law, John, to hear his thoughts about buying land in Ashland County?"

"Not yet, but we plan to make a trip to Loudonville in the next few weeks. Gretly needs to see Anna Barbara every few months, and we haven't seen them since Easter," Will replied.

✦

"Mama, I want to sit by you," begged seven-year-old Sophia as she walked down the aisle of Passenger Car 418. "I don't want to sit with my brothers." She did not like the idea of a train trip to Loudonville. Margaretha understood this trip held little appeal to Sophia.

"Your cousin, Eliza, is about your age. Soon we will all be in Loudonville, and you will be able to play with her, because we will stay with Uncle John and Aunt Elizabeth. Do you want to stay in Eliza's room?" asked Margaretha in an effort to change the focus of her older daughter's attention. Eventually, the motion of the train lulled Sophia and Louisa to sleep.

"Gretly, I'm thinking about going into farming, if I can find a farm for sale at a good price. How would you feel about moving to Ashland County?" asked Will with a twinkle of mischievousness. While holding her sleeping daughters, Margaretha was reluctant to speak her true feelings. Her smile said all that was in her heart. She would enjoy raising their children in a small town, perhaps even on a farm. The thought of moving close to Anna Barbara made her heart soar and her mind race. Will cherished the moments when he put that infectious smile on Margaretha's face.

"I will meet with John to see what he has to say about land for sale near Loudonville," whispered Will.

"It has been eight years since we moved from Mansfield. I would very much like to be near my sister again," sighed Margaretha.

Will and Margaretha moved their family of two boys and two girls to a farm near Loudonville in the summer of 1865 when prices for grains were high, and yields far exceeded local expectations. That first year farming was highly lucrative, affirming to Will that he should follow his business hunches. Similar to what he had done while running the Cincinnati wholesale cigar business, Will assessed the risks of weather, costs of equipment and seeds, and the plans of neighboring farmers, then made decisive calculations that paid off in high yields and generous profits.

On the first Sunday in July of 1865, Carl and Anna Barbara hosted a family gathering at their home following morning church service. They enjoyed Sunday dinner and having time to visit. The cousins split off into older and younger ones to play while the men settled into chairs on the front porch. The women visited while they tended to the pork roast, potato salad, and apples with onions.

Will brought a jug of beer, and Gretly baked apple strudel like Grossmama Schiedt used to make. Elizabeth Schiedt insisted on making sauerbraten to celebrate Will's and Gretly's move to Loudonville. Dinner was served from the kitchen to each group who then found a comfortable place to eat outside. John set up a table with folding legs in the back yard for the women and younger children. The older boys took their plates to the front porch steps near their fathers.

After Sunday dinner, Paul George (eleven), Henry (nine), Fred (seven), Charles W. (nine), and J F (seven) headed out to play a backyard version of the new craze of baseball in the empty lot across the street. Meanwhile, the younger children played inside the picket-fenced backyard. The younger group included Otto (three and a half), Louisa (two), August (five), John (three) and Eliza (one). Sophia, and her cousin, Eliza S., took charge of Louisa and baby Eliza to play "house" while August led Otto and John to play games of chase until they fell on the ground, exhausted and laughing.

"Oh Gretly, 'tis wonderful to have you back in Loudonville with John and me. There is always someone to work with and play with," exclaimed Anna Barbara. "And now I have my baby girl, Eliza. I thought we would never have a girl, but finally, we do. I hope this next baby is a girl to keep Eliza company. Mama would be so happy to learn of the children, you know?"

Anna Barbara smiled remembering her mother. *Having Gretly back in town is the next best thing to being with those we left in the old country. Often, I feel as if I am living two lives. One life is in my memories of family and friends in Ehningen, the people and the surroundings of my upbringing. My present life here in Loudonville dominates my mind, while memories of my Bavarian life are never far below the surface. A child's smile, a turn of phrase, a song in church, or the smell of baking bread triggers memories of loved ones I left in the old country.*

Elizabeth Schiedt understood how close her two sisters-in-law felt to each other. At the same time, they had warm relationships with her, too. "I agree. It is wonderful to have Gretly and Will back in Loudonville. The twins enjoy having more cousins to play with," she chimed in.

"I am glad to be back here where we can share our babies. I feel much safer here than in Cincinnati with the bad feelings against immigrants. Our new neighbors have welcomed us warmly. Will enjoys the farm, and the children are doing well in school," responded Gretly gratefully. *The last thirteen years in America were more difficult than I imagined before I boarded the packet ship from the old country. Civil war is finally behind us and Anna Barbara is back in my life.*

Anna Barbara cut the apple strudel into slices for mid-afternoon dessert and coffee just as her niece, Sophia brought in a fussy baby Eliza for her mother's attention. At her aunt's suggestion, Sophia took over serving strudel and coffee to her father and uncles on the front porch. Eliza S. led the younger children into the kitchen for strudel and milk at the table. The oldest girl cousins, Sophia and Eliza S., embraced their roles of caring for younger cousins just as they observed their own mothers and Aunt Anna Barbara. They imagined themselves as mothers someday, too.

✦

"Will, how is your new farm? Is the weather cooperating? Are the spring crops in the ground?" asked Carl as he sat on the front porch with Will and John. They oversaw the older boys playing baseball across the street while they compared perspectives on their occupations and happenings in Loudonville.

Will struck a match and lit a cigar. Not only had he savored his old cigar business, he savored smoking a cigar, especially on a Sunday afternoon on his brother's front porch. "Here, would you like one, John?" he offered. Carl did not smoke cigars.

"Thank you, Will. I enjoy a cigar now and again. These are fine quality," John replied. Gatherings with his sisters' families satisfied John's longings to speak German and feel at home in this foreign land. He believed immigration to America was best for his family, but his thoughts wandered back home often. Sometimes he wished he had been the one to stay home in Ehningen to care for their father rather than their sister, Anna Marie, and her husband, Jacob Schwan. Jacob could have brought his tailoring business to America and done quite well. But John was here and he would make the best life possible for his family. Already he had purchased property from pioneers leaving quickly to move west, and sold it to others eager to seek their fortunes in tilling the land. It was a lucrative business, and he was able to provide well for his family as a land trader.

"A farm is an exciting challenge," continued Will with a smile of deep satisfaction. "The prospects for a good crop and high prices are both strong. And Gretly is mighty happy here. We are doing fine."

"Speaking of farms, I heard the Martin property was for sale just north of town," mentioned Carl. "They decided to move to Iowa for spring planting and sold in a hurry. Even with hills and gullies, they received a price way above what they paid a couple of years ago. I heard that price will bring them half again as many acres in Iowa."

"I'm not surprised. The price of grains here and the cost of land out there lure people to sell quickly. They want to grab up the best land out west before it is gone," replied Will. Although Carl was interested in farming and read and learned much about agriculture, Will was the one who calculated the incomes possible given the prices of wheat and corn and cost of land. He knew a good business when he saw one, and farming was a very good business in northeast Ohio in 1865.

"I'm thinking the same. It might be time to look for some land this week," stated Carl. "I will keep my ears open for any news of land sales, and you do the same. John, have you heard of any land coming on the market recently?"

"Ah, yes, the Tannenbergs have forty-three acres northwest of town. It may be worth your time to take a look before they put it on the market. Then again, they may not decide to sell right away," replied John. "I heard the Wilsons are getting restless, maybe ready to move west before long."

Carl listened carefully to his brother-in-law, John, talk over land offerings in the Loudonville area. John had a knack for analyzing the local land market, noticing patterns of interest in buying and selling. Now he was positive about buying land in Ashland County. The post-war economy was booming and immigrants continued to arrive seeking opportunities to take up farming. The prices for properties increased steadily with increased demand creating a favorable environment for a land trader.

In 1866, Elizabeth and John Schiedt welcomed baby Charlie to their household of eight-year-old twins. The twins both doted on their beloved baby brother. After giving up ever having another child, the Schiedt family were surprised and deeply thankful to be so blessed again.

Carl and Will prospered after the end of the Civil War. With the assistance of their brother-in-law, John Schiedt, they found good land for sale. In 1867, Will and Gretly sold their farm in Hanover Township and bought another farm in Vermillion Township, west of Hayesville, Ohio.

Carl considered property as an investment, and he needed a larger home for his growing family of nine before he bought a farm. To that end he bought four lots in Loudonville in 1869. On one of them he built a four-bedroom house with a large garden for vegetables and an orchard with apple, apricot, and cherry trees. Finally, they had the house and space for animals and a garden for their growing family. Each of the children helped tend the garden and feed the animals.

"Boys, boys, come quickly," called Anna Barbara. "The chickens are out again. Come help catch them." Henry, especially, enjoyed using the chicken hook to capture the hens and return them to the chicken house. His mother kept two hooks on a nail next to the back door. When the chickens were back inside their fence, the captors each received a snickerdoodle cookie. Even so, the family grew weary of chasing chickens on a nearly daily basis. Carl turned his attention to solving the problem of escapees from the chicken yard.

"Anna Barbara, I hired Sam Wilson to build a chicken house and a loafing shed for a sow ready to produce a litter of piglets," announced Carl a week later. When eleven piglets arrived, each child chose a piglet to care for. They took turns, morning and evening, feeding the animals and making sure they had plenty of clean water. The following week, Carl brought home a cow about to deliver a calf. His children were very interested in the grand event and thrilled to dote on their new baby calf. With all of the animal life on his property, Carl hired Mr. Wilson to build a picket fence with chicken wire around the backyard to keep out rabbits and stray dogs and to keep in their animals and young children.

April 23, 1869

Dear Carl and Anna Barbara,

Greetings from the prairie surrounding Abilene, Kansas. I hope you and your seven children are well. Now that Will and Margaretha have purchased a farm near Hayesville, you will have much to share. I hope you have the opportunity to begin farming when the time is right for you, too.

Since I last wrote to you, a cattle trail has been established for herds of longhorns coming up from Texas to the trailhead in Abilene. Last year some large herds of longhorn steers arrived in June. The new stockyards were used to corral the cattle until they were loaded onto railroad stock cars bound for markets in Chicago and further east. It seems like overnight Abilene has grown into a rowdy frontier town with the cowboy businesses of livery stables, saloons, dance halls, hotels, and restaurants. The sheriff has his hands full trying to keep the peace.

Earlier this spring, I joined a buffalo hunt west of Abilene to replenish our meat supply. Herds roam where the prairie rises and rolls toward Coronado Heights. My friends, Ezra and Henry, rode out to that high point of lime-

stone outcroppings where they could see more than 20 miles in all directions. They brought back word of a buffalo herd as far as they could see toward the setting sun. When they asked for a dozen men with rifles and wagons, I volunteered. We were out of meat in Abilene, and our hunting party rode the next day to harvest several head of American bison.

We were not the only hunting party out to kill buffalo. There are groups of Indians and white hunters killing hundreds of buffalo in a day. Some hides were taken and some meat was harvested for consumption. Even more carcasses were left on the ground to rot.

In two days, we had four bulls and three cows skinned and gutted. Thankfully, the days were cool and windy, not sultry heat waves like we have had this summer. We brought back buffalo hides along with meat in five wagons. The meat we couldn't eat fresh we dried in smoking sheds much like the Indians dry their fresh meat.

From the rowdy Great Plains, State of Kansas,
Herman Roth

✦

Following the close of the Civil War, Carl, Anna Barbara, Will, and Margaretha reflected often on the opportunities offered by Kansas statehood in 1861 and the Homestead Act in 1862. *Should we move out west to purchase land? Are our prospects for success sufficient to justify moving our families so far away from family in Cincinnati? If so, when should we plan to do so?*

chapter 15

UNITY AND TRAGEDY

July 29, 1870

Dear Carl and Anna Barbara,

I am writing you from the wild frontier town of Newton, Kansas. It is an altogether new town being built from the ground up. Right now everyone lives in canvas tents. The railroad is being built from Abilene south toward Newton, scheduled to arrive next summer. Then Newton will be the shipping point for thousands of cattle coming up from Texas along the Chisholm Trail.

For now, Newton is a wild frontier town. There are very few women, and the men who come are rambunctious and eager for adventure. They drink and gamble and fight all the time. From living in Abilene when it was the railhead, I know this town will attract wild cowboys, saloons and thousands of cattle being herded onto cattle cars. I hope we hire a sheriff soon. People call Newton "bloody and lawless—the wickedest city in the west."

How is your family? Your five older boys and two beautiful daughters? I enjoy your letters about your new home in Loudonville, the pigs and cow and chickens. Of course, I will always remember the fine times the three of us had over sauerbraten and potatoes with onions and apples when your boys were small. Do you think there will be another time we see one another in this life?

Well wishes from this infant frontier town,
Herman Roth

The five years following the Civil War were the happiest of Carls and Anna Barbara's immigrant lives in America. They welcomed a second daughter, Matilda in 1866. Eliza and Matilda were playmates and best friends, just like Anna Barbara and Gretly had been in their childhoods. In 1869 Carl and Anna Barbara basked in the relief that she had survived the dangers of childbirth. Seven pregnancies in a rhythm of two-year cycles of being pregnant and nursing left Anna Barbara happy with her brood of five sons and two daughters, yet physically weary. Another child was not forthcoming when Matilda passed her second birthday, and they believed their family was complete.

◆

LOUDONVILLE, 1869

Although not as close to his sisters as they were to each other, John Schiedt was a beloved brother and a welcome part of their lives since his move to Loudonville from Cincinnati after the war. His wife, Elizabeth, was a reliable friend to her sisters-in-law. Their twins, Eliza and John F., were age-mates and favorite playmates of their cousins, Sophia and Fred. In their daily lives, Elizabeth Schiedt often joined Anna Barbara for gardening and cooking. When Gretly visited from the farm, the three women quilted together in Elizabeth's parlor where there was plenty of space for the frame.

On one particular day in May, Elizabeth's three-year-old Charlie was playing at the end of the garden with Matilda and Eliza when Elizabeth offered, "Anna Barbara, may I help weed the lettuce and carrots?"

"Thank you. Those weeds have been neglected all week," answered Anna Barbara. She tended her garden less than she wished. She was grateful for Elizabeth's help and time to share with her sister-in-law. "Elizabeth, I received a message from Cincinnati. George's wife, Elizabeth is close to her time of delivery. George, Elizabeth and Charles O. are all anxious to welcome their new baby. After waiting so long, they are very excited," said Anna Barbara.

Blushing with her face turned away from Anna Barbara, Elizabeth decided to share a confidence. "Anna Barbara, I, too, am expecting another child," she said. She was glowing with happiness. "When Charlie was born we were so surprised after waiting so many years. John is thrilled to have another child on the way."

"Elizabeth, I am so happy for you," said Anna Barbara. She was pleased both of her sisters-in-law were having the families they longed for. "Thank you for the help with my garden. Let's take a break for a glass of water." The two women talked of babies and tent dresses while they watched Charlie, Matilda, and Eliza play in their pretend gardens.

In the fall of 1869, apples and squash ripened in the days of lengthening shadows. Anna Barbara waited another month to be sure before she announced her pregnancy to Carl, then a few days later, Gretly. When she first suspected, she did not accept her pregnancy. Her lack of acceptance was merely a temporary state of mind. Up to the moment she disclosed her condition to Carl, Anna Barbara believed Matilda was her last-born. Anna Barbara was unsettled, reluctant to accept the reality of her changing body. *This pregnancy feels different from the others. Is there a problem with this child? I feel the aches and pains like never before. Will this pregnancy never end?*

"Carl, I'm so glad you are home. John came over a few minutes ago to let us know Charlie is sick. He is running a high fever. If you can stay with our children, I will go over to help my brother's family," said Anna Barbara.

"Of course, my dear, we will be fine. Whatever they need, we are glad to help," replied Carl.

When Charlie's fever did not come down right away, Margaretha and Anna Barbara took turns staying with Charlie overnight to give his parents the opportunity to sleep. For eight nights a high fever raged through his pale body. Charles Harry Schiedt died at the age of three. He had been dearly loved by his parents and older brother and sister. Whenever they thought of him, they missed his loving nature and playful countenance. In spite of the grave loss of Charlie, Elizabeth kept her pregnancy and delivered a healthy baby, Henry, only a few weeks later, on November 15, 1869.

The Schiedts and Tangemans pulled together as they mourned the loss of Charlie and celebrated the birth of Henry. Children held a special meaning within this family, and the futures of their children gave purpose to this immigrant generation. That future guided their decisions to, at times, sacrifice present comforts for the prospect of future success. The loss of Charlie was felt deeply by his parents, the twins, his aunts and uncles, and cousins, yet shared sparingly.

Without warning, Anna Barbara's and Margaretha's brother, John, died two months later, on January 12, 1870, in Loudonville. Despite being in apparently good health, he passed out at home, and the doctor was called. He never regained consciousness, and died in the night. His wife, Elizabeth, and twins were in a state of shock, in need of moral and practical support. Anna Barbara and Margaretha took turns staying with Elizabeth, the twins and baby Henry while Carl and Will helped her make decisions about the funeral and interment of her husband's body in Loudonville Cemetery.

It was an unthinkable loss for Elizabeth Schiedt, sudden and disorienting. Even then she battled the competing emotions of grief for the loss of Charles and joy for the birth of Henry as the backdrop to her husband's death. She needed someone to depend on, and she called on Carl to be an executor of John's estate, along with Fred Schwan, an architect in Loudonville who had been John's good friend since they settled in Loudonville. Both men were honest, and she trusted them to look out for her business interests. Fred Schwan was also a cousin to Anna Marie Schiedt's husband, Jacob Schwan, who remained in Ehningen.

Elizabeth Schiedt felt the haze of grief over the loss of her son, Charles, followed by John's sudden death and the grief of knowing infant Henry would have no memory, no first-hand knowledge, of his father. The winter of 1870 sank inconspicuously below consciousness as bleak sun and forbidding early spring rain melted snow and ice at a glacial pace. Like a lumbering ursine, the earth slowly and laboriously shook off the lingering winter cold. In a similar manner, Elizabeth Schiedt began to shake off her shock and grief as sunny days replaced the gray mood of winter.

In 1870, Gretly and Will were pleased with their household of five children. Their youngest daughter, Clara, was three years old. As with Carl and Anna Barbara, Will and Gretly believed their family was now complete. With each child, Will appreciated at a deep level, his decidedly good fortune for having married this strong, capable woman who gave him the family he hoped would be their future. She seemed to become more self-assured over time, and her household management skills grew to handle their growing family. Will and Gretly were more than contented as parents and life partners. And they were even more in love than when they first decided their futures belonged to each other. Will did everything in his power to love and protect Margaretha. Her need to live close to Anna Barbara and the needs of their children came before any competing demands that surrounded them. The couple had a healthy, loving, supportive, and mutually committed relationship. They made married life look infinitely appealing to the unmarried and married alike.

✦

If she had a girl, this late pregnancy would prove to be the crowning reward of Anna Barbara's generative years. Carl was, again, joyful at the thought of another child to join the family, and during her pregnancy, he agreed with Anna Barbara that she carried a girl. Instead, on April 15, 1870, Gottlob David Tangeman joined the family as a scrawny, skinny, sickly baby, markedly different from his round-faced, robustly healthy older siblings.

When Gottlob arrived, he fussed and cried and slept in fitful spurts. The whole family took turns walking him and trying to comfort him through six months of colicky fussiness. Finally, the smallest of all the Tangeman babies learned to walk and talk to the delight of his brothers, and especially, his sisters. As with other children at the end of a long line of older, more capable siblings, Gottlob was spoiled. It was not the spoiling brought on by indulgent parents too disinterested or guilt-ridden or lazy to provide clear expectations. Rather, Gottlob was good-natured and seldom exhibited annoying or mischievous behavior. He was rarely reprimanded. His siblings played with him as a young child with an abundance of affection and physical playfulness, much the way they played with new kittens and puppies.

Gottlob grew through childhood, small for his age and "sickly." Consequently, he was rarely asked to do that which could cause him stress or nervous tension; rather, Gottlob was allowed to hide behind his childhood frailties. In contrast to his strapping older brothers, through his childhood years, Gottlob spent more time in the house or garden with his mother and sisters or with his sheep than in the fields of crops. His older brothers worked in the fields planting and harvesting with strengths and skills that seemed to elude Gottlob.

✦

Gretly listened as Will and Carl talked about land prices, land coming on the market and land they would like to see become available. Gretly was torn between her wish to remain in Loudonville near Anna Barbara and her desire to support her husband's plans for life on a farm. He and Carl considered parcels for sale in 1870. Most of them were near Hayesville, and she knew Carl wanted to purchase a farm near Hayesville as soon as possible, too. Even so, it was difficult to say "good-bye," knowing they would be ten muddy miles apart. During the winter months, Carl and Anna Barbara traveled the Hayesville road as often as it froze solid enough for a wagon with sleigh runners to pass. In early spring, the winter road ran to ruts, and they would not see each other for weeks at a time until the roads dried out enough to pass.

On May 15, 1870, Will purchased 110 acres west of Hayesville with a wheat crop growing in the field. His first task was to rent a McCormick Reaper to cut the wheat and a threshing machine to separate the grains. Since he and Carl had seen the demonstration of a McCormick Reaper before the Civil War, Will was convinced it was the way of the future. Until he bought his own machine, he rented such a reaper to harvest his wheat crop. One fellow rode on the reaping machine guiding the horses to pull the reaper while another person tied the shocks and another piled the shocks on a wagon to be threshed after the reaping was completed. For his second task he purchased a pair of draft horses to pull the reaper.

In early July, Uncle Will asked his teenage nephews and older son to form his harvesting crew. Carl's sons craved the opportunity to earn wages while they learned to use the reaper. And it was enticing to be away from home for a few weeks. They packed clothes to live at Will's farm during the week and returned home on Sundays to see the rest of the family and turn their wages over to their father. The work was new to the boys and their muscles felt the stretch the first few days. By the end of the first week, the stiffness turned into muscular arms, legs, and torsos.

Carl and Anna Barbara visited Will's and Gretly's home over the 4th of July weekend of 1870 to see the new farm and hear details of the harvest. With the holiday falling on Monday, festivities were planned for Sunday and Monday afternoons. Carl's family of ten loaded into the family wagon on Saturday afternoon for the hour's ride to Hayesville before supper. Anna

Barbara brought a basket filled with baked goods, hard-boiled eggs, sausages, and potato salad. Will and Margaretha were ready for their siblings' family with strudel and liverwurst sandwiches. Margaretha spread out sleeping mats for the younger children in the parlor. The older boys settled their mats on the porch where they talked of farming and girls late into the evenings. The younger children were settled before Carl, Anna Barbara, Will, and Margaretha took chairs outside to visit.

◆

Buying land had been Carl's dream since he left Prussia. To a man who lost his first family in New Orleans and lived through a near death river steamer crash on the Mississippi River, the security of owning land held great appeal. At the same time, his cautious nature prevented him from plunging into land ownership partly based on inspiration and hunches as Will had done. *Do I have enough cash to clear a sale, or am I willing to take out a land mortgage? If so, at what interest? Will I be able to secure enough property for each of my offspring to eventually have a start in farming in the current business climate? If not, should we move out west and become pioneers?* Carl grappled with these questions before he made a commitment to purchase land in Ohio.

◆

April 10, 1871

Dear Carl,

Greetings from your family in Sulingen. Hermann, his family and I are all well. I hope you, your brothers and sisters and families are well, too. Much is happening here in Prussia.

Finally, Prussian Chancellor Otto von Bismarck has created a unified Germany with Prussia and the four states of southern Germany, Bavaria, Wurttemberg, Baden and Hesse-Darmstadt. We finally came together to confront our conflict with France.

We hope this war will be over soon with a German victory. Even now, there is a new energy and pride in our new German nation. We have hoped for this moment through upheavals of my lifetime. At last we will be able to defend our German areas from the Russians, French and British. They have tramped through our mountains and valleys of German-speaking central Europe raiding fields and barns for food to reprovision their armies. Already, I see our confidence rising after so many years of feeling inferior to these other European powers.

Thank you for your letters about life in America. Now that Wilhelm has purchased a farm, perhaps you will be able to do so also. The opportunities for a good future are much better where you are than here in Sulingen.

You are in my thoughts and prayers every day. I am thankful you are in a peaceful country, now that your civil war is over. You and your family have a bright future in Ohio.

Your father,
F. T. Tangemann

✦

On the evening Paul George brought his grandfather's letter home from the post office, Carl saved it to read after supper. First he read it silently, then out loud to his family. Carl finished reading his father's letter and laid it on the dining room table. This news of the unification of Germany brought tears to his eyes as he recalled the struggles of his family and thousands of German-speaking people of central Europe. "Papa, what is wrong?" asked Mattie, his five-year-old younger daughter. "Why are you sad, Papa?"

"Come here, little one. Come sit on my lap," her father replied. "The letter I just read was from your Grosspapa Tangemann in the old country of Germany." Carl paused to swallow at the sound of saying, "Germany" out loud. "Would you like me to tell you a story of people in our old country?" asked Carl.

"Yes, Papa. I like your stories," said Mattie. She clapped her hands, then climbed onto her father's lap.

"This is a story of my parents and grandparents, and their parents and grandparents who lived in the area of Sulingen where your grosspapa lives now. He wrote the letter I just read to you."

"What happened so long ago that makes you sad, Papa?" asked August who was curious about his family that stayed in the old country.

"Children, for more than 200 years our people in the old country have had a difficult time when other countries were at war with each other. The French, Austrians, Russians, and the British have fought wars to see which country was the strongest. Have you ever played 'King of the Mountain'?" asked Carl.

"Oh, yes," was the chorus of responses.

"Those countries all wanted to be the 'King of the Mountain' of the European continent," continued Carl.

"What about Germany? Did Germany fight in those wars?" asked Fred.

"There was no country of Germany until this year, only dozens of small kingdoms and principalities of German-speaking people," replied Carl. "Do you remember where the German-speaking people live?"

"Yes," answered August. "They live in the middle of Europe."

"That's correct. What do you think happened to the people in the middle when the other countries had a war?" asked Carl. He waited for the question to sink into their brains.

"When the French marched to Russia, they marched through Bavaria and Darmstadt and Heidelberg and other German areas. When they came home, they were hungry. The French took the wheat and oats and rye from the farms. If there were horses or pigs or cows, they took those, too. And they looked in storage areas for apples, potatoes, and onions."

"Papa, why didn't our people fight back? They can't just let other countries steal their crops and animals," asked John.

"In this case, the German states had small armies, not strong enough to defend against the great French army and win. Instead, our people learned to hide and pretend to be very poor with few animals and little food. They used caves and underground chambers to hide most of the animals and grains, and, of course, the women and children. The men left a few animals and bags of grain in sight so that the foreign army would take what they saw and leave. They learned to survive with little power in the face of the great armies of Europe. Many people starved during the wars back then, but the people who used their resources wisely survived," Carl explained. He looked to the end of the table his eyes shining with gratitude to Anna Barbara for her thrifty German ways.

"Everything has now changed where Grosspapa lives. The German states have been unified, which means they have learned to work together as a whole nation. If they need to do so, they will be able to raise a large army and defend themselves from foreign invaders. Germany is finally a nation, and we can all be proud of our German heritage," concluded Carl.

117

chapter 16

WESTERN FEVER

APRIL, 1872

Winter of 1872 in Loudonville slid into spring almost unnoticed by Carl, Anna Barbara, and their household of six sons and two daughters. The cause for their preoccupation was the farm Carl and Anna Barbara had a contract to purchase west of Hayesville. Their household goods must be packed, both houses thoroughly cleaned, and the trunks and boxes transferred between them. Most importantly, the fields must be prepared in time for the rapidly approaching spring planting.

On this last day before the Tangeman family moved out of their Loudonville home, Carl arrived home from work at the foundry with a letter he waved in one hand and whispered, "Anna Barbara, we have a letter from Herman."

"Papa, papa," squealed two-year-old Gottlob who ran to greet his father. Carl opened the picket fence gate to the back yard and swooped up slender Gottlob, tossing him a few inches in the air.

Anna Barbara glanced toward the back door and smiled at her husband. She was pleased and excited with this move to a farm two miles south of Will's and Margaretha's farm in Vermillion Township.

Carl's and Anna Barbara's sons were ready to move to the farm, too. They were eager to implement all they had learned about farm machines, planting, and harvesting. Paul George and Henry were tall and strong, impatient to follow a plow, pitch hay into the hay mow of the barn, and harvest grain crops.

Carl was also anxious to apply his mental and physical strengths to his new career in agriculture. He had learned the timing for planting wheat, corn, and oats from the successes and failures of customers at the foundry and friends at church. He had examined numerous parcels of land with Anna Barbara's brother, John, and learned to judge the productive capacity of sandy and loamy soils. He followed changes in prices of grain crops and livestock compared with prices of land. He knew when a given piece of land was offered at an attractive price. He observed rainfall for northern Ohio to know what to expect on his own farm. As he anticipated owning and working the thick, dark, loamy land, he believed the ravages of famine he encountered in Sulingen would not reach his doorstep in Ohio.

Carl's enthusiasm for farming captured the aspirations of his five oldest sons like the sweet, pungent aroma of wheat berries that would soon circulate familiar fragrances through their nostrils. Through the winter of 1872, supper table talk had been lively with questions about new machines and varieties of seeds flying around the table along with tidbits of information gleaned from neighboring farmers and agricultural publications.

"Supper is served," announced Anna Barbara. She placed the soup kettle at her end of the harvest table. After washing hands, the Tangeman offspring found their seats on side benches, with Mama on one end, Papa on the other end. Carl sliced fresh bread, while Anna Barbara served the potato soup with sausages and winter vegetables.

At the end of supper, Carl stated, "I have something in my pocket. Would you like to know what it is?"

His offspring replied enthusiastically, "Yes, Papa, yes!"

"Are you ready to hear a letter from our friend, Mr. Roth?" asked Carl, a sly grin sliding around the corners of his mouth.

"Yes, Papa, yes, yes," was the boisterous reply from his brood of offspring.

◆

March 23, 1872

Dear Carl and Anna Barbara,

I decided to stay here in Newton, Kansas for another season. Last year's cattle drive up the Chisholm Trail from Texas ended at the trailhead in Newton. Most of the dusty herds arrived in June. The cowboys stayed near the banks of Sand Creek until their cattle shipped out on the Santa Fe Railroad to Kansas City, and eventually to Chicago. Each cattle drive outfit kept their cattle out on the prairie until it was their turn to ship. Part of the cowboys stayed with the cattle while the other part came to Newton for some recreation. As fast as those cowboys collected their wages, most of them came into town and gambled and drank it away. The worst incident occurred last August over an argument between lawmen Billy Bailey and Mike McCluskie in Hide Park. In the end, eight men were dead. Newton is now known as "*bloody and lawless—the wickedest city in the west.*"

Work is easy to find in a cowtown. I don't like to work in a saloon, but sometimes I help drag out the drunks to the livery stable down the street for a place to sleep it off. That's better than letting them get into fights, sometimes gun fights that get out of hand. The general store is a better place to work. The cowboys come in to buy supplies, but also some settlers stop by. Everyone needs provisions to live or work on the prairie. Last week a widow lady with two children came into the store to buy a few things. Her husband got caught in the crossfire of a gunfight and lost his leg, then gangrene set in and he died. She and the children were ready to take the next train back east. She said she could not make it out west without a husband. I agreed, this town is too wild for a woman alone. Too bad she did not ask me if I was interested in being a husband again.

If you write me a letter in care of the Newton Post Office, I will receive it. Our first post office opened this year. I would enjoy hearing about your growing family. Did you find a farm to buy in Ohio? I hope you are still thinking about moving out west.

> *Your friend,*
> *Herman Roth*

"Papa, let's move out west! There are cowboys and cattle drives and gun fights. When I leave home, I'm going west," exclaimed August Charles. He was not the only Tangeman brother thinking about the attraction of the western states. His brothers broke into a bevy of side conversations about Mr. Roth's letter and how they imagined life in Kansas.

Carl enjoyed the banter among his older sons imagining life far out west. "Boys, we will learn more from Mr. Roth and his adventures in Kansas. For now, we are moving to Vermillion Township . . . . tomorrow."

Enthusiasm ran high on the last night in their Loudonville home. Anticipation invaded their dreams and shaped this family's beliefs in their upward path of progress.

✦

On April 10, 1872, Carl and Anna Barbara walked to the train station past charred and smoldering businesses adjacent to the tin shop. Five nights earlier a fire had started in the tin shop and swept through nearby buildings on the Loudonville town square. Joining their neighbors, Carl and the older boys passed water buckets in the fire brigade that fought the fire, to no avail. The devastating fire was more than twice as destructive as the Lutheran Church fires in the previous decade. With this greater loss, citizens of Loudonville clamored to demand the town board establish a fire department.

Carl and Anna Barbara met the Ashland County Clerk at eight o'clock right after breakfast to sign papers and pay for their first farm. They returned home within the hour to the cheers and excitement of their sons and daughters. The family launched into a final whirl of preparations to move. Anna Barbara had organized household goods into wooden boxes, trunks, and barrels and marked them for rooms in their new farmhouse. Once transported, the packed containers were delivered to one of four bedrooms upstairs, parlor, large dining room, country kitchen downstairs, plus a root cellar and back porch.

The older boys shouldered the responsibility of packing beds, tables, lamps, chairs, and household goods into the buckboard. Then Carl explained how the move would proceed, "Paul George will drive the first load including Mama, sisters, little brother, and Henry to the new house. Fred will ride another horse alongside the wagon. Older boys will unload the cargo into the new house. Next Paul George will return to Loudonville for another load of goods."

Carl continued, "Henry and Fred will stay at the new house and deliver household goods to their designated rooms, and reassemble beds and tables and situate chairs. Eliza and Matilda, you will entertain Gottlob while Mama works to settle into the new house." Even though the house appeared to be clean, Anna Barbara wiped down shelves, cabinets, walls, and floors, her "nesting" ritual. She was not satisfied the house was ready to occupy until she had cleaned it herself. Then she directed her older sons to put the dishes, pots, pans, and linens in sideboard and cupboards.

On those first days living on their Vermillion Township farm, rain or shine, Carl woke up eager to tackle his farming tasks. After twenty-four immigrant years in Ohio, he now owned his own farm. He was eager to apply all he had learned, and it pleased him that his five older sons shared his enthusiasm to master the business of farming.

Following breakfast on this first Monday in their new home, Carl called for the attention of his family, "My dear family, today we begin our grand adventure in agriculture. There is much to do this week. Today and every Monday I will go over the tasks to be done and your assignments at breakfast. For everyone in school, you will continue your schooling through the next six weeks. First, Gottlob, your job is to help Mama and keep her company," Carl smiled at his youngest son on his mother's lap. Gottlob squirmed, squinted, and giggled his agreement. Then Carl turned his attention to his older sons. "Of course, Mama is in charge of the house and garden with her able helpers, Eliza and Matilda. Girls, when you return home from school in Hayesville, you will feed the chickens and entertain each other and Gottlob."

"August and John will complete the larger animal chores and garden tilling." The younger boys often followed their father and older brothers around the farm, helping a bit here and there, and "catching" enthusiasm for farm life.

"When you return home after school today, here is what I want you to do. Paul George and Fred, take the dark pair of horses and harrow the far southwest field. That is where we will plant corn in a few weeks," directed Carl.

"Papa, do we have new harnesses for that team?" asked Paul George. He and Fred were eager to show their father they could handle a team of horses as well as any man in Ohio.

"Yes, you will find them on pegs in the tack room," replied Carl.

"Henry, I need you to help me repair the corral fence," said Carl. "Mother, what is your plan for this week?" he asked Anna Barbara. Of course, Carl and Anna Barbara had already discussed the week's work for the house and garden. Her work was vital to the success of their family farm, and Carl wanted his sons and daughters to hear her plans directly and be ready to lend a hand.

Anna Barbara explained, "Today I will wash clothes and hang them out to dry. Tomorrow I will bake bread for the week, and maybe streusel or *stollen*." At this comment her sons smiled in appreciation for the fresh bread and desserts. "Perhaps I will be able to unpack the last few boxes for the kitchen today. Before the end of the week, I will need help to clean out the root cellar. There are leftover vegetables from last year and other boxes to be carried out." Then she turned to August and John who usually made a compatible work team. "The garden is dry enough to turn over the earth. August and John, if we do not have rain today, will you spade the garden this afternoon?" asked their mother.

"Yes, Mother," replied her ten- and twelve-year-old sons, displeasure showing in their voices. They wished they could do "real farm work" like their older brothers, but they dared not speak their desires openly. Every son and daughter was expected to complete assigned tasks without complaint, but August and John could not hide their true feelings of disappointment about garden work.

Carl listened to his sons' suggestions and preferences, including their facial expressions, but in the end, his decision determined how to proceed. There was little grumbling in Carl's presence. Carl considered the contributions of his sons, and, in return, they respected the fairness and the inherent wisdom in his decisions. Carl led his five older sons in a similar fashion as he had led the company of Sandstrom militia under his command back home in Sulingen, Hanover, Prussia. Beneath his disciplined demeanor, Carl cared deeply for his children, perhaps even more because they were his second chance for a loving family. Anna Barbara was especially dear to him. He admired her strength and appreciated their family. When she smiled at him from her end of their dining room table, he smiled back his deep sense of love and fulfillment.

◆

Each Monday Carl thought through jobs for his entire "crew." Older boys drove a team for spring-tooth harrowing, planting corn and oats. Younger boys usually spread manure, mucked out stables, and fed the chickens, sheep, cattle, and pigs, morning and evening. Meanwhile, Carl took steers and pigs to market, and, anyone could be asked to help Mama with the garden and heavier housework.

By mid-April, the harrowed fields were ready for planting spring wheat, followed by oats, and corn later in the month. Carl borrowed Will's planter when not in use to sow each crop in exchange for Paul George's, Henry's, or Fred's labor to re-build Will's fences. Charles W. was sixteen and old enough to do most of what Will could do on the farm. His next son, Otto, was twelve (almost thirteen) in the summer of 1872, willing but yet to develop the height and strength he needed for heavier farm work. Will often hired one of his nephews for an extra farm hand, and they were welcome companions for Charles W.

The weather cooperated in 1872 for planting spring wheat. Gentle rains fell most evenings followed by warm, mild days that dried out the soil. By the end of April a good stand of wheat grass appeared as green stripes on the dark earth. Then came the green blades of wheat wide enough to make whistles when held between thumbs and vibrated by a breath of air. Through May and June, hollow, emerald stalks emerged from the grassy blades, and eventually topped out with green heads hiding chewy bits of grain. The heavy, spidery head tips stretched straight up to the sky. Carl recognized the prospect of a bumper crop.

In mid-May, the school year finished to the great relief and celebration of the Tangeman youngsters. The six older children finished their school year in Hayesville – Eliza, John, August, and Fred in elementary school; and, Henry and Paul George at the Vermillion Institute. Paul George was especially glad to complete his studies and graduate. He was equally surprised to be offered a position teaching math at the institute for the fall term. This opportunity allowed him to help with the farm work in the summer and earn a steady salary during the winter. He gratefully accepted the offer.

The July heat and wheat harvest arrived the same week. Carl and Will checked the wheat crop almost every day for ripening heads turning yellow and bending toward the horizon from moisture gathering in the wheat berries. In this last month before harvest, sunshine and gentle rains gradually added weight and plumpness to the kernels, increasing their value at market.

Carl and Will planned how to coordinate their rented McCormick Reaper for both farms. The two brothers and their older sons took turns guiding the horse-drawn reaper and walking beside the machine, tying stalks of cut wheat into shocks. It was hot, itchy work. The men worked long, sweaty days to bring in the harvest. The proceeds from this wheat harvest would support both families for the coming year.

Will rented the threshing machine with a crew to separate the grains from the chaff and prepare the wheat for market. Compared with the scythe method of wheat harvest by hand used for centuries, these modern reapers and threshing machines were highly efficient, saving both time and effort.

"Boys, for this first harvest, I want you to observe how the men and the machine work together. It is your job to learn each step of the harvest.

Next year we will complete the work even more efficiently with fewer hired farm hands."

Carl and Will were relieved and gratified with both high yields and high prices for wheat in 1872. The profits from selling the wheat brought in more than Carl's wages at the Miller Foundry for an entire year. The oats and corn were yet to be harvested for additional income.

The Monday after the completion of wheat harvest, Carl called his family together after breakfast. "Your mother and I are both relieved and grateful for our farming success. With the help of each of you, we have sold enough wheat to support our family for the coming year. This good news also gives us hope that we will be able to help each of you begin your adult lives when the time comes. Mama and I believe there is a way to accumulate the resources to purchase land, at least eighty acres for each of you. As you each earn wages from working for another farmer or other employment, you will keep one third of your wages for your personal use and give me the other two thirds to accumulate for future land purchases. With this first wheat harvest behind us, you older boys will be available to help other farmers for wages until you return to school in the fall."

When Carl and Anna Barbara began this policy, they believed they would purchase land in the Hayesville area for each youngster. However, as the price of land climbed in Ohio through the 1870s, they realized they needed to move out west to afford eight parcels of eighty acres each.

◆

November 10, 1872

Dear Carl and Anna Barbara,

Since my last letter, Newton has changed from a wild frontier place into an upstanding city. I'm pleased to announce the State of Kansas has granted Newton a charter of incorporation, and last summer an election was held for sheriff and mayor. By fall we had two churches, Presbyterian and Methodist Episcopal, and a public school.

The town doesn't need twenty-seven saloons now that the Santa Fe railroad tracks were built Newton to Wichita and Ellsworth has been connected to the Union Pacific. Now the cattle drives from Texas will arrive in

Ellsworth, a town about seventy miles northwest of Newton, or Wichita, twenty miles south. Already, settlers arrive every week looking for land or another livelihood. The new folks will need tools, clothing, housewares, dry goods, and more.

I'll stay here for a while, perhaps open a dry goods store in one of those abandoned saloons.

With best regards,
Herman Roth

On the Sunday afternoon before Thanksgiving in 1872, Carl asked Paul George to join him in the parlor. "Now that you are a teacher at Vermillion Institute, how is this job working out for you?"

Paul George had not expected this question. "I like teaching math to the older boys. Math comes easy for me. To tell the truth, I get frustrated with some of the younger students who just don't care to work hard enough to master the material. I think I would like farming more, but we can't afford to purchase land right now."

Carl observed his son's expression, then continued, "I like farming because I work for myself, instead of someone else. In a good crop year, there is a very good return on investment. Sure, we need to manage for occasional crop losses from bad weather. If we all work together and pool our resources, we may be able to purchase parcels of land here in Ashland County."

"Papa, I like your plan to accumulate enough money to purchase other parcels for us. I have a good job, and I will contribute my wages to purchase land," said Paul George thoughtfully. "I'm not sure we will be able to acquire that much land here in Ohio. What do you think about moving out west for some cheaper land?" he asked.

"Not for a few years," replied Carl, thinking cautiously about such a major move. "I read about farming on the prairie. Nebraska or Kansas might be good places to look for land. And I will keep in touch with Herman Roth about the land near Newton. After farming these hillsides a few years, I will be ready to farm rich soil on flat land," Carl said with a chuckle.

Carl realized the seed of "pioneer fever" had been planted in Paul George's consciousness, and he was receptive to the call of adventure and opportunity out west. He read newspapers about everything west of the Missippippi; crops, rain patterns, cattle drives, and locusts. Then he read and reread Mr. Roth's letters for every detail of life on the prairie.

When Paul George left the parlor, Henry was waiting in the hallway to approach his father. "Papa, do you have a minute?"

Carl was pleased to see Henry and invited him into the parlor. "Henry, come in. Have a seat," Carl gestured expectantly.

"Papa, what do you know about winter wheat? I've been reading about winter wheat in the west. Is it really better than spring wheat?" asked Henry. He was interested in farming, but he usually let his brothers take the lead in discussions when they were all together. Now he wanted to know what his father knew about planting and harvesting winter wheat on the prairie. His shyness faded from his face as he opened up to learn about agriculture from his father.

Carl looked carefully into the inquiring eyes of his second son. "Henry, I have read of winter wheat, too. It is supposed to grow roots and stems in the fall that are more likely to survive a bitter cold winter. In the spring, it grows early enough to be harvested before the drought period of July and August."

"Papa, wheat is supposed to be the best crop for the prairie. But, there are other risks besides drought, like locusts and rust from too much rain. A lot of farmers have gone broke because they didn't know farming is different on the Great Plains compared to states like Ohio and Indiana," continued Henry with a worried look on his face.

"Yes, Henry, there will be great risks if we decide to move west. For now, we must learn all we can about soils, moisture, insects, heat and cold, seeds, and markets. If we move, we will do so from a position of understanding the risks and rewards," reassured Carl, pleased to share his cautious approach to farming with his second oldest son.

chapter 17

CHRISTMAS JOY

Carl, Anna Barbara, Will and Margaretha, and their collective brood of fourteen offspring boarded the train from Mansfield to Cincinnati on December 23, 1872.

The Schiedt sisters settled into a coach seat together for the long day's ride. "Gretly, it seems like years since we gathered for Christmas. When we come to Cincinnati, it feels more like our celebrations in the old country. I feel we are sharing our German traditions with the children when we get together with our siblings and their families," said Anna Barbara, anticipation showing on her face and in the lilt of her voice.

"Louise works for weeks to prepare the foods for our meals. She and Elizabeth decided where we would all stay. You and Carl will stay with Elizabeth and George with the girls and older boys. Will and I will be with Louise and Otto with the rest of the children," explained Gretly.

Across the isle of the swaying train, Paul George approached his father. "Papa, the older fellows would like some time to explore Over-the-Rhine, and perhaps downtown Cincinnati. What do you think?" he asked. Carl looked his oldest son in the eye to read his emotions. With his son now eighteen, Carl recognized the desires of young men to scout out the city. Knowing their cousin Charles O. could show them the sights, Carl heartily supported their plan. At the same time, he replied to Paul George's request with a tone of reticence, to convey caution as he recalled his own encounters with nativists on the streets of Over-the-Rhine in the 1850s.

"All right, you, Henry, Charles W. may accompany Charles O. for some time out on the town. Of course, be sure to be back when your mother asks you to return," replied Carl. As the second generation of immigrants in the U.S., these boys no longer appeared to be foreign in speech or dress. The parents were comfortable allowing their older boys a degree of latitude to explore as long as they remained with their cousins.

"Papa, papa," called Fred urgently to his father. He leaned over the wooden seat back in front of Carl. "August, John, Otto, and I want to go out while we are in Cincinnati, too. We think it would be great to see Over-the-Rhine, maybe go to a German Club. Is that all right?"

Carl was less inclined to allow his younger sons the latitude he granted to his two older sons. At the same time, he wanted the younger ones to enjoy their holiday in the city. "Fred, I understand you would like to have an outing here in Cincinnati. Will and I have talked about going to the *Schützenverein*, a shooting club close by Louise and Otto's home. Would you and the other fellows like to come along?"

"Papa, that sounds great," replied Fred. "Will we get to shoot, too?"

"Let's go and find out if there is a shooting contest for boys your age," Carl suggested. In Prussia Carl attended a *Schützenfest* every summer in his teen years at the end of the grain harvest. He entered the shooting contest and usually competed well, ranking among the top shooters. Afterward, everyone enjoyed the food, music, and dances, Carl remembered.

Louise Otten hosted Christmas Day dinner in her substantial, two-story home as she had numerous times over their years in Cincinnati. Her sisters-in-law brought what they could from their farms near Hayesville: sausages, cheeses, and beer. With a crowd this size, Louise cooked for several days before Christmas, assisted by her daughters, Sophia and Bettie and her sister, Wilhelmina, who had married Dietrich Otten, her husband's brother. Every detail was planned to ensure the comfort and enjoyment of this celebration by the extended Tangeman family. Over forty relatives were expected to attend.

For the Christmas Day feast, there were Tangeman cousins in every room of the Otten home. The younger generation divided naturally into older cousins, middle cousins, and younger cousins.

At noon, the eleven adults who were Tangeman siblings and spouses gathered around the dining room table. They were surrounded by all of their offspring including Louise's grandchildren. "Brother Carl, will you bless us by offering thanks for this meal?" asked Otto.

"Thank you, brother Otto. I am honored to do so," replied Carl. He took a deep breath and surveyed this household overflowing with Tangeman brothers, sisters, and offspring. "Heavenly Father, we give thanks to You for bringing us safely to America. Thank you, especially, for the day my brothers and I found each other here in Cincinnati. Being with family is the greatest joy, the highest value of this life. We are blessed to be surrounded by bonds of kinship with those who support us continually, in times of joy, and times of sorrow. And we remember and pray for those who have departed this life and Grosspapa Tangeman and Grosspapa Schiedt and those in our families who continue to live in the old country. We give thanks for loving spouses and healthy children, the next generation of Tangemans in America. And we give thanks for the meal we are about to partake, for the hands that prepared it. We pray for Your continued blessings on each person at this gathering and for Your love as we celebrate the birth of Christ this Christmas. In Your name, amen."

Louise wiped away a tear with her apron. "Carl, when I heard your voice speaking this prayer, it sounded so much like our Papa. Thank you. Now, let us begin this Christmas feast. I hope you are all hungry. We will serve the children first and hope there is something remaining for the rest of us," she said recovering her sense of humor. The dining room table overflowed with traditional Christmas dishes: *katenbrot* (barn bread) with cheeses, sausages, sauerbraten, and pork roasts with potatoes and apples. As each dish was emptied, Louise and her able assistants refilled from large pots in the kitchen. Desserts of Christmas *stollen, strudel,* and *lebkuchen* were served from the oak sideboard along with coffee, beer, and wine later in the afternoon.

The Tangeman brothers and sisters remembered and spoke fondly of their parents. "Do you remember Mama's apple strudel? As much as I try, I still cannot make mine taste quite like hers," laughed Louise.

"Even so, it is the best strudel I ever tasted," commented her husband, Otto. "I could use a little more strudel." And the crowd cheered for Louise's strudel.

"At least you had so many years to work with Mama. I was young when she died. She let me make strudel only twice," commented Wilhelmina Otten. "So now I learn from you."

"Papa was so particular with his leather saddles," said Carl. "I never felt like I measured up to his standards. Then one day Mr. Nussenbaum came to have his saddle repaired, and he asked for me. It was a proud moment. Then again, perhaps Papa asked Mr. Nussenbaum to ask for me to keep me interested in saddlery." The table joined Carl in a toast, "To Papa. May you live many more years in good health."

That afternoon, the siblings shared details from Papa's letters to various family members and those from Hermann, their older brother who had stayed in the old country.

Laughter, music, games, stories, and playful jesting filled Aunt Louise's and Uncle Otto's two-story house the rest of the day and well into the evening. When the Tangeman family members left, they, too, were filled with the aromas, tastes, sounds, language, and love that blended their German heritage with the fruits of their American opportunities.

131

chapter 18

VULNERABLE

*"Kansas will be to America what the country of the Black Sea
. . . is now to Europe—her wheat field."*

— *Topeka Commonwealth*
October 15, 1874

A cholera epidemic broke out in New Orleans in early 1873. It spread up the Mississippi River and its tributaries through the spring and early summer of that year. One of the river steamers, similar to the ones Carl rode upstream from New Orleans to Girard, Missouri, in 1847, had an outbreak of cholera on board. River towns on the route upstream were infected. From Ohio, it was difficult for the Tangemans to assess whether they would encounter the epidemic if they traveled west by train to Kansas City, Abilene, and Newton. They believed cholera was a reason to listen for more news from the Great Plains and wait for a better time to move west.

LATE FEBRUARY 1873
An unexpected benefit of farming for Carl was the time he spent with his family on inclement days. He often settled in the parlor with a stack of *Ohio Farmer, Mansfield Gazette,* and *The Farmers' Magazine.* Although he spoke halting English, his command of written English was excellent. Every contemporary agricultural topic captured Carl's interest, including machines, seed varieties, crop prices, and transportation costs. By March he had also repaired buildings, fences, and leather goods such as harnesses. Carl was restless to begin this first full-year cycle of planting and harvesting their own crops on their own land. With all other preparations made for the new crop year, Carl and Will planned to secure a loan to fund farm machinery.

The rain let up in mid-February, and soon after, the dirt road from Hayesville to their farm dried out enough to be passable. Carl and Will planned to visit Haskell's Bank in Loudonville to secure a loan for the purchase of a new spring-tooth harrow, a wheat drilling machine, and a Mc-Cormick reaper. Like most farmers, the Tangeman brothers accepted that some debt was necessary to secure seeds and equipment they needed to produce crops.

"Carl, are you sure we need to borrow money for the farm machinery? Is there any other way to rent or borrow the machines we need?" asked Anna Barbara. She worried about how debt could interfere with their farming prospects. Assuming debt placed the farm and their future at risk if the crops failed.

"Anna Barbara, I want to have the machines ready before the rain stops. Now is the time to secure a loan and order our machines so that we are ready for planting. Leasing machines will cost nearly as much. This way we will have the machines for next year, too," replied Carl with a broad smile. He gave her a reassuring hug, while silently sharing her apprehension about assuming this debt.

Williams and Carl's families were early members of the McKay Grange in Vermillion Township. This local Grange joined the wave of Ohio Granges organized in the early 1870s. It was formed in 1872 at the McKay School located midway between Hayesville and Loudonville, Ohio, at the junction of Perrysville and Hayesville Roads. The purpose of Grange organizations was to represent agricultural interests and influence state and national policies in a time of rapid agricultural mechanization, greater grain production, and price fluctuations.

In early March 1873, Will and Margaretha and Carl and Anna Barbara loaded up their families and food in wagons to attend the quarterly Grange gathering on the month's second drizzly Saturday afternoon. Food overflowed picnic baskets – bread, butter, apricot preserves, *apfelkuchen*, bratwurst and cheeses.

Local Granges were organized around families. In the morning, children played games while the older girls and women gathered around the quilting frame. With needles and threads they sewed together the pieced top, a filling layer, and backing in a quilting pattern.

"Anna Barbara, is this your quilt? These stitches are tiny like yours," asked Bertha Zimmer. She admired the artistry of the quilt.

"I agree this quilt is beautifully made," replied Anna Barbara. "I wish I could claim it for my own," she smiled back to Bertha.

"I think I know who made this quilt," stated Fiona Wilson. "It looks like Margaretha Hawkey's work."

"That's right, it is mine," affirmed Margaretha as she sat down in the quilting group after checking on the children. "I started this quilt after we arrived in Ohio. Then I set it aside when baby Louis was on the way. When he was old enough to walk and talk, I picked it up again." Margaretha spread the quilt out on the quilt frame. As the conversation meandered through the afternoon, the women worked together to tie the layers of fabric together and apply a hand-quilting pattern to stitch them securely.

Anna Barbara said, "I always have at least one quilt underway. Eliza began her first quilt, a nine-patch, this winter."

"I'm surprised she is interested at such a young age," commented Bertha. "We could bring our other girls into quilting, too."

"Perhaps we should make a quilt to sell at the county fair this year or next," suggested Fiona.

"That's a good idea," replied Ann Heckman. "We could make it a centennial quilt for the 1876 fair."

Anna Barbara chimed in, "Do we want an all-over pattern or a sampler? I saw a sampler in Ashland last summer. Part of it was individual blocks, and the border area was made with matching squares."

"Two years should be enough to plan and gather the fabrics and finish the stitching," agreed Dorothee Higbee.

The women agreed to bring back sketches and fabric samples to their next grange meeting. A hand-made Centennial quilt could bring in much needed money for the Grange treasury, the source of funding for bulk purchases of seeds and smaller farm implements.

Meanwhile, on the other side of the large meeting room, the men gathered to share their experiences with new farm machines. They expressed enthusiasm for the drilling and reaper machines, while they were worried about the financial ruin of some farmers if there was a recession.

Unlike most organizations of the time, women were welcomed as voting members of Grange. During the afternoon business meeting, a heated discussion broke out about farm debt. "We bought so many plows and harrows. How are we going to pay the cost of loans with wheat and corn prices dropping through the floor?"

"If the banks managed their businesses better, we would not be in danger of foreclosure if crops fail a particular year."

"The cost of shipping has to be controlled."

By the end of the meeting, members agreed to a resolution for the state legislature to limit the shipping cost of a ton of freight to five cents a mile. (After much statewide political pressure, the measure was destined to pass into state law in 1874, to the great relief of farmers in Ohio. This temporary reprieve was real help for farmers who suffered from the recession of 1873 and a concrete expression of the growing political influence of Grange organizations of the State of Ohio.)

For the last item of business, Mrs. Steinbrenner, a visitor who represented the State of Ohio Grange, announced, "It is my pleasure to attend your spring gathering of the McKay Grange. The Ohio Grange is here to listen to your concerns and ideas and lend our help to solve agricultural issues in Ohio. Today I am also here to announce a grand opportunity for McKay Grange to participate in the Philadelphia Centennial Exposition in 1876. The State of Ohio Grange will receive cash support from the National Grange organization for representatives from local Granges to attend," Mrs. Steinbrenner smiled and paused for the applause. She explained, "Although much planning and organization must take place before this grand event, I am here to encourage you to consider attending. The Philadelphia Exposition will be a celebration of the founding of America one hundred years ago. It will showcase the progress of mining, manufacturing, and agriculture, and the mechanical revolution we see all around us. I encourage you to send a delegation to learn and bring back the latest news about farm machines and farming methods." Her suggestion was met with more enthusiastic applause and nods of agreement.

✦

In late March 1873, Carl and his sons plunged headlong into preparing fields for planting wheat, corn, and oats using a team of horses and the spring-tooth harrow. Like 1872, the farm crops promised overflowing granaries. Throughout Vermillion Township, Ashland County, and beyond, farmers were optimistic for another year of record farm yields and corresponding income.

✦

At breakfast on the last Saturday in March 1873, Carl announced this was the day to begin planting their wheat crop. Every family member felt the anticipation of beginning the crop year. They expected to watch the wheat stems grow, feel the grains ripen and harden, smell their musky sweetness, and hear the raspy brush of mature heads swaying in a summer breeze. These feelings of hopeful anticipation had come to Carl when they first planted their garden in Loudonville, and he would feel the same during every spring planting season for the rest of his life.

"Yesterday, I picked up the drilling machine from your Uncle Will. He used it to plant wheat earlier this week, and now it is our turn. Henry, I would like you to help me hitch the drill to the field team. Then, I will begin to plant the southeast field we harrowed earlier in the week. While Henry and I are planting, Paul George and Fred will muck out the horse stalls. For today, August and John are assigned to turn over the garden soil for when Mama says it is time to plant."

Hitching the horses suited Henry. He was comfortable with his assignments either in the barn or in the field. All the while he thought about new farming methods. Agricultural machines, methods, and crops were constantly on his mind.

When the horses were securely hitched to the drilling machine and the canisters filled with wheat seeds, Carl smiled to his son, "Henry, let's get this crop in the ground. I will plant the first round, then we will trade off. Keep this gunny sack of wheat at the north end of the field. That's where we will refill the seed canister."

The first round of planting began closest to the farmhouse, along the east side of the wheat field. Carl guided the team southward parallel to the split rail fence that marked their property line. At the far end of the field, Carl turned the team around and guided them north to the spot where Henry nearly danced in anticipation as he waited to refill the seed canister. Then he took over the team and followed his father's pattern directing the team to the south end and back to the north end of the field. For eight more rounds Carl and Henry took turns guiding the team, planting one round each, to the south then returning to the north end of the field. On this sloping hillside, each round required more muscle power than the previous round to keep the drill moving forward without toppling over to the downhill side.

Carl began the eleventh round of planting at an awkward angle with one of the team positioned downhill from its partner. Partway across the southward progression of the team, a few of the drill feet caught on a rock submerged in the soil. When the horses could no longer move forward and stopped, Carl snapped the leather lead straps commanding the team to move forward. The drill was stuck. Carl attempted to maneuver the drill to the right around the rock. Instead, the drill slipped downward into a low spot in the field which caused the drill to overbalance and turn over to the right, slipping several feet down the hillside. As the drill turned over, it slipped out of Carl's control. He strained to keep hold of the planter handles, determined to bring the drill upward to the left. Instead, the drill's wheels became cased in moist, sticky soil. It toppled down the hillside toward the deep ravine, bringing Carl to the ground with an agonizing wrench of his leg.

"Papa, what happened? Are you all right?" shouted Henry, running through soft soil across the field to his father. He saw Carl had fallen and slid several feet down the ravine. Carl came to a muddy stop with his right leg extended out from his body at an awkward angle. Carl leaned over and grasped his leg, grimacing in pain. Henry began shouting, "Paul George, Fred, somebody . . . . Come help. Quickly!"

"Control the horses!" Carl directed Henry. "Go! I'm all right."

Henry complied and brought the horses under his command. But his father was not all right.

Paul George and Fred ran across the muddy field. "Papa, Papa! What happened?" shouted Paul George. Carl's three older sons were frightened to see their father suffer a painful, debilitating injury. His cautious, thoughtful nature had served him well in the past to avoid hazardous situations that might bring bodily harm. This time the sticky conditions of the soil, the submerged rock, and the downward slope of the field overcame Carl's strength and caution, resulting in a serious injury.

Paul George approached his father, assessed his injury and turned immediately to Fred, "Go for Mama, Fred. We need her help with Papa." By this time August and John heard the commotion in the wheat field and approached from the barn at a dead run.

Fred shouted when he came close to the house, "Mama, Mama, come quickly. Papa had an accident with the drilling machine!"

Anna Barbara turned to Eliza and Matilda, "Girls, you must stay here with Gottlob. Take care of your brother until I return."

"Yes, Mama," both sisters replied to the urgent tone in Mama's voice. Their eyes were wide with fear at the thought of their father being injured.

As soon as Anna Barbara saw Carl's injury, she gave orders to her sons, "John, saddle a horse and go fetch your Uncle Will. August, you must take the wagon to bring Dr. Wilson back to the farm. Go, quickly." As the boys ran for the barn to follow her directions, she turned her attention to Carl. "Boys, we must bring your father to the house. Fred, go to the barn and bring back the door leaning against the back wall. I will need you to lift your father carefully, one at his head holding his shoulder, one on each side with one hand under a hip and the other holding one leg. I will help with the injured leg." In a few minutes, Anna Barbara heard a galloping horse carry John to find Uncle Will. Then August finished hitching the wagon to the grey mare and slapped the reins with a shout, leaving quickly to fetch Dr. Wilson from Hayesville. Fred found the door behind the barn and hoisted it above his head. Henry saw Fred struggle to run with the door, met him partway across the field and grasped one end. They ran with the door between them across the open field to their parents.

Will Tangeman arrived at his brother's side on the dining room table in time to hear Dr. Wilson explain Carl's injury to Anna Barbara. "The femur of your husband's right leg is broken. Fortunately, the break is clean, and it will heal." He continued to prepare Carl for setting the broken leg, leaning close to his ear, "Carl, your right leg is broken above the knee. It is a clean break of the bone and it will heal. First, I will straighten your leg and then set it in splints," Dr. Wilson explained. "I need help with this procedure. Are there spirits in the house?"

"No, I'm afraid not," replied Anna Barbara, her eyes downcast, recognizing alcohol would ease Carl's pain.

"Here, give Mr. Tangeman a few swallows of this," said the kind doctor as he held out a flask from his medical bag.

"Here, I'll do that," Will stepped forward, raised Carl's head and tipped the flask for his brother to swallow. Then Anna Barbara placed the handle of a wooden spoon between Carl's teeth.

"Now, I need one of you at each shoulder and one at the injured leg," Dr. Wilson directed as Paul George and Henry moved to each shoulder, and Will moved to Carl's foot. "When I give the sign on the count of three and 'pull,' hold the shoulders steady and grasp the injured leg for a firm pull." Carl's face was contorted with pain. Dr. Wilson confirmed his helpers were in place and directed Will to, "One, two, three, pull." Simultaneously, he maneuvered the broken segments of the femur bone to fit together in one smooth motion.

The intensity of the pain caused Carl to pass out. Quickly, Dr. Wilson asked for four straight boards and twine to secure a splint before his patient came back to consciousness. Anna Barbara motioned for Fred and August to exit the room on this errand. They were glad for a reason to breathe fresh air and avoid fainting themselves. Up to this time they had not witnessed their father with physical vulnerabilities. The ordeal left them uncertain, shaken, and afraid.

By Monday morning Carl had recovered nominally and felt somewhat better. He assumed his role of managing the farm work and making assignments for his older sons when they returned from school. This was Paul George's first year of teaching while Henry and Fred attended the high school and August, John, Eliza, and Matilda were elementary students.

Henry was concerned about planting the crops while his father was unable to work, and he was keenly aware the crops should be planted in a timely fashion. On Wednesday he asked to speak to his father before breakfast while the others were finishing morning farm chores. "Papa, I have an idea of how to finish the spring planting while you are laid up. Fred, August, and I could take turns taking a day off of school each week to plant during the day. That way we won't fall behind with our school work or the planting."

Carl saw Henry's eagerness and his sincere concern for the success of their first full year in the farming business. Carl would have felt the same at sixteen. His hand brushed over his beard as he thought through his response. "Henry, I appreciate you have thought through the challenge facing our family due to my accident with the drill. Your idea is a good one and I am grateful for your willingness to help, except for one thing. Your education and that of your brothers is more important than maintaining a strict schedule of planting the crops. I believe it is possible to plant in the evenings and all day on Saturdays in April and get the crops in the ground in a timely manner—if it does not rain too much. That part is in God's hands," Carl replied with a smile and twinkle in his eye.

Spring planting in 1873 was far from assured. It would take hard work, coordination, and weather luck to accomplish spring planting of wheat, corn, and oats while Carl's broken leg healed. At the same time Carl believed this lesson about the importance of education would leave an enduring imprint on his children and generations to follow.

Each week Carl gradually began to walk around the house with the assistance of a crutch August made from a willow branch. By the third week in May, he maneuvered his injured leg to the garden where he kept Anna Barbara company while she planted and cultivated the spring vegetables. She enjoyed his company and his help with household chores while he convalesced from the accident. Before the green heads of wheat began their annual tilt in June, Carl's leg had mended with no lasting ill effects.

The harvest of 1873 was cause for celebration. Not only was Carl's broken leg fully healed, the five older Tangeman brothers mastered the McCormick reaper and accomplished a successful harvest. As directed by Carl the previous harvest, the brothers had learned to guide the horses hitched to the reaper, stack the wheat stalks, and bundle the stalks into shocks of wheat. With the help of their cousin, Charles W., the young men energetically brought in the wheat harvest on both Tangeman farms. The harvest was as bountiful as the previous year but lower prices diminished their income. Without the cost of wages paid the previous summer to hire harvest help, Carl and Will were able to pay off their bank loans used to purchase the McCormick reaper and wheat drilling machine.

The Panic of 1873 came on the heels of a second year of bumper wheat, corn, and oats harvests. An over-supply of grains led to lower demand and lower grain prices. The combined result was much lower payments for grain crops. With lower incomes, some farmers defaulted on their bank loans and lost their land holdings. In turn, some banks, which held the debts of farmers, failed and interest rates rose even higher. The farmers who carried substantial debt suffered further from the high interest rates which pushed them to move out west or into a town or city to work for wages.

Carl and Anna Barbara and Will and Margaretha paid off their debts and were able to survive the Panic of 1873 without selling animals, machinery, or land. Even so, it was not a very good year to be in the farming business. Thousands of farmers in Ohio and other states responded to economic disaster by joining local Granges in hopes they could sway state and national policies to favor agricultural interests.

FEBRUARY 1874

From a letter written by Carl's brother, Hermann Tangeman, the siblings learned that Johann Friedrich Tangemann died on January 20, 1874 in Sulingen, Hanover, Prussia. Each of the siblings in America, Carl, George, Wilhelm, Louise, Wilhelmina, and Marie Dorothee, grieved – some quietly and privately, while others wept openly. With this loss, the Tangeman family in America relinquished their strongest human tie to those they left behind in the old country. They were not only immigrant orphans, but orphans in every respect. With the passing of this older generation, the attentions of the Tangeman siblings necessarily focused on raising their children and establishing their children's futures.

November 25, 1874

Dear Carl and Anna Barbara,

Newton, Kansas, is an exciting place to live and work. The German Mennonites arrived from Russia with Turkey Red winter wheat seeds wrapped in pieces of clothing, tucked into every vacant space in their shipping trunks. These experienced farmers came ready to buy land and take on the prairie uncertainties of too much wind and too little rain. Every year's weather is different, but the wind blows always. I know very little about these Mennonites, but I believe they will be successful, if for no other reason than they are clannish. They keep their customs and beliefs and help each other.

Including the Mennonites, Harvey County now has over seventy farms with more people arriving every week. Some establish homesteads, and others purchase land from the railroad or another owner. The cattle drives no longer come through Newton, and the farmers want to fence in their property to secure their farm animals. Instead of using trees for fence posts and cross rails, they are using wooden posts and barbed wire I helped string this new fencing last month for a farmer west of town. My hands were scratched from the barbs even with leather gloves, but then I got better at it. The whole country will be fenced in before long.

If only there was a way to fence out the locusts. They came through this fall in dark clouds, eating everything in their path. There is no way I understand why God made those pests.

Your friend,
Herman Roth

chapter 19

ELIZABETH SOPHIE HEIMERS TANGEMAN

On many occasions in 1872 and 1873, Carl, Anna Barbara, Will, and Margaretha discussed the possibility of moving their families out west to farm on the Great Plains. The sign to remain in Ohio came in the form of a surprise when Anna Barbara discovered she was pregnant in early 1874. They agreed to wait until after the baby arrived and was at least a year old. Anna Elizabeth was born to Carl and Anna Barbara on September 17, 1874. Following her sister in this way, Margaretha announced her seventh pregnancy in 1874, again delaying firm plans to uproot and move the families a thousand miles away. The birth of Emma in 1875 was followed by another pregnancy and birth of another baby girl, Minnie, in November, 1876. These last three baby girls grew up close in age, as close as sisters, known in their families as "the little girls."

For Will and Carl, these last three pregnancies were the primary reasons to postpone the move out west. In addition, Mr. Roth's descriptions of Newton's cattle drive years were too wild for their families with young children. After Mr. Roth's letter arrived describing churches, schools, and families, their move to Harvey County, Kansas, became a realistic possibility.

✦

Elizabeth Sophie Heimers Tangeman's life's purpose was to be a wife to George Tangeman and a caring mother to their children. When she announced her first pregnancy in 1854, she was confident her life would unfold as she had hoped it would unfold. Her first pregnancy was unremarkable. She identified with her mother who was pregnant at the same time as her sisters in the old country. Elizabeth enjoyed sharing details of this pregnancy with her sister-in-law, Anna Barbara. Morning sickness was minimal, and she had a glow of health. She especially enjoyed the preparations of clothing and furnishings for the new baby. Following the birth of Charles Otto, October 18, 1854, Elizabeth recovered full health in several weeks. She had every reason to anticipate successive robust pregnancies and a house full of energetic children. Motherhood was all she had imagined as a young girl growing up in the German-speaking state of Hessen. In the 1850s, her life was unfolding in a familiar and satisfying manner.

By late 1856, George and Elizabeth were expecting their second child. Following the births of Henry William to Carl and Anna Barbara and Charles William to Wilhelm and Margaretha earlier that year, George and Elizabeth were eager to follow suit. "George, I'm ready to share our news with our family when they visit for Christmas next week," proposed Elizabeth.

"So am I. I'm thinking we may be the lucky parents of the first baby girl in our family," replied George with a broad smile.

◆

George and Elizabeth would never forget the events of the following Friday. It was the day before Carl, Wilhelm and their families were scheduled to travel by train from Manchester to Cincinnati.

In the morning, shortly before George left for the cigar warehouse, Elizabeth suddenly, unexpectedly, felt sharp abdominal pains. "George, George!" she gasped and shouted for her husband.

George took the stair steps to the second floor of their home two at a time shouting, "Elizabeth, what's wrong?" When he arrived at her side, Elizabeth was on the floor of their bedroom moaning with knees curled to her stomach. She clung to her midsection, while bright red blood spread across the floor.

"No, no, no!" whimpered Elizabeth through tears of pain and loss. George felt helpless and heartbroken, as he gathered his wife in his arms.

"Mrs. Leitbaum, Mrs. Leitbaum," shouted George. She was already on her way up the steps when she heard her name being called. "Take care of Charles. I need to take Elizabeth to see Dr. Calderwood."

In the midst of their grief, Dr. Calderwood assured George and Elizabeth many women lost a pregnancy only to bring forth a healthy child in the future. He recommended rest, good food, and calm to bring Elizabeth back to full health. At that point they should try again. George optimistically believed it was only a matter of months, perhaps a year, before another child would come into their lives.

The same sequence of pregnancy, joyful anticipation and sinking loss happened again in 1859. As was the custom of the time, George and Elizabeth kept these heartbreaks under their own roof. Some women brought many healthy children into the world smoothly, seemingly without effort or difficulties. Others lost their babies, their own lives, or both in childbirth. The couple shouldered their burden of grief privately, with each other, without either outwardly celebrating a growing life or mourning a death. The light of George's optimism dimmed, but never completely went out. His hope carried Elizabeth through deep sadness and doubt that she would ever bear another child.

Whispers carried the news of miscarriages to close family who respected Georges and Elizabeth's private sorrow. Many couples lost infants. Certainly, some said, a miscarriage would be easier to bear than a living child who died. But it was not easier. Those who suffered this loss of a yearning in body and heart knew that the abrupt loss of a child at any age or stage of life was unfathomable, and for Elizabeth and George, their losses had been only barely survivable.

Before 1860, three pregnancies were lost for unknown reasons. George consulted the best doctors in Cincinnati, but to no avail. With each passing year without a baby in the crib, their hope slowly faded.

In 1865 the American Civil War ended for an exhausted nation. Perhaps, it was time for a new beginning for George and Elizabeth, too. A baby could be that new beginning. "George, can you believe the war is finally over? It is a fresh start for our country. It could be a new start for us, too," said Elizabeth in June, of that year, barely keeping the pleading from her voice. She was determined to begin again.

"Elizabeth, are you sure you want to risk another disappointment?" returned George. His heart ached for his wife, and he was not eager to face the grief of another loss.

"Yes, George. If you are willing, I am ready to move forward for another pregnancy," Elizabeth replied with tears of anticipation. After three years of trying, finally in late 1868, Elizabeth felt the familiar filling out and a thickening midsection along with her missed periods.

At first, Elizabeth did not reveal her condition to anyone other than George. She chose not to face sympathetic looks and words laced with pity she had heard when earlier miscarriages occurred. Unlike earlier disappointments, Elizabeth carried this pregnancy past her third month. By her fourth month, the pregnancy was showing to such an extent, she needed to wear altered clothing. When she felt the first movement of the fetus, she was willing to share her condition with family, friends and neighbors. George sent letters to Carl and Will and their families announcing Elizabeth's pregnancy. Their dreams were finally coming true.

Elizabeth's pregnancy marked a pivotal change in George's life, too. He felt that nearly everything he hoped for had come to pass. He was close to his son, Charles O., now fourteen. His wholesale cigar business was thriving. During the war, the income from the business had been steady. In the post-war business boom, people had money to spend, and cigars were very popular. George's income now far exceeded his expectations when he arrived in Cincinnati in 1848. He was able to pay for the best medical care in Cincinnati and extra help for household chores while Elizabeth devoted herself to rest in order to carry this child to full term.

George hired a widow lady in her 50s, Helga Butz, to live in and shop, cook, do laundry, and clean the house. She was grateful for the job, and she cheerfully did everything Elizabeth was not able to do. Now that Elizabeth's pregnancy had progressed past quickening, he believed their family would finally expand as they had hoped. He did everything in his power to insure this child be born healthy.

On May 22, 1869, irregular labor pains disturbed Elizabeth's night sleep. "George, the labor pains have begun," she announced with a smile that melted into a grimace.

"What wonderful news. What can I do? Are you in discomfort? I will send for Dr. Calderwood. Can I bring you something to eat or some tea?" George offered. *Oh, God. Please help Elizabeth birth a healthy child.*

"I'm all right. The pains are not regular and they don't last long. Let's have breakfast and make sure Charles is off to school. Then we can send for Dr. Calderwood," Elizabeth answered. George helped his wife down the stairs to the kitchen where Mrs. Butz had coffee, toast, and soft-boiled eggs ready. Elizabeth accepted a cup of coffee and piece of toast. "Good morning Mrs. Butz. Good morning, Charles. I have good news. Before long our baby will be here, perhaps later today or tomorrow."

"Mama, how exciting. Perhaps I should stay home from school, just in case you need me," offered Charles.

"That won't be necessary. I want you to go to school, as usual," smiled his mother. "Your father will be with me all day. I will see you when you return this afternoon."

By noon Elizabeth's labor pains settled into a rhythmic pace of about six minutes apart. He sent a messenger boy from next door to Dr. Calderwood's office at Commercial Hospital asking him to make a house call. Dr. Calderwood arrived within the hour. As soon as he examined Elizabeth, he instructed George to transport her immediately to Commercial Hospital where he could better care for her. George brought the family carriage to the back door and helped his wife into the back seat. Dr. Calderwood rode by her side the dozen blocks to the hospital.

Elizabeth labored overnight and delivered a small, yet beautifully formed daughter as a crimson sun rose over the Ohio River Valley. Bettie Tangeman was born on May 23, 1869. She was welcomed joyfully by an exhausted mother, ecstatic father, and amazed brother. She became the center of her loving family who were devoted to her health and happiness, all the more so for having waited over a dozen years for her arrival.

Elizabeth cared for her young daughter, Bettie, with careful attention to every detail of her baby's daily life. Bettie was a relaxed, easy-to-please child who thrived on the attention of her fourteen-year-old brother, weary mother and dedicated father. She grew steadily, and managed to avoid the health hazards that befell some other young children. Her father believed she deserved a healthy, happy childhood for her own sake and the rest of the family who had endured years of pregnancy false starts.

The Tangeman household awakened to begin each day in a predictable pattern. First, George woke up and knocked on Charles' door with, "Charles, time to wake up." Charles complied and dressed quickly. He was a good student who was eager to attend school.

Next, George went into the nursery to greet his daughter. "Good morning, sunshine," he said as he held out his arms to lift her out of the crib. By this time Elizabeth usually joined him in the nursery to change Bettie's diaper while George dressed for his day at work. Elizabeth carried her daughter downstairs to the kitchen where Mrs. Butz was ready to serve breakfast.

On the morning that marked Bettie's seventh month of life, her mother called, "George, I need your help." Rushing to the stairway, George arrived in time to support Elizabeth and take wiggly Bettie from her arms.

"Our darling has grown too big and too active for you to carry downstairs. Let me do it," George said. From that day until Bettie could navigate the stairway safely herself, George, Charles, or Mrs. Butz carried Bettie up and down the steps. Elizabeth's strength did not keep up with her growing daughter's energetic size and weight.

✦

"Charles, George, come quickly. Bettie just took her first step. I almost missed it myself," Elizabeth called to her husband and fifteen-year-old son. "She let go of the daybed while she held her favorite block." Father and son came around the corner from the dining room into the day room. Bettie looked up to her father's out-stretched arms and beckoning fingers just beyond her reach. The one-year-old looked into her father's eyes, then reached chubby fingers on her right hand toward his, while grasping the edge of her mother's daybed with her left hand. After a moment to catch her balance, she released her left hand, took one step, and fell into her father's arms to the cheers of all. This scene was replayed in a continuous chain of milestones great and small through her toddler years. Her accomplishments formed the collection of minutiae that accumulated in Elizabeth's heart and mind, seeming to permeate her blood and bones. Having waited more than a dozen years struggling to conceive, Bettie's well-being became Elizabeth's all-consuming purpose in life.

There was an implacable irony in Elizabeth's ecstasy of motherhood. As Bettie grew older, stronger, and more capable, day by day, George noticed his wife's vitality appeared to gradually fade. Initially, after Bettie's birth, Elizabeth was weak from blood loss, which slowed her recuperation. George believed they must be patient. He had no reason to believe his wife would not regain her former strength, given enough time. Mrs. Butz shopped, cleaned, cooked, and completed laundry, leaving Elizabeth unencumbered to care for her daughter.

Over time, Elizabeth learned to use her energy sparingly. Once she was up and dressed for the day, she came down the stairs only once. When needed, Mrs. Butz made extra trips upstairs during the day. Elizabeth rested on the downstairs daybed whenever Bettie slept on her napping bed in the same room.

George consulted with doctors, and Elizabeth tried everything they recommended to restore her ebbing health. Nothing was a cure. Sometimes Elizabeth temporarily gained strength and energy with a new medicine, but these moments of vitality eventually slipped further and further apart. At the same time she cherished each minute detail of her daughter's growth and maturity, crawling, walking, speaking, pretending, tea parties, and excursions out of doors on mild days. Bettie was quick to learn and easy to lead. For Elizabeth, Bettie was the child she had longed for through the lost pregnancies that had stolen her dreams. Her fulfillment as a mother percolated through layers of thoughts and emotions. And each day George witnessed Elizabeth's undying love become imbedded in Bettie's spirit.

On August 27, 1875, Elizabeth Sophie Heimers Tangeman died, leaving her six-year-old daughter, Bettie, to be raised by her husband George and son Charles. Despite the efforts of Cincinnati's best doctors, Elizabeth's life had gradually ebbed away. Her decline was like the forward and backward motion of the tides of the sea until one day she receded to stillness and silence.

Mrs. Butz continued to live in the family home. She kept house and helped care for Bettie for the next eleven years until her own health failed. At twenty-one years of age, Charles's loss of his mother was the formative event of his adolescence and early adult years. In the wake of his mother's death, Charles O. became a co-parent with his father and Mrs. Butz, attempting to fill the void Elizabeth left behind. He was hired as a railroad clerk for the Cleveland, Cincinnati, Chicago, and St. Louis Railway, also known as the "Big Four Railroad," where he worked his entire career. He continued to live at home until he married Emma Hanhart in 1882.

Carl received the telegraph message of Elizabeth's passing from Charles O., and he wept for his brother and his family. Carl remembered, and once again grieved, the loss of his own first wife and their two small children. Carl and Will traveled by train to Cincinnati and attended Elizabeth's funeral at Saint Paulus Deutsche Evangelische Kirche.

In the 1880 US Census, George Tangeman reported his occupation as at home, dressmaker. Presumably, this line of work allowed him to work at home close to Bettie in her growing up years. She was a compliant child who moved easily from child to adult, accepting his parenting, then providing support to George as he aged. Bettie never married and continued to live with her father until his death in 1905. Bettie Tangeman followed her brother and worked as a clerk with the Big Four Railway where she remained throughout her career.

chapter 20

CENTENNIAL EXHIBITION

In celebration of America's one-hundredth anniversary of independence, the Centennial Exhibition took place on more than 285 acres of land in Philadelphia's Fairmount Park May 10-November 10, 1876. Close to ten million visitors (9,910,966) went to the fair via railroad, steamboat, carriage, and on foot. Thirty-seven nations participated in the event, officially named the International Exhibition of Arts, Manufactures, and Products of the Soil and Mine. The grounds contained five major buildings: the Main Exhibition Building, Memorial Hall (Art Gallery), Machinery Hall, Agricultural Hall, and Horticultural Hall. In addition to these buildings, approximately 250 smaller structures were constructed by states, countries, companies, and other Centennial bureaus that focused on particular displays or services.

– Overview of
"The Centennial Exhibition, Philadelphia, PA" *1876*

The legislative expenditure (for a promotional exhibit at the Centennial Exhibition in Philadelphia) is justified as "a reasonable amount expended in placing [Kansas] before the country," because "We need people to fill our broad, rich valleys and to occupy the tens of thousands of acres of unoccupied land, and the opportunity to advertise the State presented by the Centennial cannot be lost."

– *The Kansas Farmer,* 1875

◆———————●———————◆

October 1875

William snapped slender leather reins across the backs of his two gray Percheron draft horses. In the bed of the farm wagon, Margaretha had spread two old quilts for their five older children. As usual, seventeen-year-old Sophia led her siblings with songs and lively conversation to entertain three-year-old Harry. The Tangeman family's lighthearted mood suffused the two-hour trip over country dirt roads to the McKay Grange building. Since this grange had been established in 1872, the Tangemans eagerly participated in the quarterly meetings, especially the fall gatherings with characteristic mild temperatures.

"Will, have you thought about attending the Centennial celebration in Philadelphia if you are asked to do so?" Margaretha asked her husband. She knew he had a great interest in the way machines were changing agriculture.

Will was ambivalent about taking a four-day trip away from his family. "I haven't been away from you since my time in the Union Army. The farm is a lot to leave to your care, and we have this new baby, too. It seems like too much," Will replied thoughtfully.

"It will be a great honor if you are chosen for the delegation, and you will greatly enjoy the new farm machines. I want you to take this trip," offered Margaretha. As she spoke, Will smiled his acceptance of her support.

Will was one of four men chosen to represent their Grange at the 1876 Centennial Exhibition, an International Exhibition of Arts, Manufactures, and Products of the Soil and Mine in Philadelphia, Pa.

Will's mind raced with enthusiasm as he thought of attending the grand, historic exhibition the following May. "Charlie will be in medical school. Perhaps he will come back to help with the animal chores and field work. Or we could ask one of Carl's older boys to come over to help Otto."

"Margaretha, thank you for understanding," exclaimed Will. "This World's Fair will be the first ever in the United States. It will be a pleasure to attend and represent our grange."

Will attended the Centennial Exhibition which celebrated the 1776 Declaration of Independence in Philadelphia. It was patterned after the Crystal Palace and the Great Exhibition of the Works of Industry of All Nations held in London, Hyde Park, in 1851. This centennial celebration was planned to commemorate the first one hundred years of the United States with a decidedly futuristic flavor. The latest industrial, agricultural, and mining exhibits revealed a glimpse of a machine-driven industrial world just around the corner. In this streamlined way, an explosion of innovations spread across the United States from this Centennial Exhibition.

✦

MAY 23, 1876

"Will, here take your lunch," Gretly handed her husband a cloth parcel filled with sliced cheese and sausage, bread spread with butter, and dried fruit. She wiped a sniffle and tears with the back of her hand and edge of her apron.

"I'll be back in four days. Charlie and Otto will help with the farm, and Carl and Anna Barbara will check on you every day, too." Will caught her hand, squeezed it affectionately and kissed baby Emma riding on her mother's hip. He glanced into her eyes, then quickly away to avoid her tears and his own. Taking up his well-worn suitcase and lunch parcel, he stepped quickly toward his horse, fastened the suitcase to the back of the saddle and buckled the saddlebag closed with the lunch parcel inside.

Although she supported Will's trip to Philadelphia, Gretly worried when Will was away from home. She was fearful again as she had been when Will left to serve in the Union Army during the Civil War. *Will he return to me safely?*

On the evening of May 23, 1876, Will and his three companions boarded the Atlantic and Ohio Railway from Ashland to Akron, Ohio, where they transferred to the 10:36 pm Continental Railroad bound for New York. At approximately 6:00 am, the McKay Grange delegation disembarked at Penn Haven Station in the deep woods of northeast Pennsylvania. They boarded the next train south that was scheduled to arrive in Philadelphia by noon.

The iron horse carried its passengers through Penn's Woodlands on tracks laid along ancient Indian hunting trails. Since colonial days when English forces vanquished local native tribes and William Penn received the land from the English king, the surrounding area was known as Pennsylvania. Will and his companions compared the passing farms, small towns and woods with their own. These farms were smaller than those in Ashland County with fewer crops, more stock, and numerous fruit trees. At each station along the railroad line, more people boarded than departed until an overflowing train arrived at the new passenger station, Thirty-second and Market Streets in Philadelphia.

Will had not seen thousands of people in one place since he left New York in 1847. Like rivers flowing through a narrow canyon and disbursing beyond a rocky constriction, masses of people poured into the train station

and out through archways to railway platforms and street exit porticos.
The voluminous expanse of the railway station stretched above the crowd
to the lofty arched ceiling. This light-filled architectural achievement lifted
spirits and voices to celebrate the first one hundred years of democracy.
Will's eye searched the ornately drawn directional signage placed for fair
goers to find the spur line connection to the Centennial World's Fair in
Fairmont Park.

The four McKay Grange members squeezed onto the spur line connec-
tor for the ten-minute ride to the entrance of the Centennial World's Fair.
Glancing left, they followed a sign to the Grange Grounds, an area of white
tents erected adjacent to the Schuylkill River and Fairmount Park. They
claimed two tents and checked their bags. Then the Ohio Grangers walked
briskly to the main centennial entrance with its Main Exhibit Hall on the
right and Machines Hall on the left. Will was impressed with the size of
the Machines Hall, the largest building in the world enclosing twenty-one
acres under Victorian spires and fluttering flags.

All afternoon the Centennial exhibits dazzled Will and his companions.
Will wondered if three days would be enough to see everything he wanted
to see.

"My first stop is the Agricultural Hall. Do you want to come along?"
invited Will.

"Sure thing," responded his companion, Henry. "I have to see those new
McCormick tilling, planting, and harvesting machines. I might even order
a harvesting machine if I find a sales representative."

Will wanted to order new machines on the spot, but he refrained from
doing so. A better time to purchase new agricultural machines would be
after their move to Kansas in a couple of years when baby Emma was old
enough to survive the move.

"Henry, come look at this," called Will. He pointed toward a display of
a molded butter Centennial Medallion several feet in diameter. Not only
was America a new country, compared to European nations, it was a country fascinated with new ideas. New machines were ready to reward those
who grasped the tail of the future with fervor.

"Henry, are you hungry? Come try a sample of Hires Root Beer. I like it
with sugar popcorn," urged Will. When he passed by the banana booth,
he tried one and decided to take a few bunches home to share with his family. Then he noticed a full-sized Liberty Bell sculpted from soap. Around
the corner, Will and Henry came upon a totally unexpected display.

Unknown to the agriculturalists from Ashland County, The Academy of Natural Sciences Museum in Philadelphia had placed a *Hadrosaurus* specimen on display on their premises in 1868. Since that time, the museum had commissioned an artist to paint the picture they now saw with their own eyes. They stared at the dinosaur painting, trying to comprehend the notion that such unusual animals lived and roamed across America in the long distant past.

Stepping outside the Main Exhibition Building, Will and Henry brought their attention back to the present at the sound of high stepping marching band music by the new composer, John Phillip Sousa. They marched in a circuitous route down Agricultural Avenue, turning left onto Fountain Avenue, then back toward the Machinery Building. A half-hour later the crowd was entertained for several minutes by a one-man band playing drums, accordion, and mouth organ all at one time. The two Grangers could hardly wait to return home with stories of the sights and sounds of the Centennial Exhibition.

On Friday, their last day at the exhibition, Will approached Henry, "Would you like to tour the displays from individual states?"

"Yes, if we can start with Ohio," replied Henry enthusiastically. After a ten-minute walk, the men found Ohio House, a two-story stone and frame Victorian house furnished by the state of Ohio. Cincinnati was well represented along with the agriculture of central Ohio. Displays highlighted that Ohio led the nation in the production of corn, wheat, and wool, and the Grange organization was part of that success.

Will was surprised when they arrived at an exhibit from the state of Kansas, the only state represented from west of the Mississippi River. He was drawn to read every word about the productivity of the land, newly planted with Turkey Red winter wheat. In addition, farmers could buy three to four times the amount of land in Kansas compared to Ohio. The photographs showed modern towns and cities thriving on the prairie and welcoming newcomers to venture out west.

Finally, Will paid a visit to the Women's Pavillion, a handsome one-story quadrangle featuring a square central hallway open above, three stories in height. It was paid for and managed by women to showcase their decades-long struggle for women's suffrage. Women's suffrage resonated when he thought of his daughters' futures. In the Grange, women and men were all voting members, and he saw that women enthusiastically participated in the work of the Grange. Similar to their quest for women's voting

157

rights, Grange dedicated time and effort to flexing the political strength of agricultural producers who were shifting from human to animal and ultimately mechanical power.

The four men from McKay Grange left Philadelphia on Saturday morning filled with new ideas and enthusiasm for America and the future prospects of agriculture.

✦

"Papa, Papa, you're home," shouted Clara as she threw up her arms and ran down the lane to greet her returning father. Her brothers and sisters were close behind. While surrounded by his noisy children, Will only had eyes for Margaretha, who smiled contentedly with Emma in her arms. She breathed a sigh of relief at his safe return.

"Papa, what did you see? What did you do at the centennial celebration?" asked Otto. In his father's absence along with his brother, Charlie, Otto, at fifteen years, had served as caretaker of the farm and protector of his family.

"Papa, what is in the box?" asked Harry, who, at four years of age, was curious to see what his Papa brought back from his trip to Philadelphia.

"Children, I have missed you. How have you been?" asked Will as he reached out arms to hug his family.

"We are fine. Did you bring us anything?" the chorus of his children responded.

"Perhaps, but first I must ask, how are the chickens?" Will inquired mischievously.

"I fed them every day," shouted Clara, hands on her hips and a frown on her face showing her growing impatience with her father.

"And how are the pigs?" asked Will with a pretend look of concern on his face.

"The pigs are getting fatter every day," answered Otto, who by now played along with his father's teasing game.

"And how are the cows? Are they still giving milk?" asked Will with wide eyes anticipating the answer.

"The cows are giving more milk than ever," answered Sophia whose chore it was to feed and milk the cows.

"If all is well here on the farm, it is time to show you what I brought back from Philadelphia," Will finally yielded to the fierce interest of his children. He sat on the front porch steps and carefully brought out a parcel wrapped with string. With the parcel on his lap, Will slipped off the string and opened the box inside.

"O-o-o, what is that?" asked Clara. She had never seen the curved, yellow fruit before.

"Bananas. Here, I will show you how to eat a banana," replied her father. He pulled down the stem then peeled the skin far enough to see the light yellow fruit standing erect. Then he took a bite and slowly chewed and smiled his enjoyment. "Who would like to try a banana?" Will asked.

A chorus of "Me" and "Yes, Papa" went up around him. In a few moments, the older children learned to peel a banana and helped the younger ones peel theirs. Then each child looked and licked and took a bite to examine this new taste adventure. The sweet softness won them over.

Later in the evening after the children were settled in bed, Will and Margaretha took a walk down their lane toward the local road to Hayesville. "Will, I have something to tell you," began Margaretha.

A look of concern spread across Will's face. "Did something happen while I was away? Are you all right? Are the children healthy?" asked Will, urgently.

"Nothing like that. Yes, everyone is fine. Nothing happened while you were in Philadelphia. It happened some time ago," replied Gretly. "I am pregnant." As with all of their children, Will would welcome this child with love and gratitude. However, this news meant they would not leave Ohio for Kansas until at least 1878. He hoped good land would still be available when they finally journeyed west.

On the Sunday after Will returned from the Centennial Exhibition in Philadelphia, Carl and Anna Barbara spent the afternoon with their brother and sister, respectively. While Will shared his thoughts about the exhibits, the women took up their piecework, stitching together squares to be added with other squares to form a tulip motif quilt top. They listened intently to Will as he explained the novel and the new in Philadelphia exhibits. Will commented, "I now have a much better notion of our adopted country. Democracy is a very different system from the kingships in Europe."

"I agree. In Europe, it matters most who has the strength to overpower other nations. Since the German unification in 1871, Germany has realized a new strength," said Carl.

" . . . and much pride," inserted Margaretha. "I have noticed a lot more pride in our German language and culture here in Ohio, too. The parades have German displays, and now there is even a German community choir in Loudonville."

"The American Constitution is based on equality. Leaders are chosen by the vote," said Will. "That is very different from Europe where we were stuck with the hereditary leaders. Some were fine, but others were selfish and cruel. At least here we can vote a bad leader out of office."

"Not everyone gets to vote, so not everyone is equal," chimed in Anna Barbara.

"And that is changing, too," added Will. "I visited the Women's Pavilion at the exhibition. Women's suffrage is coming. It is just a matter of time. Now that Africans, the men at least, have the vote, soon everyone will be able to vote." Change in agriculture, in mechanics, and in society was in the air. A swirl of exciting and challenging possibilities churned through the minds of the two sisters and the brothers they had married.

"What did you think of the new machines you saw at the centennial exhibition?" asked Carl. "I'm just getting used to the reaper and harrow. It is hard to imagine what will be invented next."

"You are right. The changes in machines are nearly unbelievable," answered Will. "The new machines are not only in agriculture. Mining and milling fellows are inventing new machines as fast as they can, too."

"In the old country, my papa used the same tailoring tools year after year. Here the new machines come so fast, it makes my head spin," smiled Anna Barbara.

chapter 21
1877

"If I went West, I think I would go to Kansas."

– Abraham Lincoln

"The plague of the grasshopper which threatens us is now an important and common question. Will the plague come? If it does, the calamity will be fearful. It would seem that God has a controversy with us . . . ."

– Newton Bracken
Gensco, Kansas, May 2, 1877

In May, 1977, August Charles Tangeman graduated from Vermillion Institute. At seventeen years of age, he felt grown up. He was excited to help his father and brothers with the farm work and hire out to other farmers whenever he had extra time. Despite his feelings of accomplishment and maturity, August already missed being in school in the upcoming term.

While a student at the institute, August saw Anna Margaret Smith on a daily basis. She was a Bavarian beauty, with dark hair, clear complexion, and hazel brown eyes that sparkled when August came calling. She had never felt this way about any of the other neighborhood boys who caught her eye at school. August was tall and good looking with wavy brown hair and resolute blue eyes. When he smiled, his firm jaw led his smile into Anna's heart. These two teenagers were smitten with the kind of love that could last a lifetime.

When August listened to his brothers talk about moving out west, he wanted to take on the challenge of life on the Great Plains, too. At the same time, he dreaded the thought of leaving Anna Smith in Ohio. In 1878 their parents said they were too young to get married at sixteen and eighteen years of age. *Will Papa and Mama delay moving out west for a few years, until we have our parents' blessing to be married?*

161

◆

September 7, 1877

Dear Anna Barbara and Carl,

Greetings from the land of bullfrogs and grasshoppers. If we had more bullfrogs, the grasshoppers would not be such a problem. Bullfrogs eat anything. Last month I went on a hunting trip with a couple of friends. A herd of elk were sighted along the Smoky Hill River outside of Salina, a few hours north of Newton. The first night we camped along the river. The bullfrogs sang for their mates all night long. The next night we fried up bullfrog legs before the main meal of elk flank. We slept a lot better the second night. Now I wish we had those bullfrogs back to eat the hoppers.

Last month the skies darkened with another cloud of devouring locusts. Fortunately, most of the wheat crop was harvested before the fearful mini-beasts flew into fields to clean up the leavings of wheat grains. The corn crop did not fare so well. Nothing is left to harvest this fall, no leaves, silk nor ears of corn.

In a very few years, Newton has turned from a wild west cow town into a bustling small city. The Atchison, Topeka, and Santa Fe train brings supplies to build schools, churches, stores, and farms. Hundreds of settlers arrive every week. The German-Russian Mennonites brought Turkey Red hard winter wheat from Russia in 1874. They arrived as whole communities with the assistance of the Atchison, Topeka and Santa Fe railroad. They bought railroad land and used their skills to help turn the prairie into the breadbasket of the nation. Newton is growing into a respectable place for a family. If you decide to come west, you will find land and the opportunity of a lifetime. There is so much excitement in the towns in this area.

I have enjoyed your letters about your family and farming enterprise. Perhaps your family is now complete with little David and Elizabeth. I miss you all.

Your friend,
Herman Roth

◆

On the Monday before Christmas, 1877, George, Charles O., and Bettie Tangeman rode the train from Cincinnati to Loudonville and joined Carl and Anna Barbara in their farm home near Hayesville. At eight years of age, Bettie was excited to play with her cousins Matilda, Gottlob, and Elizabeth and take part in farm life. She helped Matilda and Gottlob feed the chickens with table scraps. She climbed into the barn mow and threw pitchforks full of hay down to the sheep. John and August fed and milked the three cows and showed Bettie how to squeeze the cows' pink teats from top to bottom for the reward of a squirt of fresh, warm milk.

Christmas Eve morning began with glossy crystals cascading from bare twigs of the oak and sycamore trees. Will, Gretly, and their eight offspring rose early and bubbled with anticipation of another rambunctious family Christmas celebration. Will and Otto had converted their freight wagon to a sleigh with smooth wooden rails, easy for their Percheron horses to carry over the snow-covered country roads. Charles W. carried out bundles of German dishes Gretly and Sophia had prepared to feed their hungry clan. Pungent fragrances of potato salad, sauerbraten casserole, red cabbage, and bratwurst escaped the bundles securely tucked behind the driver's seat. The two-mile ride passed quickly for the family who sang songs and laughed when the sleigh jostled over bumps and skimmed over crystalized icy snow. They planned to spend two evenings, Christmas Eve and Christmas day evening, at Carl's and Anna Barbara's farm.

Charles W. reveled in the familiar pandemonium of his irrepressible siblings. "Charles, how is it being a doctor? Do you like it? What is your most difficult case?" asked Sophia as the horses strained to pull the well burdened wagon up the hill from the deep ravine of their own farm. At nineteen, she was thinking about her own future, and curious about her brother's career.

"I like it just fine. I'm still getting used to telling my patients, especially the older ones, what to do. The sense of command will come in time, I hope," replied Charles W. with a sheepish grin. He had arrived from his home in Mansfield the previous weekend to celebrate Christmas with his family. As much as Charles enjoyed his younger siblings, he was especially eager to have time with Charles O. and Paul George. These three cousins, the oldest sons of their three Tangeman fathers felt more like brothers than cousins. At twenty-one, Charles W. was the youngest of the three cousins, but already well into his career as an eye doctor. He wanted to talk with

Paul George about teaching at the Vermillion Institute in Hayesville, and he wondered how Charles O. liked being a railroad clerk.

✦

Christmas Eve began with a traditional Christmas dinner and all the trimmings served in the ample dining room. The adults sat at the dining room table with the younger children on laps and older children standing behind their parents.

As was their German tradition, the head of the household offered or invited another person to offer the blessing of the food and the gathering. Carl gazed around the room locking eyes with his brothers, George and William, and each of their family members, twenty-four in all. His eyes met each of his sons and daughters and finally settled lovingly on Anna Barbara. His smile revealed a sense of fulfillment and of thanks for each family member. "Before we begin this delicious feast prepared by many hands over the past week, let us give thanks to our Heavenly Father. We are blessed to gather on the eve of the birth of the Christ Child to celebrate His life. You have blessed us with this food for which we are grateful and a large and loving family with whom to share this celebration. May the ties that unite us to You also continue to strengthen one to another in this family. Only in unity will we have the strength to weather the storms of loss and disappointment so that we may greet the blessings as they arrive from your bounty. We remember those we have lost, George's dear Elizabeth, Mother Schiedt, Mother and Father Tangeman, and my Elizabeth, David, and Dorothee lost in New Orleans. We give thanks for Papa Schiedt who is still living, and our brothers and sisters and other family living in the old country. For our family members here in Ohio, may we always remember and cherish one another in our hearts. In the name of the Christ child we celebrate this evening. Amen."

The hush that fell over the Christmas gathering held for a few moments. Then Carl turned to Anna Barbara and asked, "My dear, how shall we begin to serve this dinner?"

"For Christmas dinner we have two geese roasted with apple and savory sausage stuffing along with a beef roast, red cabbage, and potato dumplings with gravy. First, let's serve the younger children who may need some assistance. The three little girls and Harry may sit at the dining room table. They will be followed by everyone in elementary school who will gather in the girls' room upstairs. The older ones may gather in the boys' room upstairs. Of course, adults will stay in the dining room," announced Anna Barbara. With these directions, each group proceeded to fill their plates and find their designated rooms.

Following dinner and conversation well into the afternoon, Carl rose from the table and called to the children, "Is there anyone ready for Christmas presents?" Immediately, the middle age group came thundering down the stairs toward the parlor. There they found Carl standing guard at the closed door that hid the Christmas tree. Once all of the children had arrived, Carl asked, "If you are ready, please listen. When we go into the parlor I want each of you to find a place to sit on the floor. Then each of you will receive a gift."

Carl, William, and George oversaw the giving of the gifts. The children each opened their own present in turn until all were opened. Finally, the three Tangeman fathers handed out a cloth parcel to each child.

"Oh Papa, I have a coin and an orange and candies," exclaimed Clara to her father.

✦

The Tangeman clan awoke to a sunny, crisp Christmas Day. Anna Barbara greeted her extended family, "Happy Christmas to all. We will have breakfast ready in a short while. First, Bettie, would you like to help feed the animals?"

"Oh, yes, Auntie. I very much want to feed the chickens and pigs and milk a cow. I can do it all by myself," Bettie declared enthusiastically. Today, Matilda, Eliza, John, August, and Gottlob, along with Clara and Harry, fed and milked the animals. As she predicted, Bettie milked her very own cow and carefully carried the bucket of warm milk back to the house.

"Papa, papa! I milked a cow," she called as she arrived at the house. "I did it all by myself."

George greeted his daughter at the back door. "Bettie, that's wonderful! I'm so proud of you." He planned this trip to celebrate Christmas on his brother's farm, partly to give Bettie time to feel close with their extended family. He had envisioned moments like this, his daughter basking in the love and attention of cousins, aunts, and uncles, while finding joint interests. As she grew toward adulthood, he hoped she would feel a connection to these people whose essence was imbedded deep in his bones, a closeness he felt with his parents and brothers and sisters, especially Carl and Will.

George trusted them now to be an anchor for his daughter, as he had drawn upon their strength through Elizabeth's miscarriages and her final illness.

Bettie relished the companionship of her seventeen cousins. They revealed to Bettie something of herself, common interests, talents, and with some, a similar countenance. Clara and Matilda loved animals as much as Bettie. Henry and Gottlob were fine singers, which intrigued her. By bringing Charles O. and Bettie to his brothers' families, George laid claim to a cultural inheritance for his son and daughter, their German character as forged in the American experience. Far from leaving his German sense of self in Prussia, George came through thirty years in the crucible of immigration, transformed into a nineteenth century American, and simultaneously holding firmly to his German heritage.

Through the morning hours, family members drifted downstairs to a breakfast of black rye bread, sliced cheeses, liverwurst, braunwurst, and coffee served buffet style. In the early afternoon, a buffet dinner of spatzle, German potato salad, sauerkraut casserole with apples and sausages, *schweinebraten* (cold roast pork) and an assortment of spritz, *lebkuchen* and *pfeffernuesse* cookies.

The rest of the afternoon the adults were deep in conversation while the young people played games upstairs. Their primary topic was whether to make a move "out west" or not, and if so, when. Was desirable land still available? What would be the cost of this relocation to Kansas? Carl shared Herman Roth's letters describing his adventures in Iowa and Kansas. William retold details he had learned about Kansas at the Centennial Exhibition in Philadelphia in 1876. Foremost on their minds were the price of land, crop yields, and going prices for wheat, corn, and oats. Everyone seemed to know friends or acquaintances who had made the long trek west, and they shared those stories, too.

George listened intently to his brothers and sisters-in-law speaking cautiously, yet steadily, and affirmatively about moving to Kansas. Realizing this branch of his family was poised to move west made their time together even more precious than when he had first arrived for this Christmas celebration.

Later in the afternoon, Anna Barbara announced, "It is time for Christmas *stollen*. This year Sophia has made our almond-filled Christmas *stollen*. Coffee is ready to be served and milk for the children." Sophia was both proud and shyly apprehensive to serve this traditional Christmas treat. The loaves of sweet bread communicated love and tradition braided together. Sophia accepted this role of oldest female cousin, assuring the German tradition of Christmas *stollen* would continue into the next generation.

chapter 22

RECONNAISSANCE

"There is nothing impossible to him who will try."

– Alexander the Great

———————◆———————●———————◆———————

February 27, 1878

Dear Carl and Anna Barbara,

Greetings from the Kansas prairie. I have lived in Newton through exciting days of cattle drives, wild cowboys, and now friendly settlers and farmers. I bought the general merchandise store on Main Street last year. More people come every year, and they need to furnish their sod houses or frame built homes and barns, so my store does well. Newton will be my home to the end of my days.

This winter has been mild as compared to recent snow seasons. The snow that falls here finally meets the ground somewhere north of Junction City. The snow that falls in Junction City ends up in Nebraska. The wind changes everything. When we have a day without much wind, people stop to notice and make comments. Some call it the lambasting wind. When the gale returns with a vengeance, it invades every crevice and crack of man, beast, and structure with dusty grit.

Even the better homes and stores fall victim to the dust that sifts through invisible, pin-prick cracks. Everything inside is covered with a veil of dust in a matter of hours. In a dust storm the fine particles of dust can be seen actually blowing through the less substantial structures. Some settlers decide to move back east rather than cope with dastardly dust storms.

I was glad to learn you may still move your family out to Harvey County. In spite of the hardships of dust and drought, this is a fine place to continue your farming enterprise. Turkey red winter wheat yields are high enough for most farmers to prosper even in years of little moisture.

Please let me know if you decide to come west. You will find me at my store.

Your friend,
Herman Roth

MAY, 1878

The last day of classes at the Vermillion Institute in Hayesville, Ohio was rainy – a serious kind of rain that let up now and again but never ceased. Paul George Tangeman mounted the spring seat of his family's covered buckboard. He coaxed his horse out of the carriage house behind the school and pulled his rig up close to the front door of the lower level of the school. Seeing the buckboard, Mary Ann Heckman emerged from the door beneath the portico created by the outdoor double stairway leading up to the main level of the institute. She firmly grasped Paul George's outstretched hand and quickly climbed the small metal foot steps leading to the buckboard seat. When the couple were both settled on the wooden spring-built seat, Paul George snapped the reins and clicked his tongue, a signal his horse obeyed. Paul George guided the buckboard onto the Wooster/Mansfield Road, proceeding east toward the Heckman farm.

Paul George and Mary Ann both served on the faculty of the Vermillion Institute. Paul George taught mathematics for the secondary students while Mary Ann's elementary students included Gottlob, Matilda, and Clara Tangeman. Paul George smiled broadly, "Mary Ann, thankfully this difficult year has finally come to an end. The Wilson boys and Barton Theber took the enjoyment out of teaching for me this year," he lamented.

"You worked hard to keep ahead of those three boys," agreed Mary Ann

"At least you had a rewarding year," replied Paul George. He slowed the buckboard to turn the corner a half mile from Mary Ann's family's farm "Everyone says you have a gift for teaching. Mattie, Gottlob, and Clara enjoy your lessons immensely."

Mary Ann smiled in agreement. "That is true, and I love teaching all of the children. You are a good teacher, too, very knowledgeable in mathematics. But is teaching your passion?"

"Are my feelings so easy to read?" Paul George grinned.

"If teaching is not your calling, what else will you do?" asked Mary Ann.

"To be truthful, teaching may not be my calling. I could do it for my whole life, if need be. But my mind wanders to farming, maybe moving out west. Many of our neighbors have left for land at much lower prices in Nebraska and Kansas. I heard some land has sold for as little as $1.25 per acre," said Paul George.

"Do you want to move west, too?" asked Mary Ann. They had spoken often about the challenge and excitement of farming, and the attraction he felt for lands further west. This was the first time Mary Ann had asked this question of Paul George directly.

"Not until I take a trip out west to see for myself," replied Paul George. "This may be the time to talk with Pop and Uncle Will and see what they think."

✦

Will was reluctant to make this move without a reconnaissance trip to see the land for himself. Their farm in Ashland County was thriving, and he preferred to stay in Ohio, closer to Charles W., who was an established physician in Cincinnati. On the other hand, Margaretha wanted to live in proximity to Anna Barbara and Carl. Will's interest in farming in Kansas was piqued when he attended the Centennial celebration in Philadelphia in 1876. Eventually, Carl, Anna Barbara, Will, and Margaretha agreed that a reconnaissance trip was needed with Paul George and Will chosen to make the trip as soon as possible. Uncle and nephew prepared to leave for Kansas before the end of May 1878. They packed clothing, food, rifles, and knives to deal with predatory animals and thieving scoundrels.

Will and Paul left Ohio by train for Kansas on May 29, 1878. They boarded the Cincinnati Southern Railway in Cincinnati bound for St. Louis on the kind of day that coaxed corn stalks to split the sky: full sun, gentle breeze, and a trace of a shower late in the afternoon. Paul George's mind buzzed with anticipation to see the western country he had only read about in Mr. Roth's letters along with accounts printed in newspapers and magazines. He discovered fields of grain interspersed with clumps of hardwoods. Tidy farms displayed comfort and well-being of their owners with bulky granaries, white farm houses, barns for horses, and hay mows. This trip to the center of the continent was as exciting to him as the journeys his parents described, traveling by ship from the old country to America. Thankfully, it lacked dangerous oceans to cross. Instead, in only three days, they would arrive in Newton, Kans., God willing, barring unforeseen delays on the railroads.

The Ohio passengers feasted their eyes on fields across southern Indiana and Illinois. In late May they appreciated what went into growing the promising stands of corn, wheat, and oats. Had the seeds been planted thick enough and deep enough to yield a bounteous crop? Would weeds threaten to choke out an otherwise profitable crop? How soon will the crop be ready to harvest, and how many hands will be needed to bring it in?

For Will, this trip had the potential to profoundly change his own life and the lives of his family members. Once the move was completed, they would only visit Cincinnati on rare occasions, not the regular holiday visits they had enjoyed the past ten years. Will would miss Charles W., who planned to stay in Cincinnati. Even so, if the land fulfilled its promise of large yields and lower costs, he would embrace the move with Margaretha and their seven younger children.

Will's mind returned to Hayesville, where Carl had agreed to take charge of the fields of both families. He had ample workers for the tasks at hand. Henry, Fred, August, and John were strong, healthy, and eager to tackle cultivating corn, mending fences, and doing daily barn chores. Carl would include Otto, at seventeen years, in his weekly meetings for assignments to care for both farms. Although some families relied on women and older girls to do field work, Carl and Anna Barbara depended on their robust older sons. The girls and younger boys helped their mothers with cooking, laundry, cleaning, caring for even younger children, and the garden. Will mused about the work he would miss. Most of all he thought fondly of the day he would return to Margaretha.

The Cincinnati Southern Railway moved passengers across Indiana and Illinois extremely efficiently compared to river, wagon, or horseback travel in 1878. Even so, there were numerous stops to take on coal and water, and swap out passengers and cargo for different versions of the same. Before the afternoon sun smiled and sank from the horizon, Will and Paul George catnapped in their seats. When vacant seats were available in the night, they leaned against their traveling bags and slept. The sun arose to chase the train west another day. Soon enough, St. Louis appeared on the western horizon.

The Cincinnati Southern Railway crossed the Mississippi River onboard the engineering marvel of the Wiggins Ferry Company. Passengers were invited to stay in their railway cars to be transferred from rails to ferry and back to rails again on the Missouri side of the grand Mississippi.

"Will, that must be a railroad bridge across the Mississippi. I wonder why they don't use it instead of switching to the ferry and back to rails on the other side," asked Paul George.

A passenger across the aisle overheard the question and answered, "Gentlemen, I have lived here for twenty years. The bridge was built a few years ago. Mr. Wiggins has enough pull to keep the train station small enough, so the ferries are still in great demand. Then the bridge company went bankrupt. I imagine it will be in use by trains someday, but not yet."

"Thanks for the explanation," responded Paul George. "St. Louis is a thriving city at this crossroads of rivers and railroads." The men exchanged remarks about the trip thus far, their destinations, and business interests as a way to pass the time.

By early afternoon, Will and Paul George were again progressing west by train through the tree-covered rolling hills of Missouri.

Their train stopped for passengers and cargo in Missouri only twice. The Tangemans arrived at the train depot in Kansas City, Missouri, as the sun scattered golden corkscrews of light across the broad Missouri River. Weary from the long train trip, uncle and nephew crossed the street and purchased hot meals and a hotel room. The next morning, they walked to the ferry station, crossed the Missouri River by ferry and hailed a carriage for hire to deliver them to the Union Pacific Railroad Station where they eventually boarded the Kansas Division of the Union Pacific Railway bound for Topeka.

The terrain of Kansas was alternately rolling and flat, with occasional sparse clumps of cottonwood trees along tributaries to the Kansas River, which flowed parallel to the train tracks. Following a two hour layover in Topeka, Will and Paul boarded the famous Atchison, Topeka and Santa Fe Railroad, bound for their final destination, Newton, Kansas.

Paul was surprised to see large swaths of native prairie populated by antelope and buffalo alongside cattle and horses. Where he expected to see farms and fields blanketing the countryside, he spotted a herd of pronghorn antelope being chased by two coyotes. At the same time, Paul felt a stiff south wind across his sweaty skin followed by a splattering of nickel-sized rain drops. In the sultry afternoon heat he began to appreciate how wind made life on the prairie bearable in the face of relentless heat.

Paul was intrigued by his introduction to Kansas, a state with vast hori-

zons and untold potential. His impressions of the prairie, of the land beneath the grasses and the sky above excited his curiosity like nothing in his
life up to this moment. *Will the land be rich enough to support agriculture?
How much effort will be needed to remove rocks and trees and prepare the land
for the plow? Can Uncle Will and I and our families withstand the threats of
fires and hoards of insects, tornadoes, and drought, and the incessant wind?*

✦

Will and Paul Tangeman disembarked the Atchison, Topeka and Santa
Fe passenger coach in Newton, Kansas on June 1, 1878. They entered the
frame structure that served as the Newton Depot. It was situated parallel
to several sets of train tracks, which were laid diagonally through this
county seat town. In contrast, Main Street, Broadway, and adjacent streets
were laid out true north/south and east/west. The evening breeze blew a
warm welcome from the south, no longer oppressive or intolerable as the
forceful gale had been in the afternoon.

"That's a mighty fine looking hotel," Will said, gesturing toward the
Howard Hotel at the corner of Fourth and Main Streets. Paul nodded in
assent. At the hotel, they were greeted warmly and shown to the dining
room, a modestly furnished room appreciated by guests for scrumptious
steaks and hearty breakfasts.

On June 2, Will and Paul began their day feasting on eggs, bacon, grits,
and gravy. "Uncle Will, I'm anxious to see the countryside. What do you think
about hiring a couple of horses and exploring the fields and farms and towns
surrounding Newton today?" Paul could hardly contain his excitement.

"I'm up for that. I noticed a livery south of the train tracks," replied
Will. They hired horses from the Cleary Livery and rode out to peruse the
leading-edge towns that were prospering in Harvey County. He wondered
how they had been transformed from wild cow towns to prospering agricultural settlements in a few short years.

On their first day on horseback, the two visitors rode westward along
the Santa Fe railroad tracks to the village of Burrton, an agricultural town
twenty miles west, midway between Newton and Hutchinson. Seeing the
surrounding fields mostly under cultivation, Will and Paul George proceeded southeast toward the village of Halstead.

By noon, they stopped in Halstead to eat ham sandwiches in the shade
of an ancient cottonwood tree overhanging the Little Arkansas River. The

frame storefronts and houses being built in Halstead were still fragrant with the smell of fresh lumber. Every spare hand was busy building, planting, or hauling goods to stores, farms, or homes. There was an air of forward movement, expansiveness, hopeful anticipation of a flourishing economy. The horseback tour progressed to the town of Sedgwick, near the southern border with Sedgwick County, home of the raucous, bustling cow town of Wichita. On their ride back to Newton, Will commented, "All of the fields we saw in the afternoon were being tilled, and there were only small patches of native prairie near Burrton."

On their second day of exploration, Will and Paul George followed the Atchison Topeka and Sante Fe railroad tracks northeast to Walton, a bustling hub of railroad and agricultural enterprise with a post office, grocery store, two-room school, and livery. "From all we heard from Mr. Roth about the abundance of land, do you think we have already missed a chance to own land in this county?" asked Paul. He thought about the hundreds of Mennonites sponsored by the railroad to emmigrate from Russia since 1874. And many others had responded to the land agents eager to sell farm land to settlers. He continued, "It looks like this land is similar to what we saw near Burrton."

"You may be right," replied Will. "Let's finish our tour today, then look up Herman Roth. He may know more about land sales."

On the long ride from Walton to Hesston, Will and Paul George were surprised by how sparsely settled they found the land along the norther border of Harvey County. About half of the land had yet to be turned by a plow.

"Will, this is the best land that is still available in Harvey County," exclaimed Paul George. For the first time since their arrival, the uncle and nephew felt optimistic for the possibility of acquiring enough land needed by both of their families.

At the urging of their riders, the horses fairly flew over the uneven paths that served as roads. They stirred up a covey of quail huddling together until forced to take to the air for safety. In contrast, the jackrabbits ran in a scatter pattern at the first sign of intruders. On this ride Paul identified meadowlarks, mourning doves, sparrows, and crows. Noticing a low bump on the northern horizon that looked manmade, Will pulled to a stop and asked, "Do you see that low building? Do you think people live there?" asked Will.

As they approached the people moving about the place, Paul George replied, "I think it is a dugout. Mr. Roth wrote to us about how farmers cut blocks of native sod, then built walls up above ground. Even the roof is made of sod blocks laid across log beams," replied Paul George. "I can't imagine Mama living in a sod dugout."

Will smiled, "Neither Margaretha."

Paul George pondered whether Mary Ann would keep house in a dugout, and he concluded they would need another residence as landowners in Kansas.

In the lobby of Howard House that evening, Herman Roth recognized Paul descending the stairs with his Uncle Will. "Paul George, welcome to Kansas. It is good to see you after all these years," Mr. Roth exclaimed as he shook Paul's hand and grasped his arm. Stepping back to take in Paul's full height – greater than six feet – he said, "You look like both your father and mother, but so much taller. I have much to ask about your family, and you must have questions about Newton, too."

"Thank you for joining us for supper. Yes, we are anxious to hear your perspective on frontier life in person." Stepping aside, Paul introduced Will. "Mr. Roth, this is my uncle, Will. We are both very interested in land for sale and learning about farming here on the plains," Paul said. Mr. Roth smiled broadly his welcome to these new Tangeman family friends.

Over a pot roast dinner, questions flew across the table about the weather, hunting game, crops, threshing machines, the families back in Ohio, and their plans to move out west.

To close out the evening, Will asked Herman what he knew about the land in the Larned, Kans., vicinity. Herman confirmed that land there was as rich as the Newton area. Similar to Newton, Larned was built along the Atchison Topeka and Santa Fe Railroad. "I have not been out that far, but I have heard it is a fine small city. There are more cattle ranches than farms. And there is Fort Larned. It was an important outpost during the Indian Wars. Most of the forts are being closed down. If you want to visit Larned, it is a few hours west by train on the Atchison, Topeka and Sante Fe."

The following morning Will and Paul boarded the morning train west-bound for Larned, and arrived by lunch time. Will led the way to explore the downtown area, including three hotels, two dry goods stores, a livery and two saloons. Although both men had formed a favorable opinion of the Newton and Harvey County community, they were curious to survey agriculture in the Larned area. They reserved a room in the Farmers and Central Hotel for the night and the next morning engaged horses at the livery to explore the surrounding countryside.

Uncle and nephew rode first to the confluence of the Pawnee and Arkansas Rivers. The slow-moving rivers braided blue and brown liquid, light with shadow. Most of the land adjacent to the rivers was occupied by cattle. They noticed a few fields, but more of the land was devoted to grassy pastures. Ranchers fattened up their cattle and shipped the animals east on the same railroad that had brought the Tangemans to Larned.

Next, Will and Paul rode up to Fort Larned, five miles west of town. They found the gates wide open and a small contingent of soldiers who maintained the fort. Obviously, they were not in a defensive posture toward Pawnee villagers camped in a dozen teepees near the fort. Their presence was a reminder of the history of the native plains dwellers.

Where native prairie had been tilled, they noticed dark, rich soil blanketing rolling hills. The farming prospects appeared to be similar to Harvey County. Shipping prospects were much the same as both Newton and Larned had been built in close proximity to the Atchison, Topeka and Santa Fe Railroad.

On their trip back to Newton, Will and Paul agreed Harvey County held more prospects for farming. In addition to proximity to a railroad town for shipping products, Newton was near the larger town of Wichita. Dark, rich, flat farm land was available for farming and railroad land was for sale. The Mennonites had introduced Turkey Red winter wheat, and it was transforming Kansas into "the breadbasket of America." As in Ohio, some land was affordable for purchase from those who had recently departed. And Newton was one hundred miles closer for those moving to Kansas from Ohio.

Paul and Will returned to Newton, satisfied with their decision. Harvey County held the best promise for farming on the Great Plains of Kansas. Before they returned to the Howard Hotel, Will walked the frontier town to familiarize himself with who had already arrived and what facilities were available for his family. At the same time, Paul rode his rented horse north of town to survey the land in Highland Township once more before they boarded the train back to Ohio in the morning.

✦

As he approached Dutch Avenue, Paul George pulled in reins to pause his rambunctious black stallion on the east-west country road that split Highland Township. A stiff south wind cooled his back from the sweltering day. Before the quivering golden sun brushed the tips of tall grasses, Paul George considered who had preceded this generation of settlers. Who had lived on these nutrient rich grasses that blanketed the undulating prairie? What was the meaning of fossils that seemed to show the prairie had once been the floor of an ancient sea? The mystery of the past and the magnitude of possibilities led him to want to explore the people, plants, and animals of the prairie. The indigenous population had followed bison and antelope herds widely across the broad plains for hundreds of years. Trail drovers, called cowboys, looked after processions of longhorn cattle from Texas. Steam trains belched smoke into virgin skies. The prairie had been branded with buffalo wallows and native encampments long before settlers like the Tangemans arrived. More recently, doggie hoof prints, and iron rails etched a record of cowboys and settlers on the prairie.

Paul felt the wind on his back and the winds of change in every corner of the countryside. He imagined farms, schools, and churches dotting the grasslands, connected by roads built over native trails. He believed the commercial bedrock of these new communities would be successful grain production.

In the last minutes before the sun reached the horizon, Paul leaned forward, loosened the leather reins, and urged his stead into a gallop. He streaked across the prairie as if skimming over a glassy sea of grassy possibilities. The prairie appeared smooth, endless, flat, and straight. He perceived no impediments only endless promise. On his left, the wind kicked up a dust devil, smaller but turning in a similar fashion to a tornado. The winds of the plains were alive with invincible spirits, playing across the sun-splashed summer skies.

He began to appreciate Kansas, the pure smell of pelting rain, the taste of dust between rain storms, and the tumbling heaps of sky-scraping clouds. He revered the episodic landscape of thunderstorms buffeted by commanding winds. He reined in his mount, and shivers of excitement rippled across his skin. Finally, as his horse pranced to a stop, Paul Tangeman planted his heart in the beguiling future of the Kansas prairie.

chapter 23

WESTWARD

HAYESVILLE JOURNAL: 06 March 1879, Vol. 4, No. 36
*MARRIED — On Wednesday the 5th. inst., at (Vermillion Institute)
East Hall, by the Rev. S. Dieffendorf, D.D., Mr. Paul* **Tangeman** *of
Kansas and Miss Mate* **Heckman** *of Hayesville, Ohio.*

Paul Tangeman boarded the train in Newton, Kansas and returned to
Ohio a week before he and Mary Ann (Mate) Heckman were to be married. For the last few months Paul had lived above Mr. Roth's hardware
store while he searched for land, farm machines, and supplies to build a
house and barn.

He reflected on his approaching marriage and their upcoming move to
Kansas. For the past five years he had been certain of his feelings about
Mate. He was committed to her and their future on the prairie.

Paul Tangeman and Mate Heckman were joined in holy matrimony on
the afternoon of March 5, 1879, in East Hall of Vermillion Institute. Following the wedding ceremony, Mr. and Mrs. John Heckman hosted a dinner reception for family and friends in the lower level dining hall. The event
was well attended by faculty, staff, and students and their families associated
with the institute, as well as other friends and family of the couple. Women
in the community contributed traditional German dishes for the dinner,
which was followed by German accordion music. The newlyweds danced
the first *schuhplattler*, the traditional knee slapping dance. Soon the dance
floor was crowded with joyful well-wishers. Among their wedding gifts,
Paul and Mate would always cherish the double ring patchwork quilt made
for them by Anna Barbara.

The following day, the newlyweds left by train to "spy out the land" in
Harvey County, Kansas. Based on Paul's previous trips, their mission was
to purchase land and establish a farm in preparation for the rest of the family to join them the following year. Paul carried a power of attorney and
cash to purchase his family's first parcel of land on his father's behalf. On

April 3, 1879, Paul purchased a quarter section one mile south of the intersection where the Highland Church and Highland Cemetery would later be established. That intersection was situated on Dutch Avenue, approximately midway between the frontier towns of Walton and Hesston.

Nearly two weeks after the wedding of her oldest son, Anna Barbara and her sister, Margaretha, received word of the death of their father, Johann Heinrich Schiedt, in Ehningen, Boblingen, Wurttemberg, Germany. The Schiedt sisters were devastated to learn of his death. He had lived with his daughter, Anna Maria, and her husband, Jacob Schwan, a tailor, in Boblingen since their mother died twenty-one years earlier. With that news Anna Barbara was forced to face the bittersweet knowledge that her parents were gone at the same time she "lost" Paul, her mischievous, inquisitive first-born, to marriage.

After Paul and Mate moved to Kansas, the remaining Tangemans had one more growing season and harvest in Ohio. Ohio's spring of 1879 fluctuated among drizzle, drips, and downpours. Clouds weeped buckets of slate gray ambiguity for growing crops, while farmers expended backbreaking labor behind their ponderous work horses. It was a grueling planting season, as wet as 1873 when Carl's leg had been broken. The Tangeman families and most of their neighbors were exhausted as they planted crops in April and May. As soon as crops were in the ground, the Tangemans were inclined to share time with friends their last summer in Vermillion Township.

As a Civil War veteran, Will was asked to serve on the Committee for Decoration Day, May 30, in Hayesville. This day had been celebrated since the end of the Civil War in northern and southern communities to honor the war dead. The main event of the day was placing flowers, especially geraniums on the Vermillion Cemetery graves of soldiers lost in the Civil War. At noon the ceremony began with an honor guard that presented the American and Ohio flags, followed by speeches by Dr. S. Dieffendorf of Vermillion Institute, and Republican gubernatorial candidate Charles Foster. The ceremony concluded with a twenty-one-gun salute to honor the fallen. Attendees ate their picnics on quilts spread near the graves of family members. Throughout the afternoon, youngsters played games among the gravestones while adults circulated the cemetery, visiting with friends and neighbors.

Inheritance certificates for Anna Barbara and Margaretha were issued in Germany on September 15, 1879. This inheritance was payable in November, 1879, and arrived from Germany before the end of that year. Although a modest amount of money (about $800 each at that time), it was significant at a time land in Kansas could be acquired for approximately $11/acre. Along with the proceeds from their sale of properties in Ohio and other savings, the two Tangeman families prepared to move west with enough resources to purchase land and build houses and barns in a timely fashion. They acquired land through purchases rather than homesteading. They had enough money to do so, at a time when desirable native prairie was no longer available for homesteading in Harvey County.

In December 1879, the extended family of Tangeman siblings met to celebrate Christmas for the last time together in Cincinnati. Since 1850, Carl, Wilhelm, George, Wilhelmina, and Marie Dorothee and their families had met at the home of their sister, Louise Tangeman and her husband, Otto Otten, for large gatherings. In 1878 Louise had been reluctant to commit to the family get-together going forward. "This may be my last Christmas celebration," she announced. "I enjoy having all of you gather in our home, but I'll be seventy soon. It may be time for someone younger to take over, with my help, of course," she said with a warm chuckle.

Several events in 1879 convinced Louise to reconsider her announcement the previous Christmas. First came the news of Carls and Will's plans to move to Kansas, probably in 1880. They had spoken of the attraction of moving west for opportunities to acquire land. Next, Paul and Mate were married in March and left immediately to begin their lives in agriculture in Kansas.

Louise felt drawn to host this gathering of the immigrant generation of Tangemans and their flourishing families one more time. And she surmised she was the only one who could successfully host this parting celebration. Her house was large enough, though just barely. Everyone helped prepare dishes for the Christmas feast, but someone needed to direct the table setting, timing of the oven for roasting meats and vegetables, calling for the blessing, and serving. In this well-ordered family, there were plenty of volunteers who wanted to do their part, but a general was needed to turn the wheels of culinary production. Louise was their beloved head of the kitchen, a position of leadership she learned from their father, Friedrich, and mother, Anne Sophie Elizabeth Luers Tangemann in Sulingen.

The bounteous buffet was ready to serve at noon, and Louise asked her next oldest brother, "Carl, will you please lead us in our Christmas blessing," as she dabbed a tear from her eyes with the corner of her apron.

Carl had anticipated this moment and thought he was prepared. Momentarily, his emotions were close to the surface as he felt the reality of this last Christmas with all of his Tangeman siblings before their move to the Great Plains. He took a deep breath, then replied, "Yes, my dear sister. . . . Heavenly Father, we are gathered today to celebrate the birth of Your son. We arrive at this table grateful for Your blessings on our lives, especially the many hands who have prepared this meal under Louise's kindly oversight. . . . You have richly blessed this family with food in abundance, secure homes, healthy families, and work to provide for these blessings. We are grateful our lives in America are even better than we had hoped when we left our home in Sulingen. At this time we remember those who have departed this life: our parents and brother Hermann and George's beloved Elizabeth, and my first wife, Elizabeth, and children Dorothee and David . . ." Carl paused to allow the emotion of speaking the names of his first family out loud to pass. "May You bring comfort as we mourn our losses and accept our sincere thanksgiving for our abundant blessings. May we all carry this time together far into the future and remember one another throughout the journeys of our lives. In Your name we ask that You continue to look favorably upon us as we carry You, Your son, and all who are gathered here in our hearts. Amen," Carl completed his Christmas blessing and parting prayer.

The room was somber and silent. Even the youngest Tangeman children sensed the seriousness of this moment. The families preparing to leave relished the optimism inherent in this move to Kansas as well as the apprehension of venturing into the unknown. The older generation relived how they felt when they left family and boarded ships from the old country

Both generations witnessed their painful memories of parting with characteristic emotional reserve.

"Papa was reluctant to let us leave for America," said Will. "He delayed his blessing for over a year, because he thought we were too young. When other fellows were pressed into army service, he finally said, 'Yes,' and we left the following month."

"The day my cousin, Sherze, drove us to Bremen to take the train to Brake, everyone in both families gathered to say 'Goodbye.' I'll never forget them standing and waving through the mist," shared Carl. Up to now, he had never spoken of that moment when he separated his physical self from his history, language, and culture in Prussia. At the same time, his heart was never far from the life he left in Sulingen.

Through the afternoon the extended Tangeman family enjoyed their traditional German Christmas fare. At the same time conversations that circulated among adults conveyed an unspoken, yet deeply satisfying communion of love and respect they felt for each other. At the end of the evening, their handshakes were firmer and their embraces longer than usual while they donned coats, hats, and scarves and prepared to leave. Unlike their normally reserved demeanor, the older generation of siblings and their spouses shed tears over final hugs. For Carl and Will and their siblings, this parting was as emotional as when they had left the old country for America thirty years earlier. Kansas was not an ocean away, yet they would not see one another nearly as often as when everyone lived in Ohio. For the Tangeman siblings, family connections were more than sentimental. Their feelings ran deep to a bedrock of family interdependence for mutual survival that reached back through precarious generations in Prussia. When faced with threats to their families' safety and well-being, these siblings depended on people with whom they shared flesh and blood.

◆

In January 1880, serious preparations began for the Tangemans' exodus to Kansas. Instead of the usual lower activity level in the winter, family members commenced non-stop sorting, packing, and selling. Anna Barbara organized the household goods while Carl was in charge of deciding which tools to pack and selling farm implements, equipment, and animals. On Wills and Margaretha's farm, a similar process was underway.

"Anna Barbara, we have three shipping trunks. Do you think that is enough?" Carl asked.

"I think we need at least three more," replied Anna Barbara. "We need enough space for two or three outfits per person, bed linens, medicines, towels. From the kitchen, we need dishes, two of the better pots, and a few knives. I will leave the dish pans. Some of the children's shoes have been worn thin, so I will give them to the church for children without any shoes at all. I have checked the mud boots and passed them down to feet that fit them. We need new pairs for August and Gottlob."

"Whatever we need to replace, we will be able to purchase in Newton. We need to take what we will need right away to set up housekeeping," offered Carl. "Paul's letter described the house he built for Mate. It is small, but I hope we can stay with him until we can buy more land and build another house and barn."

"Oh Carl, won't it be wonderful to see Paul and Mate again? It has been nearly a year since they left. By the time we arrive in the spring, their baby – our first grandchild –will have been born," Anna Barbara exclaimed. There would be many others, but this first child would always hold a special affection reserved for the first-born grandchild of a new generation.

Paul sent a telegram announcing the birth of Carl Henry Tangeman on February 1, 1880, as soon as he could make the five-mile trip to Newton. On the third day after the birth, the blizzard finally let up. Paul drove a buckboard converted to a sleigh into Newton for supplies, then filed his message at the telegraph office.

Carl inquired in Mansfield, Ohio, as to the costs and schedules for train travel west of Ohio. They would travel across Indiana, Illinois, and Missouri and finally to Kansas to board the Atchison, Topeka and Santa Fe railway. He purchased tickets for the move for the four parents, fifteen children, and a dozen trunks. Those missing from the entourage were Charles W., who would remain in Cincinnati with his medical practice, and Paul and Mate who already were living on the farm they had purchased in Carl's name in Highland Township the previous year.

✦

Carl and Will spread the word of their plans to depart and items they had for sale in the spring of 1880. Henry and Fred sold the animals, implements, and large wagons, mostly through word-of-mouth to area farmers. By March in Vermillion Township, Henry and Fred made the sales with buyers for their last few pieces of farm machinery. They also checked with their immediate neighbors to determine who may have an interest in expanding their land holdings. Adjacent land was more convenient and easier to farm than land at a distance. Buyers lined up with offers to purchase both farms. Meanwhile, neighbors arrived daily to purchase and remove the larger household goods, including tables, chairs, sideboards, bed frames, and chests.

"Henry, when you go to work at the foundry tomorrow, I need you to stop by the Heckman farm to pick up a package for wee Carl Henry. Last Sunday Mrs. Heckman told me she had some things for us to take to Mate for the baby," Anna Barbara asked her second oldest son.

"Yes, Mama. Mr. Miller has an order he wants me to finish tomorrow. I may be late, but I will pick up that package on my way home," replied Henry. His mother's smile at the thought of baby Carl Henry was the first time he had seen her so happy since the news of his grandfather's passing last year.

✦

Carl and Anna Barbara sold their two parcels of land in Vermillion Township on March 29 and April 1, 1880, while Wills and Margaretha's farm sold on March 29, too. They transported their families in four wagons bound for Mansfield on their bold adventure of moving "out west." The following day nineteen Tangemans arrived at the Mansfield train depot with tickets for cargo and passengers in hand. Will signaled the boys to roll the trunks on trolleys to the cargo car. "This way, boys."

Carl led the rest of the family to their designated passenger car and helped them get settled before he sat on the oak bench seat next to Anna Barbara. "My dear Anna Barbara. This is the day of our grand adventure to the Great Plains. Are you ready?" His eyes met Anna Barbara's, overflowing with memories and gratitude for their life together.

"Oh Carl. This is the day we have planned for and worked for. It is almost unbelievable this day has arrived," responded Anna Barbara, her mixed feelings about leaving showing plainly on her face to her husband of twenty-six years. They would meet this new beginning together as they had each step of their marriage. They were both better prepared to begin again, having lived in Ohio for more than thirty years. They could read, write, and speak English, and their children could help them if need be. They brought with them a considerable cache of wealth from the sale of their land and possessions, inheritance payments from Grosspapa Schiedt's estate, along with their savings. Their family was complete; God had blessed them with nine healthy sons and daughters and their first grand-child awaited them at the end of this journey.

Carl remembered the way he felt when he departed Liverpool, England, with his first family: Elizabeth, Dorothee, and David. He felt eager for ad-venture, filled with unaffected anticipation. At that moment, the future shone brightly amplified by confidence in his own ability to master the unknown. Parallel to his excitement to embark on a voyage across the At-lantic Ocean were his feelings of sadness and loss at leaving his family in Sulingen knowing they might never see one another again.

Similar to his departure from Sulingen, Hanover, Prussia, in 1847, Carl again felt the anticipation of a new beginning along with the sorrow of leaving his siblings and their families in Cincinnati. Uppermost on his mind was one question: *Will we find success on the Great Plains?* He would devote the rest of his life to the land, seeking to purchase eighty acres for each of his nine children in the western country. He believed it was possible and he wanted to establish an egalitarian future for each of his children, not just his oldest son or a few sons.

The balance of anticipation vs. misgivings tipped in favor of anticipation for Carl and Anna Barbara. Uppermost in their minds was the prospect of meeting their first grandchild when they arrived in Newton, Kansas. Even so, they ached for their siblings who remained in Cincinnati, like they missed those left behind in Sulingen over thirty years earlier.

Will and Margaretha, on the other hand, left more of their lives in Cincinnati. Their devoted son, Charles W., was a well-established physician who chose to stay in Ohio. His decision left them sad, yet proud of his success and future prospects. Unknown to Charles' parents, he had been seeing Anna Geier, the young lady who would eventually become their daughter-in-law. They turned their attention to beginning their lives in Kansas and raising their younger seven children.

The Atchison, Topeka and Santa Fe train arrived in Newton, Kansas the late afternoon of April 4, 1880. With relief overflowing, all nineteen Tangemans spilled onto the platform of the train depot.

"Papa, are we really here?" asked Gottlob, rubbing his eyes to wake up.

"Yes, Gottlob, this is our new home town," replied his father with an affectionate tousle of his youngest son's hair. "Henry, will you be in charge of transferring all of our bags and trunks to the front of the depot? Fred, August, John, and Otto, you need to help Henry with the luggage."

"Will, would you like to join me on a short walk to Herman Roth's general store?" suggested Carl.

Mr. Roth met the Tangemans at the hotel dining room for breakfast the following morning.

"Hello, Anna Barbara, and you must be Margaretha," Mr. Roth greeted the Schiedt sisters warmly, grasping both sets of hands in turn. "How do you find our fine town?"

"Mr. Roth, the town is charming, a small town something like Loudonville," replied Anna Barbara. "We are so glad to see you again after all of these years. We have read your letters many times, and our children are anxious to meet you in person." Anna Barbara lined up her offspring from oldest to youngest for the introductions. In turn Margaretha asked her children to line up and speak their own names as Mr. Roth moved down the line and shook each youngster's hand.

"Now that you have all met Mr. Roth and had your breakfast, would you like to hear a letter from Paul and Mate welcoming us to Newton?" asked Carl with a broad grin.

A chorus of "Yes, yes," erupted at the prospect of hearing the letter.

Dear Papa, Mama, Uncle Will, and Aunt Gretly,

Welcome to the prairie town of Newton. If you read this letter, it means you have arrived on your frontier adventure. We hope your trip was comfort-

able and all of you are in good health.

We are anxious to see all of you. Perhaps you will rent wagons and venture out of town to our (your) farm. Take Main Street north out of town six and one-half miles. Turn left one-half mile and you will find us.

Affectionately,
Paul and Mate and Carl Henry

◆

Carl folded the letter and slipped it into his shirt pocket, then announced, "We have rented wagons to transport all of us to Highland Township." He rose to a round of cheering and declared, "Follow me."

Carl and Anna Barbara led the way out of the Howard House and across the railroad tracks to the Cleary Livery. Will and Margaretha followed at the end of the group scooping up their daughters, Emma and Minnie, and counting to make sure all of the youngsters were accounted for. Everyone was eager to make the wagon trip out in the countryside. They had not seen either Paul or Mate since their wedding over a year ago.

The two wagons left the town and rolled past fields and fenced prairie grass in pastures not yet turned by a plow. Henry accepted the reins of one wagon while Otto guided the team of horses pulling the other wagon. Their parents joined them on the wooden seats. Cousins and trunks filled up the wagon beds.

"Gretly, be careful with the little girls. If they venture out in the tall grass, we may never see them again. It is as tall as my waist," commented Will with a grin. The gusting wind blew billowing clouds high overhead.

"Papa, those clouds look like wandering giant snowballs," said Clara. This comment led to a lively game of names for other shapes of the dynamic cloud forms.

To their right, cottonwood treetops were visible half-way above the surface of the land, no doubt overhanging a meandering creek. Will pointed out a dugout house on the left side of the roadway. It appeared to be abandoned. In the following mile two more dugouts were visible on the right. A barn had been erected between the two dugouts. The morning passed in a mood of curiosity and excitement to see the environs of their new home in this strange new land.

When the two wagons finally turned west on the last half mile to the farm, the Tangeman families began shouting, although they were too far away to be heard. Paul was watching for the caravan of wagons. When he saw them, he waved his hat in the air, throwing words into the wind. As soon as the young people saw Paul, they climbed out of the wagons and ran over a quarter mile to greet him, everyone except Minnie, who clung to her mother's skirt. Anna Barbara had waited more than a year to see her son and daughter-in-law; she could barely stay in the wagon to ride the final twenty minutes to Paul and Mate's place.

At last the drivers stopped the wagons near a hitching rail. Carl helped Anna Barbara; Will helped Gretly; and Minnie jumped off the end of the wagon. Shouts of greeting and hugs were passed around and each family member accepted a generous helping. "Paul, how are you? Do you like farming?"

"Mattie, when did you get so tall?" Paul asked, and she blushed.

"Gottlob, how did you like the train trip?"

The noisy, joyous reunion reminded Will of his feelings when he, George, and Carl were reunited thirty-two years earlier in Cincinnati. The sounds of pure happiness wrapped them all in blankets of bliss. After several moments of noisy joy, Paul glanced toward the door of their home.

Mate stood in the doorway holding her firstborn son. He was wrapped in an unbleached cotton blanket, one corner hanging down, draped across her left leg, confirming the infant had been lifted hurriedly at the sound of commotion in the yard. First one, then another of the crowd noticed and stopped saying or doing anything more. For a few moments, only the sound of the wind and the sighs of the horses could be heard as all eyes were on Mate and her baby.

At once, Paul turned and took a few proud strides across the yard to join Mate on the doorstep. As if performing an ancient, practiced ritual, they deliberately stepped off the stone doorsill, then proceeded in lockstep to greet Carl and Anna Barbara. In a moment too deeply felt for words, Paul gently lifted his son from Mate's embrace and placed him in his mother's arms. Gladness, relief, contentment, and ecstasy all filled the space in their hearts that Carl and Anna Barbara had prepared for their first grandchild.

In this moment the Tangemans were no longer strangers in a distant land. They had come home.

Epilogue

In 1879 when Paul and Mate Tangeman moved to Kansas, the family of Carl Tangeman began to sink roots into the fabric of Highland Township in Harvey County. The five oldest sons of Carl, along with Will's son, Otto, shared their fathers' interests in agriculture. They raised crops and livestock on farms they inherited and expanded in Highland Township. Three of the brothers, Henry, August and John, loved and raised horses. Henry raised shetland ponies; August, draft horses and John, pure-bred Percherons.

After Carl passed in 1899, his oldest son Paul and his family moved to California. Henry, Fred, August, John, Eliza, and Matilda lived out their lives in Harvey County as farmers and small business owners who each benefitted from their inheritance of eighty acres each. Gottlob attended seminary, then moved to Nebraska to pastor a Congregational Church. When his health began to fail, Fred and Paul helped him and his wife sell his land in Kansas and move to California to be near Paul's family. Elizabeth graduated from Emporia State Teachers College and married Frank Agrelius, who later became a biology professor at their alma mater. She spent many summers with her family in Newton and lived out her life in her family home in Emporia, Kansas.

In their quest to acquire acreage for each of the Tangeman siblings, Carl's sons formed a family bank led by Fred to accumulate the capital necessary to buy, sell, and expand their land holdings. Before Carl's death in 1899, Carl and Anna Barbara fulfilled their dream to provide each of their off-spring with "an eighty" (acres), a secure beginning for their adult lives. It is unknown the origin of those egalitarian values. Perhaps they reacted against the European practice of primogeniture, the firstborn legitimate child, more often the first born son who inherited the parents' estate rather than sharing an inheritance among some or all of the descendents. For example, Carl's brother, Herman, inherited their father's property in Sulingen. The practice of providing a land bequeath to female children was not common at the time. Perhaps Carl and Anna Barbara were influenced to do so by the cash inheritances Anna Barbara and her sister received from their father in 1879.

Another theme of this story was the closeness and interdependence of the Schiedt sisters, Anna Barbara and Margaretha. They shared their childhoods in Ehningen, Boblingen, Wurttemberg, and their early adult years in Cincinnati. As wives of Carl and Wilhelm Tangeman, they gave birth and raised their combined seventeen children largely in tandem. Their families' moves were influenced by the sisters' desire to live in close proximity and support one another; Cincinnati to Loudonville, Loudonville to Hayesville, Ohio, and Hayesville to Highland Township, Harvey County, Kans. They even died in the same year, 1913, in Newton, Kans., at the ages of eighty-three and seventy-eight, respectively. There is little doubt this relationship was a buffer against threats to immigrant safety and success, such as loneliness, despair, and deprivation common among some female immigrants on the isolating prairie.

Paul and Mate continued to live on the first parcel Paul purchased for Carl and Anna Barbara, situated one mile south of Highland Church. This property has been in the Tangeman family continuously since 1879. Currently, Larry (Carl's great-great grandson, also Henry William's great grandson) and Margaret Goering live on and farm that property. The second parcel Carl and Anna Barbara purchased became their "home place," catty-cornered across from Highland Church.

William and Margaret Tangeman lived on their successful farm in Highland Township. William died in 1887 following a long battle with stomach cancer. According to census records Margaretha remained on their farm with her children, Louisa, Clara, Harry, Emma, and Minnie. In 1907 she moved to Newton where she lived until her death in 1913. Their oldest son, Charles W., practiced medicine in Cincinnati, Ohio, and served as an occulist for the Four Railroads Company where his cousins Charles O. and Bettie worked as clerks. He visited Newton regularly. In 1884 Charles W. married Annie Geier (see below). She was expecting their first child when their fathers both died a few days apart in the spring of 1887. Charles W.'s next oldest sibling, Sophia, died of consumption, July 15, 1886, only months before their father passed away. Louisa married Al Heilman; after his death, she moved to California to keep house for Paul. Otto and his wife, Lillie May Egy, operated a grain elevator in Moundridge, Kans., then moved to Hutchinson, Kans., and he died in 1922 on a visit to their daughter in Oklahoma. Harry remained a bachelor teacher in Newton until he moved to Denver, Colo., to practice law. His sister Clara was also a teacher in Newton and lived with their cousin August's family for a time. After August died in 1920, Clara moved to Denver and kept house for Harry. Emma married Edgar Krehbiel and lived at 225 East Eighth Street, Newton. Minnie married Dr. Frank Mahan, and they lived out their lives in

Dow City, Iowa.

Following the death of his wife, Elizabeth, in 1875, George Tangeman stayed in Cincinnati and raised his six-year-old daughter, Bettie. She lived with her father until his death in 1905. Charles O. and Bettie Tangeman both worked for the Four Railroads Company as clerks. The first child of Charles O. and Emma Hanhart Tangeman, Martha Sophie, was born in 1883 and died in 1884. Subsequently, they were parents to one son and two more daughters who lived in Cincinnati.

The Tangeman sisters from Cincinnati, Louise and Wilhelmina, married the Otten brothers, Otto and Dietrich, respectively. Louise and Otto were the parents of four children born in Prussia; Friedrich (born 1840), Sophia Louise (1842), Bettie (1845) and Otto (1848). Louise's older daughter, Sophia Louise married Phillip Otto Geier in 1861. The Geiers's oldest daughter, Annie, married Wilhelm's son Charles W. in 1884. When Phillip Geier (Annie's father) died in 1887, his oldest son, Fred A. Geier, age twenty-one, took over his father's company and established the Cincinnati Milling Machine Company in 1889. It became the largest machine company in the world in the 1930s. It eventually became the Milacron Company, an international mill works company. Wilhelmina Lenore Tangeman and Dietrich Otten were the parents of one child, Eleanor E. Otten (born 1869), who married George Adolphus Mayer in 1904. Marie Dorothee Tangeman remained single and lived out her life in Cincinnati, Ohio.

Through the last half of the nineteenth century, the Tangemans prospered through hard work and mutual support while learning to adapt to life in the United States. Their children were first generation Americans, the beneficiaries of their immigrant parents' propensity to take risks, work hard, realize material success, and contribute time and effort to community life. The older immigrant generation bridged the old country and the new. They remembered their parents, told stories of life in Sulingen, and grieved as each one passed. Those were the grandparents their children would never know except through the stories they heard at holidays and evenings around the dining room table.

The Tangeman thread of my life came through my parents, Fred and Hazel Dudte, who were born in Harvey County early in the twentieth century. They farmed and lived in Highland Township until they retired to a new home in North Newton, Kans. Their lives unfolded much as their Tangeman ancestors had hoped and imagined for their family when they arrived in 1880. They embraced the opportunities to raise wheat, corn, oats, alfalfa, soybeans, cattle, and sheep on their farm located on Kansas Highway 15. Every spring, numerous times, Dad walked several paces into one of his fields, reached down and picked up a handful of dirt. He firmly pressed the spongy, black humus soil with his practiced hands and breathed in the dark, pungent sweetness. This ritual informed Dad's decisions of when and what to plant in each field as his grandfather, Fred Tangeman, and great-grandfather, Carl Tangeman had surely done.

A few years ago in June I visited my parent's graves in Highland Cemetery, Highland Township. Across the ripening wheat fields I recalled how they had farmed the land, raised our family and routinely supported community organizations. Shadyside and Golden Plains Schools, Highland Grange, Highland 4-H Club, churches, and others benefitted from their time and commitment to their community. While in this place of crops and wind and fully open skies, I reflected on the turning of seasons, the rhythm of planting, harvesting, and preparing for next year's crops. After nearly a century on the land, my parents chose Highland Cemetery to return to the sheltering earth. They now rest several paces from the grave markers of Dad's forebears, Anna Tangeman Dudte (his mother), Fred Tangeman (his grandfather) and Carl and Anna Barbara Tangeman (his great-grandparents).

Barn in which the Tangemans lived for a time. Left: Tillie Tangeman.
Right: Anna Barbara Tangeman. circa 1890

Home place of Carl and Anna Barbara Tangeman diagonally across the
intersection from Highland Church in Highland Township, Harvey County,
Kansas circa 1890

193

Johann **Friedrich** Tangemann m. Anne Sophie Elizabeth Luers Tangeman

- Elizabeth **Louise** Marianne 2/12/12–10/13/1890 m. Otto Otten 1810–1897

  - **Friedrich** Otten 11/2/1840–1/16/1900
  - **Sophia Louise** 9/7/1842–1922 m. (9/8/1861) Phillip Otto Geier 1839–5/6/1887

    - Annie 12/1/1862–1/1/1932 m. (8/20/1884) Charles W. Tangeman 1856–1922
    - Emma (Cone) 1884
    - Fred A. 6/23/1866–3/29/1934
    - Matilda E. 1868
    - Louisa S. 1870
    - Otto Philip 1874
    - Phillip Otto 1877
    - Walter Henry 1878
    - Norma Elizabeth 1880

  - Johanne Elisabeth (**Bettie**) Otten 2/2/1845 m. Henry Ahlers
  - Otto Otten 8/5/1848–1/28/1949

- Marie Sophia 6/7/1815 (died as a child)
- **Hermann Friedrich** 8/9/1817–7/4/1876 (cared for Johann Friedrich, remained in Sulingen)
- **Carl Heinrich** 2/16/1821–1899 m. **Maria Anna Barbara Schiedt** 12/26/1853

  - **Paul George** 9/6/1854–11/20/1938 m. Mary Ann Heckman
  - **Henry William** 5/26/1856–1/7/1925
  - **Frederick** 4/5/1858–10/17/1938
  - **August Charles** 4/5/1860–9/5/1920
  - **John Herman** 2/21/1862–8/30/1936
  - **Wilhelmina Marie (Eliza)** 10/2/1864–12/19/1929
  - **Matilda** 6/16/1866–10/22/1922
  - **Gottlob David** 4/15/1870–10/15/1922
  - **Anna Elizabeth** 9/17/1874–4/26/1967

- **George Heinrich** 12/1/1822–12/28/1905 m. Elizabeth Heimers

  - Charles Otto 10/18/1854–1/38/1939 m. Emma Hanhart
  - Bettie 5/23/1869–5/7/1932

- Johann Hermann 8/25/1813– (no children)
- Auguste Charlotte 12/10/1824 (died as a child)
- **Marie Dorothee** 4/5/1826–2/1903 (died in Cincinnati)
- **Wilhelmine Lenore** 12/1/1828–1915 m. **Dietrich Otten** 4/17/1814

  - Eleanor E. 1869 m. George Adolphus Mayer

- **Wilhelm** 12/31/1830–4/25/1887 m. **Margaretha Schiedt**

  - **Charles W.** 9/10/1856–4/2/1922 m. **Anna Geier** 1863
  - **Sophia Louise** 1858–1886
  - **Otto** 8/27/1861–1/17/1922
  - **Louisa** (Heilman) 1863
  - **Clara** 1867–1953
  - **Harry** 1/1872–1946
  - **Emma** (Krehbiel) 11/1875
  - **Minnie** (Malin) 1876

194

Johann Friedrich Schiedt 1788–1879 m. Maria Barbara Klein 1792–1858

- Johann **(John)** Friedrich 1/23/1819–1/12/1870 m. Elizabeth
- Johann Georg 7/21/1821 m. Margaretha Reichert (1823)
- Maria Barbara 1824–1826
- Anna Maria 1825–1826
- Magdalena 10/15/1826–1870
- Johannes **Heinrich** 4/20/1828–12/17/1888
- **Anna Barbara** 9/10/1830–8/21/1913 m. Carl Tangeman (see children previous page)
- Anna Maria 1/15/1832–7/2/1871 m. Jakob Schwan
- Maria Agnes 1/25/1834–12/7/1907
- **Margaretha** 4/18/1835–1/18/1913 m. Wilhelm Tangeman (see children previous page)

195

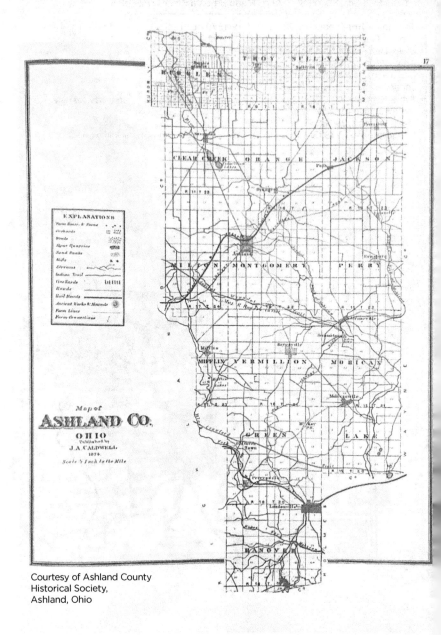

Courtesy of Ashland County
Historical Society,
Ashland, Ohio

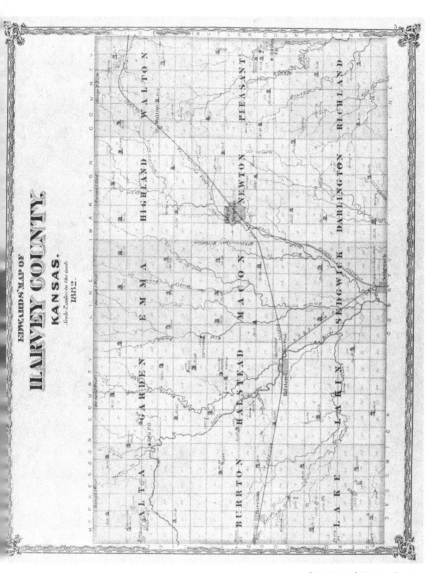

Courtesy of Harvey County
Historical Museum,
Newton, Kansas

197

Historical Events

CHAPTER 1

Marriage of Carl Heinrich Tangeman to Anna Barbara Schiedt, December 26, 1853.

Marriage of George Tangeman to Elizabeth Helmers, July 29, 1853.

Over-the-Rhine was the area of Cincinnati where German newcomers moved for inexpensive housing in the mid-nineteenth century.

Heinrich Schiedt (brother of Anna Barbara and Margaretha) was a pastor in Cincinnati along with his wife, Wilhelmina.

Saint Paulus Deutsch Evangelische Kirche and St. Mary's Church were located in Over-the-Rhine in the 1850s.

German immigrants faced negative nativist attitudes by residents of Cincinnati, especially the Irish.

Carl served as a Prussian soldier in Sulingen, Hannover, Prussia in the 1840s.

CHAPTER 2

Friedrich Tangemann was the father of Carl, George and Wilhelm Tangeman. He remained in Sulingen, Hannover, Prussia when his sons and daughters left for America in the mid-nineteenth century. He wrote a parting letter of blessing and encouragement to Carl and Elizabeth which they received in Brake, on the Weser, River in 1847.

"Running of the meat" through Cincinnati meant livestock moved from trains, boats and wagons to the meat-packing plants that made Cincinnati famous as "porkopolis."

Carl and his first wife, Elizabeth, and two children left Sulingen for New York in 1847. They were blown off course and landed in New Orleans where Elizabeth, Dorothee and David perished.

Carl became a naturalized citizen on September 16, 1852.

Anna Barbara and Margaretha grew up in Ehningen, Boblingen, Wurttemberg in Bavaria.

CHAPTER 3

Anna Barbara was pregnant in 1854.

Anna Barbara and Carl moved to Loudonville in 1854 as evidenced by the birth certificate for Paul George Tangeman who was born September 6, 1854.

Friedrich Tangemann maintained a saddlery shop in Sullingen.

CHAPTER 4

Cincinnati, Columbus and Cleveland Railway began service for cargo and passengers in 1851.

Crestline Station was the crossroads for the CCC Railway and trains traveling between St. Louis and Cleveland.

Loudonville was founded on the the Blackfork of the Mohican River.

CHAPTER 5

Wilhelm and George Tangeman were tobacconists, wholesale tobacco merchants in Cincinnati.

CHAPTER 6

Oak, hickory, and birch trees were native to the Black Fork of the Mohican River in Loudonville, Ohio. Meadowlarks and mourning doves were common, too.

CHAPTER 7

Hanover Evangelical and Reformed Church was found on North Union Street in Loudonville.

Paul George Tangeman was born on September 6, 1854.

CHAPTER 8

Charles O. Tangeman was born to George and Elizabeth Tangeman in Cincinnati, October 18, 1854.

CHAPTER 9

Wilhelm Tangeman and Margaretha Schiedt were married in Mansfield, Ohio, April 14, 1855.

In Cincinnati, abolitionists assisted African slaves escape to freedom in Canada, also known as the Underground Railroad.

The Kansas-Nebraska Act of 1854 created a contentious struggle for residents of each state to determine slavery or free status when each territory became a new state.

Federal legislation authorized slave owners to enter free states to capture their escaped slaves.

Henry William Tangeman was born to Carl and Anna Barbara Tangeman, May 26, 1856.

Charles William Tangeman was born to Wilhelm and Margaretha Tangeman on September 10, 1856.

CHAPTER 10

The winter of 1856-1857 was bitter cold in Ohio.

Maria Barbara Klein Schiedt (Anna Barbara's and Margaretha's mother) died in October, 1858.

Sophia Louise Tangeman was born to Wilhelm and Margaretha Tangeman in 1858.

Fredrick Tangeman was born to Carl and Anna Barbara Tangeman on April 5, 1858.

CHAPTER 11

A railroad bridge was built from Rockland, Illinois to Davenport, Iowa.

"Prairie fever" was prevalent in in prairie states, especially for women on isolated frontier farms.

CHAPTER 12

August Charles Tangeman was born to Carl and Anna Barbara Tangeman on April 5, 1860.

Otto George Tangeman was born to Wilhelm and Margaretha Tangeman on August 27, 1860.

Civil War in the United States broke out on April 12, 1861.

Millions of Europeans immigrated to the United States in the 1840s and 1850s.

Kansas became a free state, January 29, 1861.

"Bleeding Kansas" was the term used to describe the armed conflict for the territory to become a slave or free state prior to statehood. Quantrell's Raid was perpetrated by Missouri militia in Kansas in 1856.

Hanover Evangelical and Reformed Church and Zion Lutheran
Church burned to the ground in Loudonville, Ohio, in 1860.

Sophie Louise Otten (daughter of Louise Tangeman and Otto Otten)
married Phillip Geier on September 8, 1861.

The Homestead Act was signed into law by President Lincoln on
May 20, 1862. Citizens (or intended citizens) who lived on a
parcel of land for five years, made improvements, and paid an
$18 filing fee could establish ownership of up to 160 acres.

CHAPTER 13

William Tangeman was drafted into the Union Army, 4th Militia,
8th Regiment, Company G, in the summer of 1862 and ordered
to report for duty on September 3, 1862.

Company G participated in the Battle of Antietam, September 17-18,
1862. President Lincoln issued the Emancipation Proclamation
freeing slaves in Confederate States on September 22, 1862.

William Tangeman and his fellow soldiers in Company G
were mustered out of the Union Army, October 3, 1862.

George Tangeman was drafted into the Union Army in June, 1863;
he did not actively serve.

John Tangeman was born in 1862 and Eliza Tangeman was born in
1864 to Carl and Anna Barbara Tangeman.

Louisa Tangeman was born in 1863 to Wilhelm and Margaretha
Tangeman.

The American Civil War ended with the surrender of
General Robert E. Lee at Appomattox Courthouse, April 9, 1865.
After the end of the war the thirteenth, fourteenth and fifteenth
amendments were added to the Constitution of the United States.

CHAPTER 14

Half the men in Ohio aged 20-45 served in the Union Army
of the Civil War.

William and Gretly sold their farm in Hanover Township and bought
a 105-acre farm in Vermillion Township, west of Hayesville,
Ohio, in 1867.

Carl and Anna Barbara bought four lots in Loudonville.

Buffalo herds roamed the prairie around Coronado Heights west of
Salina, Kansas.

Matilda Tangeman was born to Carl and Anna Barbara Tangeman on June 16, 1866.

Clara Mary Tangeman was born to William and Margaretha Tangeman, October 1, 1867.

CHAPTER 15

Charlie Schiedt (three-year-old son of John and Elizabeth) died in 1869.

Henry Schiedt (son of John and Elizabeth) was born on November 15, 1869.

In the 1870 census, Carl Tangeman's occupation was listed as foundry and machinist. George was listed as a bookkeeper and clerk for Four Railroads, and Wilhelm was a farmer in Vermillion Township.

John Schiedt, (brother of Anna Barbara, Margaretha, and Heinrich) died on January 12, 1870.

Carl Tangeman and Fred Schwan were executors of the estate of John Schiedt.

Gottlob David Tangeman was born on April 15, 1970.

Will purchased 110 acres west of Hayesville on May 15, 1870.

In 1871 the Franco-Prussian War ended with the unification of Germany under the leadership of Bismark.

CHAPTER 16

Harry H. Tangeman was born to William and Margaretha Tangeman on January 19, 1872.

Carl and Anna Barbara Tangeman purchased and moved to their first farm in Vermillion Township, 1872.

Newton, Kansas, was the railhead of the Atchison, Topeka and Santa Fe Railroad 1871-1872. A gunfight in Newton's Hide Park between Billy Bailey and Mike McCluskie ended in eight men dead, and a reputation as "bloody and lawless—the wickedest city in the west" in 1872.

First post office was opened in Newton, Kansas, in 1872.

A fire in Loudonville on April 5, 1872, began in the tin shop and swept through nearby buildings.

Paul George was hired as a teacher at the Vermillion Institute after he graduated high school.

CHAPTER 18

Kansas was predicted to become the "breadbasket of America."

Agricultural machines in use in Ohio in 1873 included spring-tooth harrows, wheat drilling machines, and McCormick reapers.

McKay was a town midway between Hayesville and Loudonville, Ohio, with a school in the early 1870s.

The Ohio Granges supported legislation to limit the shipping cost of a ton of freight to five cents a mile in the State of Ohio.

Carl and Anna Barbara Tangeman moved from Loudonville to a farm in Vermillion Township west of Hayesville, Ohio in 1872.

In 1872, Ohio farmers realized bumper crops, high prices and huge profits.

The Panic of 1873 occurred as a result of oversupply of grain crops in 1872, lower prices, lower yields, and much lower farm incomes. Farmers unable to meet mortgage payments were forced to default on their loans, which in turn led to banks going out of business, too.

Johann Friedrich Tangemann, Carl's, George's, and William's father, died in Sulingen, Hanover, Prussia, January 20, 1874.

Mennonites arrived in Harvey County, Kansas, and introduced Turkey Red winter wheat in 1874.

CHAPTER 19

Bettie Tangeman was born to George and Elizabeth Tangeman on May 23, 1869.

Elizabeth was born to Carl and Anna Barbara Tangeman on September 17, 1874.

Emma Tangeman was born to William and Margaretha in 1875; Minnie was born to them in November, 1876.

Elizabeth Sophia Heimers Tangeman died on August 27, 1875

In the 1880 US Census, George Tangeman reported his occupation as at home, dressmaker.

Bettie Tangeman lived with her father, George, until his death in 1905. She worked for the Big Four Railway along with her brother throughout her career.

CHAPTER 20

The Centennial Exhibition took place in Philadelphia, Pennsylvania,

May 10-November 10, 1876, to celebrate the 100th anniversary
of US independence.

Bananas, Hires Root Beer, and sugar popcorn were introduced at the
Centennial Exhibition along with McCormick Reapers
and other agricultural and mining machines.

In 1875, the Kansas legislature authorized an expenditure for a
promotional exhibit at the Centennial Exhibition in 1876.

CHAPTER 21

August Charles Tangeman and Anna Margaret Smith fell in love in
Vermillion Township, Ashland County, Ohio leading to
their marriage, March 16, 1882.

Grasshoppers invaded Kansas in the 1870s.

CHAPTER 22

William and Paul Tangeman made a reconnaissance trip to explored
land in and around Newton, Kansas and Larned, Kansas in
1878. They chose Harvey County as the most favorable location
for farming in their upcoming move to Kansas.

The Howard Hotel was situated across the street from the train
depot in Newton, Kansas.

CHAPTER 23

Paul George Tangeman and Mary Ann (Mate) Heckman were joined
in marriage March 5, 1879. The following day they left by train
to "spy out the land" in Harvey County, Kansas.

On April 3, 1879 Carl Tangeman purchased the north 80 of the
NW quarter of Section 20, Highland Township, Harvey County.

Johann Heinrich Schiedt, father of Anna Barbara, Margaretha,
Heinrich, and John Schiedt, died in 1879 in Ehningen,
Boblingen, Wurttemburg, Bavaria.

Carl Henry Tangeman was born to Paul and Mate Tangeman
on February 1, 1880.

Anna Barbara Schiedt Tangeman and Margaretha Schiedt Tangeman
received an inheritance from their father's estate in 1879.
in Ehningen, Boblingen, Wurttemburg, Bavaria.

Acknowledgements

"I come from a family that keeps track of our history," I have replied when asked how I know so much about my Tangeman family background. This book would not be possible without the detailed genealogical records compiled over generations by previous and present Tangeman family members. Immigrants Land is based on the real lives of Carl and Anna Barbara Schiedt Tangeman, William and Margaretha Schiedt Tangeman and George and Elizabeth Heimers Tangeman, their children, and to a lesser extent, their siblings in the 19th century. The factual details of the Tangeman and Schiedt families were largely drawn from the The Carl Heinrich Tangeman Genealogy, 1821-1971, a treasure trove of documents, photos and records compiled over decades by Bonnie Tangeman Goering and Peg Tangeman Wickersham.

In the spring of 2019, I visited Ohio to delve into the state where the Tangeman immigrant generation of siblings lived during the period of my book, 1848-1880. Thanks to The Ohio Genealogical Society, Ashland County Historical Society, Ashland County Clerk's Office, The PL Of Cincinnati And Hamilton County, Wayne County Public Library, Ashland Public Library, Loudonville Public Library, National Underground Railroad Freedom Center in Cincinnati, Ohio for their generosity. The Kaufman Museum at Bethel College, North Newton, Kansas, Newton Public Library and the Harvey County Historical Museum, Newton, Kansas also generously shared their resources.

John Scheidt and his family were real people. He purchased and sold properties that were documented in real estate records in the Ashland County Clerk's Office. His wife, children and death were also documented. He may have been a cousin rather than a brother to the Schiedt sisters. In any event, Carl Tangeman and Fred Schwan were close to him as evidenced by their appointments as co-executors of his estate.

Herman Roth is a fictional composite character who represented the westward flow of newcomers through Ohio in the mid-1800s. He was created to show how pioneers lived out promises and perils in the formation of western states of the United States.

About the Author

Cheryl Clay is a veteran educator who has taught at the preschool, elementary and college levels. In her professional career she wrote journal articles and books and presented at numerous conferences and training events for early childhood and elementary staff.

The author grew up on her family's farm in Highland Township, near Newton, Kansas, the same township where Carl and Anna Barbara Schiedt Tangeman and William and Margaret Schiedt Tangeman moved their families to the Kansas prairie around 1880. She writes from an intimate understanding of the Tangeman family and as a granddaughter of Anna Tangeman Dudte.

Cheryl Clay and her husband, Jim, live on the Pine River along side the abundant wildlife who enhabitat the river environment near Bayfield, Colorado.

CPSIA information can be obtained
at www.ICGtesting.com
Printed in the USA
LVHW042251220922
729060LV00003B/505